ANGEL

close to the ground

Jeff Mariotte

An original novel based on the television series
created by Joss Whedon & David Greenwalt

POCKET PULSE
New York   London   Toronto   Sydney   Singapore

Historian's Note: This story takes place during the first half of *Angel*'s first season.

An *Original* Publication of POCKET BOOKS

POCKET PULSE published by
Pocket Books, a division of Simon & Schuster Inc.
1230 Avenue of the Americas, New York, NY 10020

ISBN: 0-671-04147-9

First Pocket Books printing August 2000

10 9 8 7 6 5 4 3 2

POCKET PULSE and colophon are registered trademarks of
Simon & Schuster Inc.

For Maryelizabeth Hart and Nancy Holder
My Angels.

***Angel breathed a sigh of relief and headed
back toward Sunset.***

"Just playing it safe," he explained. "That's what we bodyguards do."

"I think you bodyguards are all whack jobs," Karinna suggested.

"That may be, but—"

The car blasted out of nowhere, no headlights on, and slammed into the GTX. There was a sound like an explosion. The Plymouth went into a skid and stopped ninety degrees from the way it had been headed.

Angel was reaching for the key to restart it when he saw nine men on the street, coming toward them from every angle.

"We're not here for you," one of them said. He was tall, with steely gray eyes and black hair slicked close to his scalp. "You could go. Take your car. We'll take the girl."

"No deal," Angel said.

"Didn't think so," the guy said. "Thought I'd offer, though."

"Appreciate it."

"Kill him," the guy instructed calmly.

Angel™

Available from POCKET PULSE

Acknowledgments

For this one I have to thank Joss Whedon and David Greenwalt for creating these characters, and David Boreanaz, Charisma Carpenter, and Glenn Quinn for giving them life.

Thanks also to the publishing commandoes: Caroline Kallas, Debbie Olshan, Liz Shiflett, Micol Ostow, and especially Lisa Clancy.

And the ground crew: Maryelizabeth, Nancy, Chris, Scott, Holly, Dave, and Belle. Couldn't have done it without you.

PROLOGUE

Ireland—four weeks ago

The island rose from the waters off the west coast of Ireland like a great beast thrusting its head up from the surf. Waves had pounded the island's sheer rock walls since time began, scouring them clean and smooth. Thick tall grass carpeted the island's interior, dotted by the stunted, twisting trees that were all the strong winds and heavy mists would allow to grow.

No visitor but the winged ones had ever set foot on this island, and even those were soon driven off—if not by the elements, then by the sense of foreboding that blanketed the place as surely as the ever-present fog. Ireland, they said, had been rid of snakes by Saint Patrick, but that man was simply redundant here. No natural creature that *could* leave the island would stay on it more than a night.

1

According to legend, a force of Celtic warriors had once tried to claim the island because where it sat, off the end of Blacksod Bay, might have strategic significance to anyone invading that part of Ireland. Climbing the rocky cliffs, they found in the center of the island a strange assortment of huge rocks, standing at angles to the ground, as if they would fall down at any moment. In the middle of this arrangement they discovered a broad, flat rock, and on that rock an old man's severed head. As the warriors approached, the eyes of the head opened and gazed upon them. The head then called each warrior by name.

By morning all the warriors were dead, and each of the big, leaning rocks was topped by a fresh human skull. The island was left alone after that.

It was never given a name.

So when a castle was built on the island, no one saw its walls go up, its roofs covered over. It was constructed of the same gray stone as the island itself, and from a distance—which was as close as anyone came—it looked like simply another rock outcropping.

The castle belonged to Mordractus.

Mordractus sat in a chair made of massive antlers, with deerskin stretched between them, watching as P'wrll shoved a tape into the VCR. The room was vast and dark, with the only light coming from small electric sconces set high up on the cold stone walls, and the glow from the rear-projection TV.

"The quality ain't great," P'wrll said. His voice rasped like two rocks scraping together, and Mordractus thought that his accent was a bizarre cross of Irish and Faerie. P'wrll was an odd-looking thing, too, his body all bent and twisted, his skin chalk-white with narrow black lips and cavernous red eyes, strands of long white hair that reached halfway to the floor from his patchy scalp, and limbs that seemed made from random branches of different trees. It was a good thing he had masking spells which enabled him to pass among humans. "It was all shot at night," he went on, "mostly from a distance. And we couldn't exactly announce ourselves, you know, 'ad to shoot it all from 'idin'.'"

Mordractus waved an impatient hand at the bogie. Goblins and fairies in general were typically bad with modern machinery, and he'd half a mind to do it himself, or at least to summon one of his human minions to operate the thing. "I've no interest in your excuses," he said. "Just show it to me."

P'wrll fiddled with the remote, his long, gnarled fingers finally locating the right button, and the widescreen went blue. "I think I've got it," he announced. Sure enough, the screen flickered and went dark, and then Mordractus could make out a wide, urban street, at night, lit by streetlights.

"I dinna like it there," P'wrll said. "Too many folks." His word for humans.

Mordractus watched the screen for long moments. The street was empty. "This is useful," Mordractus commented. He was never sure if sarcasm was lost on fairies and bogeymen. "You didn't edit?"

"We thought you'd want to see this as soon as you could," P'wrll said. *Another quality common to bogies,* Mordractus thought. *Always with the "we," as if to dilute any blame for anything that might go wrong.* They were mischievous, occasionally malevolent, but they dodged responsibility as efficiently as the laziest human.

Mordractus surrounded himself with both. Humans had their uses, but for some jobs, a bogie or another type of fairy or goblin was more effective. Sometimes he just had to laugh at the modern world's fascination with fairies, and the perception of them as innocent magical creatures fluttering gaily about the woods and fields.

A fairy would as soon rip a human's head off and have it for dinner as pose on the petals of a flower. People had forgotten that—forgotten so much about magic and the old ways.

But Mordractus hadn't. He'd lived it, for three centuries now.

Which is, he reflected, *part of the problem.*

A skilled sorceror could extend his life for a long

4

time. But no magician had ever lived as long as Mordractus already had—not even the great ones of old, not Merlin, not Gilles de Rais, not Agrippa. Mordractus had studied the works of the greats, had learned from each of them, and had, at last, surpassed them in knowledge and skill.

And yet, in spite of all his efforts, even he was tiring. He had tried everything to rejuvenate himself, to restore his strength, to ward off the effects of age. Spells and rituals that had worked in the past failed him now. And there was the big one, the Summoning, which sapped more of his life force than anything he'd ever attempted, at every stage.

Mordractus was dying, and there seemed to be nothing he could do to stop it.

Still, he didn't give up. He sent his followers far and wide, looking for anything he might have missed, any sign or sigil, any clue to a new treatment, an untested technique. Most of them came back empty-handed, unable to turn up anything he hadn't already tried.

But P'wrll and two humans, Currie and Hitch, had returned with this tape, which they claimed revealed something quite unexpected, and possibly helpful. They had gone to America; more specifically, to the city of Los Angeles, in the United States. What they found there was, they claimed, remarkable.

On the screen a man walked out of a doorway and

onto the sidewalk. At the curb he looked both ways, as if checking to see if he was observed, and then opened the door of a car and climbed in. He was tall, young, and handsome, with spiky dark hair and intense eyes that seemed to glare right into the camera. He wore a black leather overcoat over dark clothes.

"There 'e is," P'wrll said. "That's 'im now, gettin' in the car."

"Amazing," Mordractus said dryly. "A man gets in a car. Who'd have believed it?"

"There's more," P'wrll protested. "Just wait."

The tape cut then, and started again someplace else. A different street, still outdoors, still in the city. The same man filled the screen. This time he was closer to the camera, but he still didn't seem to see it. His attention was focused elsewhere.

And while Mordractus watched, the young man changed.

His forehead swelled, becoming thicker, almost plated. His eyes narrowed. His teeth grew and his lips pulled back in a grimace.

He was definitely a vampire.

The camera swung around, following him as he went past it.

Two men had a woman pressed up against a concrete wall. Probably this vampire had chosen her as his victim, and these men were interfering, Mordractus thought. The men were shadowed—it was possible they were vampires as well. Hunting together? Unusual, but stranger things had happened.

The young man—*young vampire,* Mordractus corrected himself—waded into the men. His fists flew, he lashed out with a mighty kick, and in a moment both men were running away at top speed. The vampire let them go.

Then he turned to the woman. Mordractus was expecting him to take her there, but he didn't. In fact, in the dim light, Mordractus could see that his face had taken on its human demeanor again. He looked at her with concern in his eyes as he helped her to her feet. He picked up a fallen purse and handed it to her, and then he escorted her to a nearby car.

She gave him a wave as she drove away.

"Is he a vampire or a Boy Scout?" Mordractus asked.

"That's just it," P'wrll replied. "According to the rumors, 'e's a vampire, but 'e does good things. 'E won't feed on folks. And 'e's got a soul."

"A soul?" Mordractus echoed.

" 'S'what they say," P'wrll said. "Immortal, sure, but wi' a soul."

"Indeed," Mordractus said, his mind already racing, considering the implications.

"There's more tape."

"Let it run," Mordractus told him. "Did you happen to get the vampire's name?"

"They call 'im Angel."

Angel.

Angelus? Could it be?

"Warm up the helicopter. And book some flights," Mordractus instructed. He watched the tape roll on, a new optimism suddenly filling him.

"We're going to California."

CHAPTER ONE

Los Angeles—now

"I could do this," Cordelia Chase said. She walked into Angel's office from his downstairs apartment, waving a glossy magazine in her hand. Angel glanced away from the TV. She seemed to be showing him a society section—dozens of small photos of L.A.'s social elite were flapping at him.

"I really could," she went on. "I mean, what are the qualifications? To be pretty? Look at me."

Angel did. Even wearing a casual tank top and track pants, the brunette was definitely pretty. Angel thought she had, even in the short time since graduating from high school back in Sunnydale and moving here to L.A., seemed to grow into herself more, becoming more elegant and lovely with each passing week.

"And I guess you have to be able to talk for hours about nothing in particular, but, hello. High school? If they'd scored on meaningless conversation, I wouldn't have that whole grade-point-average thing hanging over my head. And I mean that in the best possible way—meaningless conversations are so much more interesting, really, than the kind that are about deep psychological issues, aren't they?"

"News is on, Cordy," Doyle announced. A little more brusque than he usually was with her, which Angel figured meant that he was so distracted by the tube he had forgotten he was still hoping to date her someday. Angel thought he sometimes played the Irish brogue up more, too, as if hoping that the Irish side of him would camouflage the demon side. She didn't know yet that Doyle was half-demon, and Doyle hoped she never did.

"See, that's what I mean. What good ever comes from watching the news? I'm talking about more than a career choice here—becoming a trophy wife is more of a lifestyle choice, with the added bonus that then you don't really need a career."

"Right now," Doyle said, "the good that'll come from it is that I've got some money down on the Padres, and I'm waitin' to see if Tony Gwynn's gonna come through for me again. It's a sure thing, but I wanna see just how sure."

"Quiet a minute, both of you," Angel said. "I want to hear this." Cordelia and Doyle both shushed.

". . . another daring overnight bank robbery," the local news blow-dry said, "but this one resulted in the deaths of three innocent bystanders who happened to be on the street in the early hours of the morning, when the heavily armed robbers left the bank. A witness says the alleged robbers came out through the front door, surprising Los Angeles residents Ford Gilmore and Tomm Coker, and a third, unnamed minor. The bystanders were between the bank door and their getaway car, and when the alleged bank robbers left the building, they opened fire with automatic rifles, killing the three instantly. . . ."

"Listen to that," Doyle said. " 'Alleged robbers.' Like it ain't pretty clear when they come out of the bank carryin' stolen money, shootin' people, that they really are robbers."

"Kate told me about these guys," Angel said. "They tunnel into banks overnight, load up their bags from the vault, and then go out the front door into waiting cars. She was afraid things might escalate some day, and someone would get hurt."

"Looks like it has," Cordelia said. "Does Police Woman have any clues?"

"She said she thinks so, but wouldn't tell me what they were."

"Guess she don't want you goin' Batman on them," Doyle said.

"Something like that."

"Hey, that reminds me, man. Those guys jumped

you, a couple weeks back? I've been asking on the street, see if anyone knows anything. No dice so far."

"Well, thanks for trying, anyway," Angel said. "It's not a big deal."

He'd been out late—when one is a vampire, it beats being out early—and four thugs had come out of a car as he walked down the street, not far from his office/apartment. The car had pulled up at the curb, and the passenger door opened—letting someone out on the sidewalk, Angel assumed. No reason to think differently.

Until the guy spoke to him. "Hey, pal," he said. Angel glanced at him then. The man was dressed all in dark clothes, like Angel himself—black jeans, a dark long-sleeved tee, and a Dodgers cap pulled low on his brow.

"Hey," Angel replied, not even breaking his stride.

Then the back doors opened and two more guys came out of the rear seat, dressed similarly. Angel saw that they were carrying weapons—a black police-style billy club in one's hand, and a baseball bat in the other's. He looked back toward the first guy, and saw a knife in his fist now.

"What's going on?" Angel asked.

None of the men said anything. They spread out, surrounding Angel on the sidewalk. Angel heard another car door open—the driver, he figured, but he didn't lift his gaze from the guys nearest him.

"I think maybe you've got the wrong man," Angel said.

Still no response.

The guy with the baseball bat swung it lazily through the air in Angel's direction. It wasn't a threat, so Angel ignored it. Then the billy club came whipping toward him, fast and hard. Angel dodged the blow, felt it whistle past him.

Knife guy lunged at him then. Angel caught the man's wrist, tucked it up under his own arm, against his ribs, and brought his arm in fast.

There was a snapping sound, and the guy let out a scream. The knife clattered to the walk.

And the baseball bat slammed into his kidney from behind.

He let go of the man with the broken wrist, turned to the bat wielder.

"There's still time for you to get out of this without getting hurt," Angel said.

"Don't think that'll be a problem," said the fourth man, the driver. Angel saw him now. He was huge, six-five easy, and well over two hundred and fifty pounds. A big gut spilled out of his black T-shirt and over his belt buckle. Heavy motorcycle boots peeked from beneath his jeans. He had long dark hair, streaked with gray, and a bushy beard.

In one massive hand he held a ball-peen hammer.

He advanced on Angel. Angel figured this one was the most dangerous, but couldn't turn his attention from the others, either. A bat and a billy club were still in play. He decided that a quick finish to this whole encounter would be for the best.

When the billy club came swinging at him again, he caught it in the palm of his hand. He closed his fist around it and yanked. The wielder lurched toward him, and Angel met him with a sudden kick to the chest. The guy dropped back, winded. With the same motion, Angel spun, dropping beneath the arc of the swinging bat. He came up under the bat guy's hands, driving the billy club into the man's throat. The man dropped the bat and fell to the ground, clutching at his neck.

Now it was just the big guy with the hammer. He looked at Angel with a half-smile on his face, as if looking forward to the matchup with delighted anticipation.

Angel stood in a partial crouch, billy club still in his grip. He watched the hammer guy's eyes, ready for any signal that he was ready to charge.

Instead, he surprised Angel. "Okay," he said. "You win." The other guys piled back into the car, and the driver, gaze locked with Angel's the whole way, went back to the driver's door. He got in, and they drove away.

Angel made no attempt to follow, figuring they were just muggers who had mistaken him for an easy target. They were human, that much was certain. And that fact made it not overly worrisome.

He'd practically forgotten the incident by now, but was strangely touched that Doyle hadn't.

Sometimes Doyle acts like the only thing in the world he cares about is himself, Angel thought, *but then he surprises you with unexpected depth.*

Since moving from Sunnydale—and away from Buffy—Angel had found that Doyle had proven to be a big help in his activities. So, oddly, had Cordy, pushing him to "legitimize" his quest to help those in need, in the form of a business that, once in a great while, paid real money.

Angel had been a vampire for a long while. But for the last hundred years or so, he'd been a vampire with a soul, thanks to a Gypsy curse. Having a soul meant having a conscience, and having a conscience was naturally followed by feelings of incredible guilt for the many lives he'd taken during his vampiric days. Now he refused to feed on humans, restricting himself to pig's blood from a butcher shop.

But no longer killing humans wasn't good enough. He had many deaths for which to atone. He remained immortal, which was a good thing, because he figured it would take him that long to make up for all the misery he'd caused. And, if he wanted to get right down to it, he was still trying to make up for not having been such a good guy before he became a vampire.

It took, he thought, Buffy to help him see that. She allowed him to understand that a person got to choose between being good, and being something else. And to value the choice for good.

Unfortunately, some choices were harder to make than others. Such as Buffy. Being with her, and then leaving her behind. Moving to Los Angeles. But they had to be made, and he made them and tried not to look back.

Anyway, his apartment was cool, and had access to underground tunnels, which came in handy for moving about in the daytime. And it came with the upstairs office space, which Angel didn't want to let go to waste. So the detective business seemed like a reasonable compromise.

"Bank robberies, killings, general meanness, that's all the news is ever about," Cordelia said, sinking into Angel's dark blue couch, next to Doyle. "If there's so much bad stuff happening in L.A., what I want to know is, why aren't we profiting from it? I mean, how come business has been so slow lately? You'd think some of these people in trouble would come to Angel Investigations to get help, right?" She looked hard at Doyle, who turned away from the screen when he felt her gaze on him.

"Maybe it's you," she went on. "Maybe that vision radar of yours is out of whack or something. Have you had it tuned up lately?"

"I don't need to—"

"Because if you're supposed to be having visions

of people who need help, you're falling way behind," she interrupted.

"The Powers That Be don't exactly explain how they work to the likes of me," Doyle said. "All I know is I get 'em when I get 'em, and if I don't get 'em, then I don't get the excruciatin' headaches that go along with 'em, and that's just fine with me."

"Well, maybe we should think about renting a billboard or something. Or those benches at bus stops. Because if we're relying on your visions to grow a business, and you're not having visions, then we're in trouble."

"Maybe that'll be my next vision," Doyle said. "Angel Investigations in fiscal crisis. But what do you care, Cordy? You'll be on the arm of some ninety-year-old discount store billionaire, escortin' him from the nursing home to the opening of a new location in Wichita Falls."

"Eew," Cordelia replied. "Old guys. I hadn't thought of that. I can get a young, handsome, successful rich husband."

"It seems like the young, handsome, successful ones are seldom in need of trophy wives," Angel pointed out.

"You could be right," Cordelia said, stifling a yawn. "Maybe there's a flaw in my plan after all. This'll require some more thought." With a flutter of pages she tossed the magazine onto a table. "It's too late to think tonight. Try to remind me to do it sometime tomorrow, okay?"

"Quiet," Doyle snapped. "Sports're on."

"I don't know why I'm so sleepy," Cordelia continued. "It isn't that late. Remember when I could stay up until all hours and still look beautiful in school the next day? Well, of course you don't, Doyle, you didn't know us then. And I guess staying up late is not an especially impressive skill, to a vampire. So never mind."

"Cord . . ."

"Okay, quieting here."

". . . Padres were swamped," the sportcaster announced, "twenty to seven by the Kansas City . . ."

"Sorry, Doyle," Cordelia said.

"No big," Doyle replied. He looked crestfallen. "Just, if the phone rings, I ain't here, all right?"

"You gave our phone number?" Angel asked.

"Hey, these guys aren't the kind I want callin' me at home, if you know what I mean."

"Got it," Angel said. *Sometimes he's a help,* he told himself. *Other times I have to remind myself why I let him stick around.*

Then the sports was over and a wrap-up of international news came on. Heartbreak, greed, danger, and violence weren't confined to the L.A. city limits, and Angel found himself wishing he could do more, be more places at once. He had to remind himself that he was only one vampire, and he did what he could.

Sometimes that was all one could ask.

CHAPTER TWO

The Beverly Mortuary was on Pico, not really even in Beverly Hills but not far enough outside to matter. It was well known in the business, and it was run by professionals who were known to be caring, compassionate, and discreet. There were less expensive funeral homes, but when the price didn't matter, it was hard to do better than the establishment run by Mr. Moy and Mr. Carani. Those two men, both lean, white-haired, and solemn of demeanor, took good care of their clientele—even the ones who could walk out the door after the service instead of being carried.

Today's service was very private. Family only, and not much of that. It was held in the Green Room because that was the smallest, most intimate setting they had. Everything was green—wallpaper with the subtlest floral print, carpeting, the cushions on the four pews. But even there, it was obvious that there were only a tiny handful of mourners.

And usually the green was broken up by sprays of flowers. Not this one. There was a single bouquet that the mother had brought in her hands. It rested now in a vase on a table at the head of the casket.

During the brief ceremony, Mr. Carani, watching from the back of the room, had noticed that the father seemed almost distracted. His grief was real, Mr. Carani was sure. But he kept glancing about the small room as if to remind himself of where he was. And he fiddled with something, almost incessantly. The one time Mr. Carani got a good like at it, it looked like a small rectangle of paper. A business card, perhaps. Not the Beverly Mortuary's, which had a tasteful band of embossed gold around its perimeter.

But a business card, just the same.

"Your cappuccino, Mr. Willits," Amber said. She put a ceramic mug down on the top of his vast expanse of desk. "Double shot, extra hot."

"Thanks," he muttered without really looking at Amber. Her title was administrative assistant. To Jack Willits, that meant she got coffee when she was told to, and did any other duties that occurred to him during the day. His wife had complained that he didn't treat her with respect, so he tried to remember to say "please" and "thank you." Even though, according to him, she was just doing what she was paid for.

"Can I get you anything else?" she asked.

"I need a copy of that script," he said. "The one by that Hart woman, you know. What's it called?"

"*Taken by the Wind?*"

"That's it. And then get me Peter Delano on the phone."

"The script is right here in your in-basket," Amber pointed out. "I'll get Mr. Delano right away."

She walked out of his office and to her own desk, sat down, and touched a key on her computer. The screen came to life, and she pulled Peter Delano's number from her database. She dialed the number, and Roxanne, Peter's admin assistant, answered.

"Hi, Rox," she said. "Jack wants Peter."

"He on the line?" Roxanne asked.

"Not yet. When I have Peter."

"I think it's Jack's turn to get on first," Roxanne countered. "Didn't Pete go first last time?"

"Maybe, but, Rox—Jack runs a studio."

"Pete runs IFM." Internationally Famous Management. Dumb name, powerful agency. With all the bad blood and in-fighting between the old, established agencies over the past few years, maybe the most powerful agency.

"I know, but—"

"Jack first."

"He'll hate it. He may not even take the call."

21

"He'll take it."

Jack Willits had the power to give work to actors, producers, directors, and writers. He could green-light any movie he wanted, for any amount of money up to sixty million dollars, without taking it to the multinational corporation that really owned Monument Pictures.

But Peter Delano controlled the actors and directors that Jack needed, if he wanted to have a hit.

And Jack wanted, Amber knew, to have a hit. Needed to.

She buzzed his desk. "Mr. Willits, please hold for Mr. Delano," she said.

He held.

The Monument Pictures lot was located in Burbank, down the hill from Universal but not as far down as Warner Bros. They had a couple of square miles of land, all tucked away behind high walls, with access through seven guarded gates. Inside those gates were soundstages, a big back lot, production offices, a mill, crafts shops, a commissary, and all the assorted offices and warehouses and incidental space it took to create movie magic.

Above it all, in the tower of the Gleason Building, was Jack Willits's office. Jack liked his office. It was big and spacious. The bleached hardwood floor was partially covered by an Oriental rug. The thick adobe walls were whitewashed and glowed in the sun that came through nine-foot-tall double glass doors open-ing onto his private balcony. Massive wooden beams ran up the walls at wide intervals and were echoed in the support beams that crossed the high ceiling.

Jack's desk was really a huge, flat table, the kind that would have seated a dozen easily, and sixteen in a pinch. It was also made of bleached wood. There was always a laptop computer on it, and a few stacks of scripts and other papers, but there was also room for him to spread out papers or cards or the trades when he wanted to. His chair was an upscale ergonomic desk chair in butter-soft black leather. Against one wall was a comfortable soft couch, and before that, three big overstuffed chairs and a low wooden coffee table. Bookshelves lined another wall. In one corner was a state-of-the-art sound and video system with a plasma-screen monitor.

He spent most of his waking hours in this room, and he wanted it to be comfortable. It was.

He didn't want to lose it.

There was every danger that he might.

"Jack?"

"Peter."

"What's shaking?"

"You know, same. You?"

"Never better, my friend."

"Glad to hear it." *I hope you go down in flames, "friend,"* Jack thought. *But not as long as you can do something for me.*

"Talk to Geffen lately?" Peter asked.

"Tennis, last week. He won."

"He wins at golf, too."

Jack chuckled.

"So," Peter said. "You called me."

"Just figured it had been too long, Pete. Wanted to shoot the breeze, you know."

"Sure, of course."

"What've you got going on?"

A slight pause. "You know how it is. Warren's in pre, Julia's in post. Kevin's on location somewhere. You got any idea how much it costs to feed horses? And Jimmy's looking for a big project that has nothing to do with boats or water."

"Can't blame him there."

"So what about you? Anything we can do together?"

"I'd love to. I've got a couple of powerhouse scripts here. I've got guys lined up around the block waiting to get at them, but I could push someone to the front of the line if you had anybody interesting."

It was the same old dance. If Jack looked like he needed a hot director or a big-name actor, he'd never get them. If he didn't need them, they'd fall all over themselves to work with him.

But Jack needed them, and bad. Monument Pictures was hemorrhaging money. The studio hadn't had a real hit, a significant earner, in a couple of years. But that didn't mean that things ground to a halt. Pictures greenlit two years ago were still in production. The studio had released forty movies the year before, and would release thirty-seven this year. Of those, at least twenty would lose money. The others might break even. There were one or two that had a chance of earning.

Jack needed a hit. His corporate masters had made it abundantly clear that if he didn't deliver a hit within the next twelve months, he'd be looking for a new job. Twelve months, in terms of producing motion pictures, was not a lot of time, and he knew that nothing in the works was going to be satisfactory to them. Therefore, he had to bring something together fast. He had to have a star who could open a picture, and he needed a script that would give it legs.

Peter Delano could deliver both of those items.

If only he could just ask.

"Send me something," Peter said. "I'd love to take a look. I'm looking for a script for Rob to direct, for one thing."

"I think I have just the thing. It'll be on your desk tomorrow."

"Looking forward to it," Peter said.

"What's Blake up to?" Jack asked. Blake Alten could open a picture and keep it open. He was, at last count, the biggest action star in the world. His name on a movie was a guarantee of a hundred million in ticket sales, minimum. He was one of those people that Jack couldn't come right out and ask for.

"He's considering options," Peter said. "You know, he's always got a pile of great scripts in front of him. We'll be picking something soon. Why, you got something?"

"I think of anything, I'll send it over," Jack said. "Talk to you soon, okay?"

"You got it," Peter said. He hung up first.

But at least he'd taken the call, Jack reflected. There was a rule in Hollywood, and he was dangerously close to becoming personally impacted by it. If you called someone three times and they didn't call you back, they were a jerk. If you called four times, you were the jerk.

It was a tightrope walk.

And the ground was a long way down there, with no net.

Jack Willits didn't want to take that fall.

Los Angeles was an amazing place.

Mordractus had not left Ireland in more than a hundred years. He kept in touch with the world through television and magazines and movies and the Internet. But to actually drive down the wide boulevards in a rented Rolls-Royce convertible with the top down; to see palm trees reaching into the sky like grasping hands at the ends of long skinny arms; to pass the HOLLYWOOD sign in the hills overlooking the city, and the stacked disks of the Capitol Records building, and the famous names of Sunset and Santa Monica and Doheny and Vine . . . *it's all a remarkable experience,* he thought. He was sorry he hadn't done it earlier.

Even though he rarely left the castle, he considered himself a fairly modern man. While he had once worn robes of silk, now he was more comfortable lounging about the drafty castle in a heavy sweater and a pair of jeans. He mail-ordered from a variety of sources, and his waist size hadn't changed in more than a hundred and fifty years.

For L.A. he'd left the heavy sweaters behind. He wore a soft cotton polo shirt, dark linen slacks, a lightweight jacket of white nubby silk, and deck shoes with no socks. He'd pulled his longish white hair back into a ponytail. He figured that he looked about sixty, which was upsetting because until he'd begun this whole business with the Summoning, he had been stalled at a healthy thirty-five, in physical appearance. The only part of him that hadn't seemed to age were his eyes, which, he'd once been told, looked as if they'd been plucked from clear blue sky.

But that compliment hadn't earned his victim even a second's hestitation.

The sun on his forehead felt glorious.

"I should have done this years ago," Mordractus said. He was walking up Beverly Drive with David Currie, one of the humans who'd accompanied P'wrll here in the first place. Andrew Hitch, his partner, had stayed with the car. P'wrll was back at a rented house in the Hollywood Hills, with the rest of the staff he'd brought over. Since arriving in the city three weeks before, he'd gotten into the routine of taking an afternoon stroll through one of the neighborhoods. Yesterday it had been Brentwood, the day before that, Santa Monica's Third Street Promenade. Today, Beverly Hills.

"It's right nice, isn't it?" Currie said. He was English, not Irish, but loyal and resourceful, so Mordractus kept him around. Anyway, his unruly hair was red enough, and his cheeks rosy enough that he could almost pass for Irish. Mordractus had a general distrust of the English, and it was more common for him to kill them than hire them, if they happened to cross his path.

They won't be a problem for much longer, though, he thought. *No one will. Forget about giving Ireland back to the Irish . . . they can just give it to me.*

But time enough for that later. For today he was just enjoying the sunshine and the beautiful girls on the streets, actresses or would-bes, he assumed. Everyone was well dressed, everyone seemed to be wealthy and footloose.

Ireland had never been like this, in his memory. Certainly not during the years that he had spent time in the company of humans, before retreating to the privacy of his island sanctuary to commune with more powerful beings.

A pair of shoes in a shop window caught his attention. They glowed with the sheen of fine leather, and looked as if they'd be supremely comfortable.

"In here a moment," Mordractus said to Currie. "I've a mind to try those shoes on."

"Right," Currie agreed.

They stepped into the shade of the shop. It was cool inside, air-conditioned, as Mordractus had learned most of Los Angeles seemed to be. The shop was empty except for a single salesclerk behind a broad counter, talking on a cordless telephone. Mordractus spent a few moments looking at the shoes on display, all very pricey and seemingly of high quality, and located a pair of the ones that caught his eye in the window. He picked them up and waved them at the clerk.

"Excuse me," Mordractus said, when the clerk gave no indication that he was finishing his call.

The clerk—a young man, barely out of his teens, in a snug suit with very narrow legs and a four-button jacket, looked at Mordractus through yellow-tinted glasses. He gestured toward the telephone.

"I can see that you're on the phone, young man," Mordractus said. "However, I'm right here in your shop, with cash in my pocket, and I'd like to try these shoes in my size."

The clerk gave a loud sigh. "Customer," he said into the phone. "So anyway, on Saturday night Gus said he never wanted to see her again, and by Sunday he was knocking at her door, you know, carrying flowers and candy and going on and on. . . ."

"Excuse me," Mordractus said again.

This time the clerk turned away from him, showing his back. ". . . and she opened the door, can you believe it, and welcomed him in with open arms. But then Sunday night . . ."

Mordractus put the shoes back down.

"Let's go," he said.

As Currie opened the door, Mordractus heard the clerk call from the counter, "Have a nice day."

"And you, as well," Mordractus said quietly. "It'll be your last."

He stopped on the sidewalk outside the store. The late summer sun was hot after the chill inside, but he didn't feel it. He closed his eyes, and concentrated for a moment. He muttered something unintelligible, even to Currie, who stood right beside him. As he spoke, he traced a pattern in the air with the index finger of his right hand.

A moment later he was finished.

Beads of sweat had appeared on his brow, and he wiped them away with a quivering hand. That had taken a lot out of him—more than he anticipated. *Growing weaker, then,* he thought. *Must get this business wrapped up soon.*

Inside the shop the clerk droned on into the phone, barely aware of a headache that was just beginning to expand behind his eyes.

30

By closing time it would blossom into a migraine. By midnight he'd be dead.

Walking slowly back to the car, leaning on Currie's arm for support, Mordractus chuckled to himself.

Maybe he'd come back tomorrow and see if the *new* clerk would be willing to find his size.

CHAPTER THREE

Late that night Mordractus saw Angel for himself.

His minions had staked out the vampire's place of business. *Angel Investigations*. Mordractus stifled a chuckle. *If this is indeed the Angelus of old*, he thought, *his clients had better count their rings after shaking hands on a deal*.

Mordractus sat in the back of a rented van with tinted windows. Hitch and Currie had taken it to a construction site and thrown dirt at it to make it dingy-looking enough that it would not stand out in Angel's neighborhood. Now it was parked down the street from the doorway that Angel and his friends had been seen using on occasion.

There was also a back door, accessed from the carport area where the vampire parked his black convertible. But there must have been another entrance as well, Hitch had explained, because sometimes he seemed to come and go without using the front door. Try as they might, they had not been able to find any other way in.

It was well past dark now. Mordractus had been driven back to the house in the Hollywood Hills, where he'd taken a long, hard nap for several hours. Angel wouldn't come out in the daylight, Hitch had assured him. Of course, Mordractus knew that anyway. Suicide, for a vampire to come out during the day. Especially someplace like Los Angeles. Back home one could get away with it for short periods because the fog often blocked enough of the sun's rays. If there was ever fog in Southern California, though, Mordractus had yet to see it.

They'd been waiting outside the office for five hours. It was somewhere past two in the morning. Mordractus was stiff from sitting in the van. What good is a vampire who won't go outside? he wondered. Doesn't he have to feed?

"He's never coming out," Hitch said, as if reading Mordractus's mind. Which was impossible, of course—Mordractus made a point of not hiring people with such talents.

"Then we'll draw him out," Mordractus said after some deliberation. For the second time that day he shut his eyes and began to mutter an almost silent incantation, describing patterns in the air with his hands.

After a moment of this he opened his eyes again

and peered at a window facing into Angel's office. A vague shape appeared nearby, like a puff of greenish smoke. It drifted toward the window. When it reached the window, there was a soft tapping noise that Mordractus could barely hear from inside the van. When they were over, the puff vanished.

Mordractus sat back in his seat, exhausted from the effort.

And after a moment a blind over the window pulled back and a face appeared inside. Someone stood looking out, a man with black hair. He looked up and down the street, as if trying to find whoever had knocked. He said something Mordractus couldn't hear.

But it was not Angel.

The man started to walk away, and then the blinds fluttered again and another man came into view. A taller man, lean and powerful-looking. This one opened the window, sticking his head out. He also looked both ways.

"It *is* him," Mordractus whispered. "Angelus. Awfully long way from the Auld Sod, aren't ye, boy?"

Angelus, he thought. *Scourge of Europe. Here in the United States, after all these years, and with a soul.*

Amazing.

Angel stood in the window. No one on the street. A few cars parked up and down the block, but nothing unusual. Doyle had answered the strange tapping on the window, but after glancing outside and seeing nothing, he'd given up, shaking his head.

Then something struck Angel, and he sniffed the air.

The faintest whiff of ozone hung there, like the aftermath of lightning.

Or magic.

He started to step farther out when he heard a bloodcurdling scream from inside.

He spun, shoving the door closed behind him.

Doyle was on the floor, hands clasped to the sides of his head. He writhed in pain.

Cordelia watched, wide-eyed. She and Doyle had been playing Hearts, just a few minutes before. She'd been stalling about heading back to her apartment, and the "one more hand" thing had gone on for a couple of hours now.

Another vision.

"It's about time," Cordelia said.

Doyle moaned. "A little sympathy please, Cord," he said. "You have no idea. . . ."

"So it hurts your pointy little head," she said. "If there's a paycheck at the end of it, I think it's worth it, don't you? Come to think of it, never mind— what you think doesn't enter into it. You're not exactly an impartial observer here."

"Give him a break, Cordy," Angel said. He watched Doyle roll back and forth on the floor. "That looks like it really hurts."

Cordelia sighed. "I suppose."

With a final groan Doyle relaxed his death grip on his own head.

"Ohhh," he moaned. "A bad one, that was." He pushed himself to his knees, and Angel helped him to his feet, steadied him.

"What was it?" he asked.

"Girl," Doyle said. "Very pretty, but young."

"Oh, and you didn't even have to leave home to stalk her," Cordelia said. "Lucky you."

"Cordy," Angel warned.

She mimicked pulling a zipper across her lips.

"She's in trouble, Angel," Doyle went on. "Couldn't tell what, for sure."

"Did you get a name, a location?"

"She's at a club. There was loud music, dance music. It was horrible—everything was pink, and there's something—sugar, like, on the walls. Even the light fixtures are shaped like big sugar cubes, frosted-like."

"Sugar Town," Cordelia offered. "It's the hottest after-hours club this month. So hot I've even been there. By next month it'll be completely over—does this girl know what she's doing, going to a place on the way out? No wonder she's in trouble."

"Where is it?" Angel asked her.

"Hollywood," Cordelia replied. "One of those side streets, just off Sunset."

"I'll find it," Angel said. He poured Doyle a cup of

water from the big cooler standing against the wall. "What about the girl, Doyle. What can you tell me?"

"Like I said, young," Doyle said, his face ashen. He took a sip of the water, then a gulp. "Thanks. She's sixteen, maybe, or seventeen. Red hair, piled up on her head. A grown-up's hairstyle and makeup, but a kid's face underneath it all. She's wearing green, I think, a dark forest green maybe. Clear skin, blue eyes. Beautiful girl."

"I'll find her," Angel said.

One never knew about the traffic in Los Angeles, day or night, but fortunately it was pretty light and Angel made it to Hollywood in about twenty minutes. There were lots of cars on Sunset, of course— there always were. And parking was tight. But he found Sugar Town, on a side street a couple of blocks off Sunset, up the hill. He tucked his car into an alley, illegally. He ran inside the door, threw a bill at the bouncer.

Doyle had been right. The place was hideous. It looked like something that had been decorated in the 1960s by the person who designed Barbie's Dream House. Angel had never seen so many shades of pink, especially all in the same place. The only relief from the pink—and "relief" was used in the loosest possible sense—were the various oranges and light purples that covered some of the Naugahyde seating areas. Fortunately, the lights weren't bright—if they had been, he wasn't sure he'd have been able to take it.

But they were, as Doyle had described, shaped like sugar cubes. Angel shook his head, but the image didn't go away.

Amazingly, it was crowded, even after two-thirty. Cordy had been right about that—the place seemed to be enjoying some heat. People were dancing on a packed dance floor, and others sat at tables sipping drinks as colorful as the decor—nonalcoholic, this time of night. Alcohol couldn't be served after two. Many of the glasses were decorated with umbrellas. The crowd was mostly young trendoids, wearing dark clothing that contrasted with the bright interior. Lots of goatees, lots of shaved heads, lots of thick-framed glasses. Angel didn't see anyone who fit Doyle's description—but then here, just inside the door, there were lots of people he couldn't see. Taking the mental equivalent of a deep breath, he pushed his way deeper into the club.

The thrumming techno music pounded him and the colors and lights assaulted his eyes. But through it all, he moved, looking at every face, especially if he caught a glimpse of red hair. He bumped into someone with practically every step, and said "excuse me" more times than probably in the last four months combined. He circumnavigated the whole club, twice.

She just isn't here, he thought. *Doyle missed something. Or she was here, and I missed her.*

He turned to look for the door.

And saw her.

As Doyle had said, she had a thick mass of orange hair worn up on her head, and a tight dress of a shimmering, rich dark green fabric. She was on her way out the front door. Two men were gripping her arms, hard enough to hurt, to make sure she went.

"Hey!" Angel said. He started to run for the door. But there were too many people—he had to thread his way through them, the "excuse me" bit forgotten now. He spilled someone's drink and was called an obscene name.

He didn't look back. The girl was outside now, completely out of sight. *If there's a car waiting out there,* Angel thought, *she's gone.*

And I will have been useless.

While the club had seemed crowded before, now it seemed positively jammed—with every step, there was someone in Angel's path.

If he'd arrived and not been able to find her, he might have been able to tell himself that they'd misinterpreted Doyle's vision somehow, that there wasn't really a girl needing help here tonight. The fact that she was really in the club—not to mention being strong-armed toward the door by two body-builder types twice her size—meant that Doyle's vision, as usual, had been accurate.

He had to find her.

Finally he made it through the crowd and shoved his way through the door. The street seemed oddly silent after the raucous din inside. Nothing moved, except the almost silent lights of cars whishing by on Sunset, two blocks away.

Angel was still. Instead of rushing in the wrong direction, he centered himself, listening.

Then he heard it. Voices. He couldn't see the source, and they weren't on the street. So they must have been around the corner between here and Sunset, or in an alley, or in the parking lot across the street on the corner of the next block. There was a big illuminated sign that said U-PARK $5.00 in front of it, but otherwise the lot was dark.

". . . don't care if you like us or not, we have a job to do, and it don't help when you give us the slip like that," a man's voice was saying.

"We don't like you all that much, either, you want to know the truth," a second voice said. Also male.

"I don't care," a third voice responded. This one was younger, and female. Petulant. *Has to be the redhead,* Angel thought. *Sounds like a scared kid.*

Angel headed toward the voices, at a sprint.

". . . time someone taught you a lesson . . ." the first voice was saying.

He darted into the parking lot. It was full of cars, parked in numbered slots. A tall black Jeep Cherokee stood at the back, and there was motion on the other side that he could barely see through

its tinted windows. He saw a blur, and heard the
smack of a hand on flesh.

"Hey!" the girl shouted. "My dad's gonna—"

"You'd have us fired anyway," one of the men
scoffed.

Angel came around the front of the Jeep.

"And you'd deserve to be."

Both men whirled at the sound of his voice.
"Who—?"

One of them had stopped in mid-swing, winding up
to take another shot at the girl. She was leaning against
the Cherokee, blood trickling from her mouth, her
cheek already reddening from the blow. Probably just
a slap, Angel figured. But still, these guys were in their
late twenties, and strong. She was seventeen or eighteen, from the looks of her. As Doyle had intimated,
she looked like a kid playing dress-up, with sophisticated clothes, hair, and makeup that couldn't disguise
the youthfulness of her face or the terror in her eyes.

"What's going on here?" Angel asked.

"These guys are hitting me," the girl said quickly.
"They're supposed to be guarding me, but instead
they're beating me up."

"One light slap," the first guy insisted. He was
dressed in a black silk long-sleeved shirt and blue
jeans, with expensive running shoes on his feet. His
head was shaved close. His partner looked about the
same, but his shirt was Hawaiian and multicolored,
and his hair was longer, straight, and surfer-blond.

The second one raised his hands in Angel's direction. "No problem here, dude. We're in charge of the girl, we're taking her home. We're on the job here."

"Please don't leave me with them," the girl sobbed.

"I don't think so, *dude*," Angel said.

"Man," the first guy protested, "you don't know what we're dealin' with, here. Chick puts us through hell, tryin' to keep up with her. She was in a place six blocks away, said she was going to the women's room. We're just lucky the bouncer saw her slippin' out the door, told us."

"So you caught up with her, figured you'd just knock her around a little bit," Angel said. "The fact that she's just a kid and you're professional muscle doesn't enter into the equation?"

"Fact is, dude, it just ain't any of your business," the surfer hissed. "You try to make it yours, you'll regret it."

Angel knew what was coming. There was a moment that this could all have blown over, without violence. That moment had passed, though, and now there was only one way this could go. He saw it in the surfer's eyes, which had narrowed to slits, and in his stance, coiled and tense. "You could very well be right," Angel said. "I've done foolish things before. Guess I'm not finished doing them."

At least one of them hit a teenaged girl, he remembered. *That'll make it easier.*

He let the surfer make the first move. The guy

closed fast, driving multiple short, sharp punches at Angel's midsection. Angel took them, trying to get a sense of the surfer's strength and skill.

He was strong, and he was good. His punches avoided the ribs, squarely aimed at Angel's solar plexus. Any mortal man would have had the wind knocked out of him.

After taking a few, Angel caught the surfer's fist in his hand, tugged the guy right up to his face. The surfer's eyes widened in surprise at Angel's strength. Angel squeezed until he could feel some of the small bones of the hand break.

"Don't ever go near her again," Angel whispered. "If you do, I'll hear about it. And you'll be the one with regrets."

He let go of surfer dude, who stepped back, cradling his hand and shaking his head. There were tears in his eyes, from the pain. Angel was briefly sorry he'd taken it so far, but it seemed to work. The fight was gone from the surfer, and his partner didn't look willing to take up where he had left off.

"D-dude." There was a hitch in the surfer's voice. "He broke my freakin' hand, dude."

The surfer's friend backed away from Angel. "You want her, man, you got her," he said. "She's all yours. Jeep's mine, though."

"That true?" Angel asked the girl.

She nodded her head, wiping tears off one cheek with her right hand.

"Take it," Angel ordered. "And get out of my sight."

The two men piled into it. The bald one got behind the wheel, cranked it up, and pulled out of the lot. The last Angel saw of them was their taillights turning onto Sunset.

"You okay?" Angel asked.

She sniffed. "I guess so." Her eyes began to fill again, and her head snapped around at the sound of a car engine on the street. "Please don't leave me here," she pleaded, clutching at Angel's arm. "What if they come back?"

"Don't worry," he assured her. "Want to tell me what that was all about?"

She looked very young in the faint light from the U-PARK sign. Her eyes were wide, her round cheeks glistening from the tears. Doyle had called her pretty, and he was right. *In a few years*, Angel found himself thinking, *she'll be a knockout.*

And, this being Los Angeles, she'll be very skilled in using her looks to get what she wants.

"Like Dave said, they were supposed to be watching me. Daddy calls them bodyguards, but they're more like chaperones or baby-sitters. It's not like I'm in any danger or anything, he just wants to make sure I don't do anything he doesn't want me to do."

"How old are you?"

"Twenty-one," she said. She seemed to be relaxing now, getting a handle on her terror.

At least enough to lie.

Angel just looked at her. *Right,* he thought, *and I'm only a hundred and ten.*

"I have ID."

"I'm sure you do. And I'm sure it's a great fake."

"Nineteen," she offered. Angel looked at her some more. "Well, almost eighteen. In November."

"Which makes you seventeen now. It's almost three in the morning. Your father seems pretty permissive as it is."

"He knows I'm not going to stay home on a Saturday night, so he figures he can sic the watchdogs on me to keep me from having any real fun."

"I don't blame him a bit."

"Gee, thanks. And I thought you were on my side."

"I'm not on anybody's side here," Angel elaborated. "I just don't think grown men should slap around young ladies."

"Well, there's something we can agree on," she said. She seemed to be gaining in confidence as they spoke—she carried herself now with the air of someone older than she really was, maybe even older than she liked to pose as being. "They were mad that I made them earn their pay," she went on. "And I guess they figured, after I gave them the slip, that they'd get fired as soon as Daddy found out anyway, so they had nothing to lose by taking their aggressions out on me."

45

"Well, they're gone now, so I guess I'll deliver you back to Daddy. I don't think you should be out here alone, not at your age. What's your name?"

"Karinna," she said. She smiled politely and stuck out a small-fingered hand, like a toddler learning manners. Angel shook it. "Karinna Willits."

"Pleased to meet you, Karinna Willits. I'm Angel."

"Angel," she repeated. "How very apropos. That means 'fitting.' "

"I know what it means," he said. "Let's go. Unless it's been towed, my car's in the alley."

"Oooh," Karinna said. "You live dangerously."

CHAPTER FOUR

"So what's he like, your dad?"

They were in Angel's car, heading toward Bel Air. The top was down and cool night air rushed into the car, and Karinna was kind of huddling against her door, staying as far away from Angel, and as protected from the wind, as she could manage.

"I don't know, he's a dad, you know. Likes to make rules, likes to set limits. Home by midnight, no boys with piercings, don't make the school have to call home more than twice a year, stuff like that."

"Home by midnight?" Angel repeated. "Not tonight."

"Yeah, well that one kind of fell by the wayside a long time ago."

"The boys with piercings, that seems like a good one to stick with. At least for now."

"He used to include tattoos in that, until Mom made him get one."

"Your father has a tattoo?"

Karinna smiled. "It's cool. It's a rose with a thorny stem, and one of the thorns looks like it's sticking into his arm, and there's a drop of blood where it stabbed him. It's on his bicep. I'm trying to get him to pierce his eyebrow, but he won't even talk about it."

"Imagine my surprise," Angel said. "He sounds like an okay guy."

"I guess he is. Like I said, for a dad and all. He's not like my friend Jasmine's dad, Albert. We all call him Albert, and he lets us hang out in his basement, watch videos, kind of do whatever we want, you know? He and Shyla, that's Jasmine's stepmom, they're like the really cool parents everybody else wishes they had."

"I know I'm going to sound really old saying this," Angel began. "But I think it's true. As you grow up, you'll realize that parents who care enough about you to set some limits and let you know their expectations are probably the best kind to have."

"You're right."

"I am?"

"You do sound old. Are you?"

It was Angel's turn to smile. "You wouldn't believe me if I told you."

He slowed to turn into the guarded entrance to

Bel Air, one of the wealthiest communities in one of the wealthiest regions of one of the wealthiest countries on Earth. There was probably more money within Bel Air's walls than there was, total, in half the countries on the planet, he guessed. Angel had never had occasion to go behind the walls that surrounded this enclave of privilege, and he anticipated some problem with the guard.

But the uniformed man simply stepped out of his little guardhouse, tossed Karinna a smile and a smart salute, and said, "Morning, Ms. Willits."

As if it wasn't almost four o'clock in the morning and she wasn't seventeen and arriving in a stranger's car, Angel thought. *Who is this girl?*

"Hi, George," she said to him. As Angel drove by with a small nod of his own, Karinna said, "That's George."

"Figured that out from the clue," Angel said. "That's what we private detectives do. We get clues, and from those we deduce the answers to the really tough mysteries like that one."

"You're kind of a smart-ass, aren't you?" Karinna asked.

Angel looked pensive, or tried to. "No, I don't think anyone's ever called me that before."

She laughed, for the first time, and Angel liked the sound of it. She sounded her own age, when she laughed. Like she had forgotten she was trying to appear older.

Past the gate, Karinna directed Angel up a broad avenue that swept past magnificent estates, mostly hidden from the road by trees and vast lawns and, frequently, walls and fences of their own, as if the ones that protected everyone else weren't sufficient shelter.

"What does your family do?" Angel asked.

"Mom doesn't have, like, a job, but she's on the boards of like eighteen different charity organizations and stuff. Dad runs Monument."

"Monument?" Running through his mind, trying to think of any businesses with that word in the name.

"Monument Pictures? The movie studio?"

He was impressed. "Oh, that Monument."

"Better than being a private investigator."

"Oh, I don't know," Angel said.

"You live in a place like this?"

Angel looked at the enormous mansions, or the bits of them he could see from the road. He thought about his apartment in a section of L.A. most people wouldn't even want to be caught in after sunset. In Sunnydale he had lived in a mansion, but it wasn't necessarily any better than the downtown apartment. Bad things still happened. Good ones, too. "Not recently."

"Yeah, I didn't think so. And what's up with this car, anyway? What is it?"

Angel glanced at the broad hood of his 1968

Plymouth Belvedere GTX. "It's a classic," Angel replied. "Anyway, money isn't everything."

"There you go sounding old again," Karinna said. "And anyway, don't try saying anything like that to my dad. He'll have you committed."

"He likes money, huh?"

"If you ask him what he loves in life, he'll say me, my mom, movies, and money. Just don't ask him what order they come in." She thought a moment. "No, I take that back. Making movies would come at the top of his list. The others are a toss-up."

At her direction Angel pulled the convertible up to a locked gate. She reached over him to punch numbers on the keypad that operated the gate, pressing uncomfortably close as she did. Angel could smell remnants of the perfume she'd put on that evening, before leaving the house for her Hollywood expedition. It was a grown-up woman's perfume, not a trendy teen one. He found it a strange choice for her.

But then, he thought, *how many of us really look our own age here? Talk about the pot and the kettle.*

Karinna's code entered, the gate swung open and Angel nosed the car through it, then up a tree-lined drive as wide as most city streets, and more smoothly paved.

"You think he'll be angry?" Angel asked, glancing at her. "You coming home so late, and without your regular bodyguards?"

"That's why you're here," Karinna replied. "If I

came home by myself, I'd catch some hell. With you here, he'll be polite. Especially when I tell him about how you saved my life and maybe my virtue."

"I see." Angel returned his attention to the driveway, which began a graceful arc as it broke through the trees into a clearing. A huge expanse of lawn stretched from the clearing to a house that might have been better described as a palace. Floodlights hidden in the trees and in bushes that edged up against the mansion illuminated its sides, arches of light extending almost to its distant roofs.

The place was Spanish-style, with clean whitewashed walls and slanted red tile roofs, wooden beams that Angel remembered were called vigas jutting out from the walls a little ways below the roofline. It was one of the biggest houses he'd seen in this country, and compared favorably to many of the castles he'd seen back in Ireland and elsewhere in Europe. Three or four stories tall, and seemingly as wide as a couple of football fields. Here and there, turrets or cupolas broke the roofline as if they were architectural afterthoughts.

"Nice," Angel said. "Rich" was an understatement. Filthy rich? Abominably rich? Disgustingly rich? *Why do all the words that modify "wealthy" have such negative connotations?* he wondered. Then answering his own question, he thought, *Because poor men write the dictionaries.*

"It's home."

"For three of you?"

"And the staff, of course," Karinna corrected him.

"Of course."

Angel brought the car to a stop in front of the front entrance. Five steps led up to a pair of wooden doors that must have been fifteen feet tall. They looked ancient, as if the doors had been here when California was young, at one of the old ranchos, and had just remained here until someone built a newer house around them.

"This okay?"

"Perfect," Karinna said. "You have to come in with—"

"I said I would."

She waited in her seat until he came around and opened the door for her, then held out his hand to help her out. *Well-schooled in manners or just manipulative?* he wondered. *Is she just reminding me that she's rich and female?*

Not that he needed any reminder of either.

She bounded up the steps as if it were midafternoon and she'd just had a nap. Angel followed at a somewhat more sedate pace. By the time he reached the door, she'd flung it open and stepped into the tile-floored entryway.

Inside, a fat aromatic candle sputtered in an alcove set into the thick white wall. Another doorway led away from the entry with thick wooden beams surrounding the door, and a wide stairway climbed up, the stairs also tiled, with a hand-worked wrought-iron banister. High above, a wrought-iron chandelier held a dozen bulbs.

There was no one here to meet them.

That's probably better, Angel thought. Images of a quick getaway started to enter his mind. He wasn't sure he was really done with Karinna—it seemed that merely protecting her from some testosterone cases was hardly enough to give Doyle a vision—but the sun would be up soon, and he didn't want to be caught out here in Bel Air when it rose.

He stopped at the door, waiting for an invitation across the threshold. She was inside, turning in a slow circle as if to ascertain that the entryway truly was empty.

"Looks like everyone's gone to bed," Angel said. "Guess I'll—"

"Oh, no," Karinna protested. "Come on in. I'll get Daddy. He'll want to meet my rescuer. Better start polishing up that armor, Angel."

Angel waved a hand, trying to dissuade her. "Look, if it's a problem, I really don't—"

She stepped outside, took his hand, drew him through the doorway onto the terra cotta tiles.

"You just wait right here."

Before he could speak again, she was gone, through the doorway. She let the thick door close behind her, and Angel was alone. He couldn't hear anything from the rest of the house. *Three-foot walls'll do that,* he thought. *The old ways of building had their charms.* He'd never lived anywhere quite so lavish back in mother Ireland, but he'd been in some castles that were similar in the philosophy of construction. Everything solid, stout, built to last.

He was beginning to wonder if she'd forgotten about him and went to bed when the inner door opened again and Karinna stepped through. Behind her came a man who had to be her father. He had the same red hair, except it had faded to gray and a kind of orange juice yellow. His face was deeply lined, eyes hooded and squinty like those of someone who spent a lot of time in the sun. Despite the hour, he wore tennis whites, with a canary sweater pulled over his white polo shirt.

"Dad, this is Angel," Karinna said. "Angel, my dad, Jack Willits."

"Pleasure," Angel said. "Hope we didn't wake you."

"Not at all, young man, not at all," Jack Willits said. He offered his hand, and when Angel took it, closed it in a crushing grip. He smiled broadly, animating laugh lines around his mouth. "No rest for the wicked, right?"

Jack paused as if he really expected an answer.

"Guess not," Angel said at length.

"That's right. Just reading some scripts, in the study. You like cigars, Angel? Study's the only room in the house they're allowed, anymore, but I could probably break out a couple if you want one."

"No, that's really not necessary. But thank you."

"I understand thanks are due you, Angel. Karinna says you really saved her bacon out there tonight."

Angel shrugged. He wanted to downplay the whole knight-in-shining-armor routine. "I guess her bodyguards got a little frustrated, tried to take it out on her," he explained. "I don't think they'd have done any more damage than they did."

"Not the way she tells it. Said you probably sent one to the hospital. No more than he deserves, you ask me. I hired them to take care of it, keep her safe, not to manhandle and assault her. They'll be lucky if I don't press charges."

"I did what anyone would have, if they'd seen it," Angel protested.

"But no one else did see it. I'm damn glad you happened along, Angel. You did just happen along, right?"

"Yes. That's right," Angel said. "Just on my way back to my own car."

"Karinna tells me you're a private eye," Jack said. "That a fact?"

"Yes, sir. At least, that's what it says on my business cards." He reached into his pocket to find one, and found just that—one. It had one corner dog-eared, and there was a phone number scrawled on the back of it in Doyle's handwriting. But he'd gone this far, so he handed it to Jack Willits.

"Sorry," he said. "Cordy—my executive assistant—is always after me to carry more cards. That's the last one I have on me right now."

"Angel Investigations," Jack read. "You don't mind if I keep this, do you?"

"Not at all," Angel said.

"You never know when you're going to need a good investigator," Jack said. "You don't happen to do bodyguarding as well, do you?"

"I haven't, sir. No."

"Just had to ask. There's an opening here, as you know. Karinna isn't the easiest person to keep tabs on, I'm afraid. And it's hard to find guards who'll do good work and stay on task. No work ethic anymore, you know?"

"I know what you mean, Mr. Willits. I'm kind of an old-fashioned guy myself."

"I can see that about you, Angel. I like that in a man. Sign of character."

"Thanks," Angel said. He glanced toward the door. "It's been really nice meeting you, Mr. Willits. This is a great place you've got here. And Karinna seems like a really nice girl. But it's getting late, and I really should get going."

"Sure, I understand," Jack said. He took Angel's hand in his death-grip again. "Just—thank you for bringing my Karinna home in one piece. If anything ever happened to her, I . . ." He paused, as if searching for the right words.

Apparently, they didn't come. ". . . I just don't know," he finished.

"Yeah, thanks, Angel," Karinna said. "You know where to find me if you ever feel like club-hopping."

"You be good, Karinna," Angel said. He opened the door, glanced at the sky. *Still dark. But not for much longer.* The sun would start to edge over the horizon soon, and Angel had to get back home and inside before it did.

"Good night, Karinna, Mr. Willits," he said. He stepped out onto the short staircase. In the entryway Jack Willits still held his business card, turning it in his hands as if there were secrets written on one side or the other, if only he could figure them out. But his gaze was on Karinna, his daughter. They were both silent as he closed the door behind himself.

Angel wondered, not for the first time, what kind of relationship they must have. Out till all hours, with bodyguards to keep her safe. Was that how the rich lived in L.A.? If so, what was the point of being rich?

Angel had no kids, and he never could. But if he had, he thought he'd rather be poor and spend time with them than be so rich he had to pay others to do it for him.

He descended the few stairs and got back into the Plymouth. The drive circled around and met itself and he followed it back to the estate's front gate, which opened at his approach. As he drove, he thought about Karinna sitting in the car next to him looking so young and vulnerable in the cold breeze. The way strands of her fair red hair dangled around her face, curling at the line of her chin. The way she held her arms tightly about herself, knees pulled up inside them. He realized that she reminded him of someone.

Someone from his past.

But there was a lot of that, and he couldn't draw the image out from the recesses of his mind. Couldn't place who it was. The inability to do so frustrated him.

Twenty-five minutes later he parked in front of his apartment. The sky was beginning to lighten—the precursor to the sun's first rays. He hurried inside.

And inside a darkened room in a recently rented apartment across the street, a curtain moved. The room smelled like stale coffee, pizza crusts, and burnt popcorn. The person who had been watching through the window crossed the littered floor to a plain wooden table, flipped on a tiny flashlight, and made a notation in a spiral-bound notebook. Angel was inside for the day.

CHAPTER FIVE

Angel was a little surprised to find both Doyle and Cordelia still in the office. Cordy had curled up on the blue couch, with a blanket that Angel knew had been on his bed pulled over her. Doyle sat, head back and mouth open, in one of his guest chairs. The TV was still on, showing an exercise program in miniature. Tinny voices shouted instruction and encouragement to the couch potatoes who were watching at home.

Cordelia opened one eye at the sound of the door closing, and then graced Angel with a smile. Or as much of one as she could muster at this time of day. A morning person, she was not.

"Everything okay?"

"I think so," Angel said.

Doyle stirred then, too, rubbing his eyes.

"Hey," he said. "Find her?"

"Found her."

"And?"

"You were right. Pretty girl."

"I knew it. What was her trouble?"

"Her bodyguards were taking out their frustrations with their fists."

"On a girl?" Doyle asked.

"I persuaded them to seek other avenues."

"So are we talking reward, bonus, or continued employment?" Cordelia interrupted. She kicked her feet off the couch and sat up, drawing the blanket up around her chin.

"None of the above," Angel replied.

"None? Why not?"

Angel shrugged. "Didn't come up."

"How could it not come up? Did she have money?"

"Her family has money. Her dad, I guess. You might know who he is. Jack Willits?"

"Jack Willits? The head of Monument Pictures? The guy who makes the 'Ten Most Powerful People in Hollywood' list five years running? Never heard of him."

"I'm impressed," Doyle said. "I tend to pay more attention to *The Racing Form* than *Variety*, so unless he's a jockey or has a racehorse named after him, I probably wouldn't know him."

"That's amazing, Angel," Cordelia went on brightly. "You actually met Jack Willits?"

"Briefly. He wasn't there the whole time I was

helping Karinna. His daughter, remember? The one who was in trouble? But I dropped her off at home, and she introduced us."

"You've been to Jack Willits's home? What's it like?"

"Again, briefly. Nice place. Big."

"Do you know what this could mean?" Cordelia asked.

"That's he's a successful guy with bad taste in bodyguards?"

"This could be my ticket to the big time," Cordelia said. She threw the blanket off and jumped to her feet. "My break. You get in good with Jack Willits, and then introduce me. He'll recognize my potential—I've heard he's brilliant that way." She crossed the room and threw her arms around Angel, enveloping him in a backbreaking hug. "Angel, thank you!"

Angel caught Doyle's gaze. Doyle shrugged, and Angel returned it with his eyebrows, as they were just about the only body part not being crushed by Cordy.

"My pleasure," he said.

Finally she let him go and went back to the couch, a bit of a spring in her step and a dreamy smile on her face.

"You know," Doyle offered. "I ain't so sure about this whole business."

"What do you mean?" Cordelia asked, horror

creeping into her voice. "It's perfect!" She fixed Angel with a serious glare. "Remember, you do have bills, Angel. Rent, electricity, credit cards, phone, insurance, gas, and so on. I know, because I just lined up all of mine on my coffee table so I wouldn't accidentally see one anywhere and get all depressed."

"What I'm gettin' at," Doyle interjected, "is maybe it's not as perfect as we'd like to think. I mean, sure it'd be great and all for you to hook up with this Willits guy and become a big star, Cordy. But what if the girl's problems are a little more complicated than what Angel dealt with tonight? I don't know for sure what the visions mean, you know. It could've meant her bodyguards were using her for a punching bag, but it could be something much worse. I think you need to be on your guard until we know for sure."

Cordy considered this.

"I guess maybe you're right," she finally relented. "Maybe we should research the Willits family a little."

"Might be a good idea," Doyle agreed.

"I'll start with Jack, and Monument Pictures," she went on. "You do, I don't know, whoever else there is."

"Gotcha," Doyle said. "Glad to see you're so concerned about their well-being."

"I am concerned," Cordelia argued. "I just express it differently than you."

"You got that right," Doyle said. "Just let me get a few more minutes of sleep and I'll join right in."

He closed his eyes again, and in a few moments he was snoring softly. Angel decided he could use some as well and headed downstairs to his apartment.

Mordractus paced the creaky floors of his rented house. The place sat back in the hills, and from a balcony off the living room he could see, in the narrow gap between two other hills, the brown cloud that hung over Los Angeles most days, and the sparkle of the city's lights at night. But here in the hills the sky was blue overhead, and gentle breezes stirred the curtains. The place was a little drafty, but that reminded him of home, and he didn't have a problem with it.

He paced because he was anxious, and he was anxious because he was dying.

And worse, he was dying because of the Summoning, a spell he had begun, a spell that took months to complete, was sapping him of his life essence, and could very likely kill him before he was even finished with it.

And then things would, he knew, get very nasty.

Finally, exhausted from his pacing, he sat down in a wide wicker chair with floral cushions that faced a window.

The house had been built in the 1920s by Arthur

Pennington, a magician who moved in Hollywood circles and who had been, for a time, a student of Mordractus's. It had everything a self-respecting magician might want in a house—secret passageways and trapdoors and a vast basement room with a slate floor.

But Pennington had died in the fifties, and the house had been taken over by other owners, less interested in its special properties. They had made the ritual room downstairs into what they called a "rumpus room," with games and a wet bar and a hi-fi system.

Still other owners took it over in the seventies, and they were swinging Hollywood types who held orgies on weekends and decorated with lots of hanging beads and soft fabrics in earth tones.

Now, the house was sparsely furnished. Mordractus had "persuaded" the rental agency to evict the previous tenants with no notice, and to let him move in without signing a lease. The tenants took most of what they owned, but left behind a few pieces, and there were remnants of all the previous owners remaining, too.

The place was a decorator's nightmare.

Mordractus didn't care about any of that. He was just somewhat offended by the indignity of having to sit on a floral cushion in a wicker chair that had probably been bought in the 1970s by a small-time actor wearing an orange shirt and a wooly vest and bell-bottoms, with a medallion around his neck and a thick mustache over his lip.

He could have done something about it, but he didn't want to expend the energy. Instead, he lifted his head and called out in a weak, quaking voice, "P'wrll! Water!"

The bogie's gnarled form shuffled into the room. "Reg'lar, or bubbly?" he rasped.

Since coming to California, Mordractus had become entranced by sparking mineral water, which he called "bubbly" because he couldn't remember any of the brand names. The household staff accommodated him.

"Bubbly," he said.

"Comin' up." P'wrll left Mordractus alone by the window.

Mordractus gazed outside blankly, not really registering anything that lay before him. He was thinking, instead, of Balor.

According to ancient Celtic legend, the Fomorians were a race of giants who had inhabited Ireland long before people tried to move there. Each time people came, the Fomorians drove them off—wave after wave of humans trying to gain a foothold on the emerald isle, each time turned away by the ferocious giants.

And the king of the Fomorians—the Celtic-Irish God of Death—was named Balor of the Evil Eye.

Whenever things got tough for the Fomorians, all

they had to do was bring out Balor, their ultimate weapon. He was enormous, and he had only one eye, in the middle of his forehead, which was also enormous—so big, in fact, that he needed help to lift his own eyelid, so heavy was it. But when that eye was open, it destroyed everything Balor saw. Normally, he kept his eye shut, so as not to cause mass destruction, but in battle it was propped open and he was a force to be reckoned with.

There was only one thing that Balor was afraid of— a prophet warned him that he would be slain by his own grandson. To prevent this prophecy from coming true, Balor had his only child, a daughter, kept under lock and key at all times. In spite of that precaution, with the help of druid magic, a Danaan lord made Balor's daughter pregnant with triplets. Balor ordered the triplets to be drowned in the sea. But one, a baby boy, washed up on shore and was found in Danaan territory. This baby was named Lugh.

Years later Lugh rallied the Danaans against the Fomorians. In a bloody battle at Moytirra, he challenged his own grandfather, Balor. Balor, who had been using his evil eye to cause great losses amongst the Danaan forces, accepted the challenge and called to have his eye opened. As soon as it did, however, Lugh hurled a stone with a slingshot, and it hit the eye with such incredible force that the eye flew out the back of Balor's head, wiping out a contingent of the Fomorian troops.

Balor went into the Otherworld, the parallel world below the one that we can see. When the Gaels, the early equivalent to the modern-day Irish, took over the island, the Danaans were sent to live in fairy mounds and to rule the Otherworld. Under Danaan rule, Balor kept his eye closed, but gradually, over the course of millennia, it healed.

Mordractus intended to bring Balor back from the Otherworld.

Restored to the visible world, Balor would be his to command. His evil eye would be a devastating weapon at Mordractus's beck and call. Or more likely, Mordractus knew, it would be held back as a powerful threat—give me what I want, or I'll open his eye! Blackmail more powerful than any ten stolen nuclear weapons, and it would have the added benefit of shaking the modern world's beliefs to their very foundations. They thought the stuff of legend was just that, stories told by ignorant peoples to explain their world.

It was more than that, Mordractus knew. The stories were true. The part about them being mere legend came later, to keep people in the dark. The fewer people who understood the old ways, the more power was concentrated in the hands of those who did. Mordractus had kept that faith for hundreds of years.

It was time all that changed, though. After centuries of living in the shadows, he was finally ready to become a very public figure. He would make his demands known, and he would demonstrate that he had the power to back up his demands. He could unleash Balor, and by controlling their king, could bring back a whole army of Fomorians if need be. He would be, after all these years, a political and economic force to be reckoned with, instead of an unknown working spells of which only he knew.

Mordractus considered himself the most powerful sorceror who had ever lived. By the time he was finished, history would know it to be true. The world would tremble at the sound of his name.

All he had to do was live until the autumn equinox.

Summoning Balor from the Otherworld was no simple task. It required decades of research, years of preparation, once it even occurred to him. And in his research he discovered that it could only be completed when the moon and stars were in a certain alignment in the heavens, at the equinox—an alignment that occurred only once every five hundred years or so.

This year.

Having made that calculation, he realized he had to act fast. He began the rituals, which themselves had to be spread over many months. They should have been spread over years, in fact, but that would have meant missing the deadline and waiting another half-millennium. Mordractus was patient, but not *that* patient.

So he fast-tracked the Summoning, performing parts of it that should have been months apart in weeks instead. It would still work, he knew. The preferred schedule was mainly set for the health of the practitioner. This kind of necromancy wore heavily on the one carrying it out. There should have been long periods of recuperation in between the different segments.

By the time he realized he wouldn't live through it, it was too late. Once begun, he couldn't turn back. If he stopped, if the next ritual didn't follow the last within the specified period, he would be drawn back through the veil he had opened. He would be taken into the Otherworld, where Balor and the other Fomorians would be very angry that he had disturbed them with unkept promises of a return to the visible world.

He didn't want to live through an eternity of that. He *had* to finish. The equinox was less than a month away now.

And he knew he'd never live the month. Not without help. He had grown too weak, too frail. The magic that had kept him alive for so long had run its course, used up by the stress of the Balor-recovery rituals.

With Balor and the Fomorians backing him, he would be supremely powerful, and he could dedicate himself once again to ensuring his own longevity (immortality) with all the wealth and power over petty humans that he had long deserved.

No, he thought. *I will not die. There is a way, and I know what it is.*

When P'wrll returned with his mineral water, Mordractus took the glass in a shaking hand and drank deeply. He swallowed and looked at the bogie. "Where are they?" he asked. "Bring them to me, all of them."

P'wrll nodded. "On the way," he said.

When the bogie left, Mordractus leaned over to put his glass on the floor. His chin felt comfortable against his chest, and he left it there.

A few minutes later he looked up again. All his minions were gathered around him, human and non alike. There were Currie and Hitch, Needham and Blaine, McCourt and McIver, Leary and O'Neil. Intermixed with them were goblins and bog-fairies, hog-men and howlers. A total staff of twenty. *And they haven't been able to perform one simple task,* he thought.

He looked up at them, meeting each one's gaze, in turn. He willed himself to sit up straight, to look more strong and robust than he felt.

"We all know why we're here, isn't that right? Here in California."

There were murmurs of assent.

"Then why isn't it done? There are plenty of you to do it."

McIver spoke. "We're usin' the plan you came up wi', sir," he said. "It'll take a stretch o' time for it to work, though, as you said yourself."

"I said that, did I?" Mordractus responded. "That was when I was more patient."

"It's under way now, though," McIver said. "Might as well play it out."

"Might as well," Mordractus echoed again. "You do understand that there is some urgency here, do you not?"

"Aye," McIver said. "I think we all do."

"And the rest of you? Does McIver speak for all of you?"

Again, words of assent from the crowd, in both human and fairy speech.

"That's interesting, that's good," Mordractus said. "McIver, who appointed you to speak for this lot?"

"No one, sir," McIver replied. "Just speakin' me mind, and they seem to agree wi' me."

"Speaking your mind. Taking initiative, eh?"

"Yes, sir."

Mordractus looked hard at McIver. Holding the ruddy-faced man in his gaze, he began to describe a pattern in the air with his bony fingers.

"Sir, no—" McIver started to say, but his voice caught in his throat. He brought a hand up to his neck, as if feeling for an obstruction. His eyes started to bug out of his head, and the expression in them was pure panic.

Everyone else watched silently as he fell to the floor. He kicked a couple of times, and then was still.

"I want results," Mordractus told them. "Not excuses. Not rationalizations. Results. Does everyone understand that now?"

For the third time there was a chorus of confirmation.

"Good," Mordractus said. He waved them away with a backhanded flip of his fingers. "Leave me, then. And make it happen."

When they were almost to the door, he added, in a soft voice, "There isn't much time to waste."

CHAPTER SIX

Jack Willits blew into the office, banging the door as he came.

It was a little after noon. Angel was sitting behind the front desk with his feet up, reading one of the magazines Cordy had found for him, a back issue of *Hollywood Reporter* with a profile of Jack in it. This one had come from her personal collection, but she had gone down to the library to find more. Doyle was out, too, dodging creditors or researching the Willits family, or maybe both.

"Angel, my man," Jack said when he came in.

Angel swept his feet off the desktop and stood, wondering what the studio executive was doing in his low-rent neighborhood. He took Jack's outstretched hand, gave it a shake. "Mr. Willits."

"Please, just Jack."

"Okay," Angel said. "Jack. What brings you down here?"

"Wanted to talk to you, Angel. Without Karinna around, you know. *Mano a mano,* right?"

"Right, okay. About what?"

"About Karinna. And you."

Angel was a little concerned by that. "What about us?"

"I'm a reasonably well-off man, Angel. I appreciate everything that has come my way, don't get me wrong. But it also comes with a cost. I'm a target, and that carries over to my family. We're all targets."

"I'm sorry to hear that."

"Thank you. So the long and the short of it, Angel, is that, as targets, we—especially Karinna, because she likes to have her fun—need bodyguards. Ones that I can trust. Karinna told me all about what happened last night, and I swear to you I never would have believed those guys could behave that way. If I had, I never would have hired them. You have to believe that."

Willits seemed truly distressed by the memory of it. His lips were pressed tightly together, his eyes blinking, as if trying to hold in strong emotion of some kind.

"I believe you," Angel finally said.

"I'm glad."

"But where do I—?"

"I'm getting to that, Angel. I want you to take

over security for my daughter. For Karinna. I want you to keep her safe from—from whatever might threaten her."

Angel thought a moment. "I don't know if I can do that," he said at length. "She's a very . . . active girl. I think she needs a team of guards, and I pretty much work alone."

"What he means," Cordelia announced, barging through the front door with a stack of magazines clutched to her, "is that he alone manages our staff of operatives." She put the magazines on Angel's desk and turned to Jack with her hand out. "My role is more of a figurehead one than a real hands-on partnership, since I'm so busy with other projects. Cordelia Chase, Mr. Willits. It is truly an honor to meet you."

"A pleasure, Ms. Chase. You are Angel's partner in this venture?"

"Like I said, a silent partner. I offered him some, uh, backing, when he was just getting started in the business."

"I see."

"But enough about that," Cordelia went on. "Let's talk about you. I'll bet those fourteen years at the helm of Monument Pictures have gone by really fast, haven't they?"

"Well, umm—"

"Especially the years you had the biggest box-office hits in the industry. What were they, '87, '89, and '92? You really made Monument a powerhouse, Mr. Willits. Or can I call you Jack?"

"Sure, Jack's fine, Miss Chase. You certainly seem to know a lot about the movie industry. Especially Monument Pictures."

"It's my life," she said. "I eat it, breathe it, and sleep it."

"Jack is just offering me a job, Cordelia," Angel interrupted. "Bodyguarding his daughter."

"That's right," Cordelia said. "And you were just about to negotiate a fair price for this job? Keeping in mind that you'll have to pay some of our operatives overtime to keep her under round-the-clock surveillance."

"I think you're overestimating our capabilities, Cordy."

She turned to Angel. "No, I am not. I'm simply taking all the circumstances into account. Who the subject is, and who her father is, and, uhh . . . who her father is . . ."

"I really would like you on our side, Angel," Jack said.

"I'm getting the feeling that everyone would."

"How perceptive," Cordelia said.

"I'm prepared to offer you five hundred dollars a day."

Angel started to protest. "I don't think—"

"Seven-fifty, then," Jack offered. "Not a penny more."

Angel considered it. He felt wary of Karinna Willits—guarding her might be more trouble than it seemed at first glance. But there was Doyle's vision. If she really was a soul in need, if there was more to her problem than bodyguards threatening to beat her up, then he couldn't turn his back on her. Working for the family guaranteed that he'd be able to keep close tabs without arousing suspicion.

"Like I said, Mr. Willits. Jack. I don't really have a team of guards at my disposal. What I suggest is that you keep guards you know and trust with her in the daytime, to get her to school and back, or whatever she does during the day. At night I'll take over, and stay with her until she's back home safely. If that sounds reasonable, then we have a deal."

"Deal," Jack said. He offered his hand again, and Angel pumped it twice. When he let go, Cordelia was there with her hand extended, again. Jack took it.

"Like I was saying," Cordelia began, "the movie industry? Monument Pictures? That's where I could really make a contribution, something that would benefit both of us. I think Angel has his feet on the ground now, he can function just fine without my day-to-day supervision. So if you think you have a place for me, I'm sure that I can rearrange my schedule to accommodate you."

Jack laughed. "Looking for a job, is that it? Okay, Miss Chase, you've convinced me."

Angel could almost see Cordelia's heart leap in

her chest. Her smile widened to the point that he was afraid she'd split her head in two.

Jack wrote something down on the back of one of his business cards, handed it to her. "Show up at this office in the morning," he said. "Say, nine o'clock. They'll be expecting you, and they'll get you all set up."

"Thank you so much, Jack," Cordelia gushed. "You won't regret this, I promise you."

"I doubt very much that I will, Miss Chase." He gave her a little bow. "I'll see you tomorrow. On the lot."

Kate Lockley stood before a dry-erase board in the police station's War Room. The walls were covered with maps and schematics and drawings and photos—locations and tunnel photos and shots of broken-out bank doors. Written on the white board, in Kate's neat handwriting, were the names and addresses of seven banks spread throughout the city. Underneath California Savings on Robinson, there were three names written in red: F. Gilmore, T. Coker, J. Doe. J. for Jane, the minor female.

"This is what we've got so far," Kate said, addressing her task force of a dozen officers. Some of them were in uniforms, others were plain-clothed detectives. Kate's task force. "It's not much. The crew tunnels into the banks during the night hours, when they're closed. Our experts guess that it takes them four to six nights of steady work to dig their tunnels. This also jibes with the timing of the robberies."

One of the uniforms raised his hand. "Detective Lockley?"

"Yes, Ybarra?"

"Is there any identifiable pattern to the kinds of places where the tunnels originate?"

"Good question," Kate said. "Not so far, unfortunately. At California Savings, they had rented a garage on the other side of the block and started it there. At First Western, it was a basement apartment across the street. The only point of similarity is that the spaces are always somewhat isolated, and that's probably a matter of not wanting their efforts to be heard.

"At any rate," she continued, "they dig for their four or six nights or whatever. They finish up when they're almost through the walls, usually into or adjacent to the bank's main vault. This causes us to believe that they might have some kind of inside information—who would know where the vaults were located, in all these different banks?

"On the big night they punch through the last bit of wall into the bank. They get into the vault— sometimes they've dug right into it, other times they blow the door with a little bit of C-four. This is another point to consider—where do they get the plastique, and where'd they get the expertise to do all this? Keep that in mind. Anyway, they go in, they load up big bags with cash, and then, rather than carrying the awkward bags back through the elaborate tunnel system, they go out the bank's front door into a waiting car. At this point they don't care about the alarms—they're gone.

"This is what happened to our three victims. Mr. Gilmore, Mr. Coker, and our unidentified minor were apparently out on the street, quite late. They were in front of, or close to, the bank doors when the crew came out. This is confirmed by security cameras that were taping the doorway. The crew charged through the door, and one of them, seeing the witnesses, opened fire with an automatic weapon. He fired a burst into each victim, and then they all got into the waiting vehicle and they drove away.

"The killings, as far as I can determine, were completely unnecessary. These people are cautious. They wear leather masks and gloves at all times while on the job. They carry automatic weapons even when they don't expect to be seen or heard. They have developed a very elaborate system of—"

The door to the War Room opened, and a man swaggered in, dressed in an expensive blue suit, a white shirt, and a striped tie. His black hair was close-cropped and neatly combed. His teeth were white and straight.

Kate cringed inwardly. Glenn Newberry. He was a Fed. Even if she hadn't met him before, she'd know that on sight. But she knew him, so her preconceived notion of him wasn't just based on his job, it was based on his personality. Or lack thereof.

"Thanks for gathering the troops, Detective," he said. He walked to the front of the room, shouldering Kate aside. She held her ground.

"We were just going over—"

"Yes, well, let's talk about where we go from here," he interrupted. "I want the uniforms to recanvass the neighborhood around the garage where the California Savings tunnel originated. And I—"

"Excuse me, Special Agent Newberry. This is an LAPD operation. If you'd like to observe, you're welcome to, but you're in no position to dictate strategy or assignments to my task force."

He looked at her, his green eyes holding her gaze. "Would you please step outside with me, Detective Lockley?" he asked.

"Certainly."

They left the War Room and stood close together in the hallway outside. He leaned in toward her, violating her personal space.

"These are banks, Lockley," he said. "Insured by the Federal Deposit Insurance Corporation. Maybe you've heard of it. Bank robbery is a federal crime, and that puts me in charge of this task force."

What a dweeb. She gritted her teeth, reminding herself that diplomacy with these guys was more effective than kicking the stuffing out of them.

"People are dead, Special Agent Newberry. Citizens of the city of Los Angeles. That makes this crew my job, my responsibility. You can catch the bank robbers if you want. I'm aiming to catch some killers."

"I'll be talking to your captain, Lockley, and we'll see where we end up."

"Talk all you want, Newberry. I'm confident of my jurisdiction here."

"Your jurisdiction is one thing, Lockley. The collar is something else altogether. And when I'm handcuffing these mooks, you'll be standing on the sidelines watching."

"Collar?" Kate asked. "Do you have something?"

Newberry smiled.

Smug, self-righteous creep, Kate thought.

"If you've got something on these guys, you need to share that with me," she said. "I'm running a task force here. We've got killers running around the city, and we need to rein them in."

"If I had anything I thought would help you, I'd share it," Newberry said. "You'd do the same for me, right?"

"Of course. I don't care who makes the collar, I just want this crew brought down." Which was a lie, she knew. She wanted the collar. And she wanted Special Agent Newberry to go back to Quantico and learn some manners.

Her dad had been a cop, and she'd been a cop, long enough to know that the best way to track down these bank robbers was for the P.D. and the FBI to cooperate. But she couldn't bring herself to let go of the case, and sharing anything with this slug was repugnant to her.

"Well, that's good to know, Detective," Newberry said. "I'm very glad to hear that."

The whole situation made her feel selfish and greedy. She didn't like it, didn't really care for the way it made her see herself, like gazing into a fun-house mirror and seeing someone who looked like herself but distorted and ugly.

Except the difference is, she thought, *what I'm seeing is really me.*

"I'll be counting on you, Special Agent Newberry," she said. Twisting the knife in her own heart. "You come up with anything, you know where to find me, right?"

"I'll find you," he promised. He walked away, down the hall.

She went back into the War Room. The gathered officers looked questioningly at her. "Okay," she said. "Where were we before we were so rudely interrupted?"

There was a round of laughter. Kate basked in it.

"This is a Los Angeles Police Department task force," she went on. Scattered applause. She let it die down. "And it will remain one. We should co-operate with the FBI whenever possible—the goal here is to catch these guys, and it doesn't matter who does it as long as they're caught."

"That's the spirit," someone said.

"Keep in mind that they've graduated from bank robbers to killers," Kate continued. "They should be considered armed and very dangerous. Now, here's where we go from here. . . ."

Thirty minutes later she was alone in the War Room. She'd sent the task force members out on their assignments, and she stayed behind. She walked slowly around the room, looking at the charts, the maps, the photos. Every now and then she looked at the names she'd written on the board.

There was a large map of L.A. on one wall with stickpins at the site of each robbery. She stared at the map, then let her eyes drift out of focus, hoping to see a pattern where there was none.

But the problem with that was, there was none. Whoever these guys were—and she used the word intentionally, as the bank cameras had shown that they were all male—they were smart enough to randomize their activities.

They knew that the way criminals were usually caught was by becoming predictable. So they did their crimes the same way each time, but there was nothing—besides the obvious fact that the targets were all banks—in common about where they chose to do them. It did the police no good at all to know that a tunnel was being dug somewhere, if there was no clue as to where that somewhere might be.

And they had been remarkably adept at leaving no

clues behind. No fingerprints, no DNA. Even digging the tunnels they had worn gloves and used cheap tools easily bought at any of dozens of hardware warehouse stores around the Southland. Broken tools, left behind, provided no information. She had assigned two officers to check out all the home improvement and hardware stores, just in case—these guys did, after all, seem to go through a lot of shovels and picks. But she held out little hope there.

No, when this crew was caught, it was going to be because they made a mistake. And so far, they had only made one.

Killing three people.

It was a mistake because it made Kate Lockley want them. When they'd just been robbing banks, she'd been concerned but not particularly involved. She would have been happy to let the Feds have it.

When they became killers, she was sucked in.

When she was seven and wanted a Barbie, she had insisted, begged, pleaded, cajoled, whined. Her dad had finally relented, telling her that she was as tenacious as a bulldog. For a few weeks he'd called her that. It wasn't a nickname that stuck, and they'd moved on to others.

But the bulldog spirit, that stuck. She knew tenacity carried the day. If others called her stubborn, so be it.

Kate wanted these crooks, and she'd have them.

Simple as that.

CHAPTER SEVEN

Dinner was at eight.

Jack Willits wouldn't leave Angel's office without a promise from Angel that he'd be there. When he did go, Angel thought he'd have to peel Cordy off the ceiling, she was flying so high from Jack's offer of a job at Monument Pictures.

In fact, she was more calm than he'd expected—so calm, in fact, that it was several minutes before he realized that what she really was, was terrified. He tried to broach the subject a couple of times, but her reaction caused him to think she needed some time to take it all in.

For dinner he chose a simple black ensemble off-set by one of his only white shirts and a black Italian silk tie. When he dressed and came out of his bedroom, Cordelia applauded.

"Now, you know which fork to use when, right?"

she asked. "Because sometimes at these fancy society dinners they have, like, eight of them or something. And they'll be eating, you know, people chow, which I know is not your favorite dish."

"I'll be fine, Cordy."

"I wouldn't want you to make a fool of yourself or anything," she continued. As she spoke, she circled him, eyeing him from all angles for anything that might be out of place. "After all, this is a big break for Angel Investigations. And for me, too, I guess, but of course I put others first. At all times."

"Of course you do."

"So just be very careful about what you say and how you pass food and don't drink too much—well, I guess if you started drinking anything that you might overdo, it'd be blood, and that would pretty much kill the whole deal right there."

"Pretty much. But I promise not to overindulge."

"In fact, maybe you just shouldn't say anything. Do you think you can get through the whole night by just smiling and nodding?"

"Cordelia, I'm older than this country. I've eaten with nobility. I think I can handle myself."

"Well, I thought so, too, but you can never be too careful about these things."

"They're just people, Cord."

"No, they're not. They're rich people. Entirely different species. With occasional cross-pollination."

"I won't embarrass you."

"Oh, it's not me I'm worried about," she said, adjusting his collar for the tenth time. "I used to be one of the rich people, remember? We know how these things work. But sometimes we get a little embarrassed for those who are beneath us."

She tossed him a smile that almost, but not quite, made him think she was kidding.

Finally he got out of the apartment and made the drive back up to Bel Air. He was waved through by the guard, and parked in the Willits family's parklike driveway a few minutes before eight. By eight-fifteen they were seated in a formal dining room. The table was set with fine china and crystal, and dinner was served by a staff of quietly efficient Scandinavians.

Marjorie Willits, Jack's wife, joined the group just as they sat down. This was the first time Angel had met her, and when he shook her hand, it was tiny and light and quaking like a bird fluttering against its cage. She was very lean, with prominent bones and blue veins that showed through her milk-white skin. *Makes me look tan,* Angel thought when he saw her. When they sat, he watched her nervously touch her hair, her lips, her chin. She looked more fragile than the crystal, as if a loud noise would reduce her to a quivering mass. He found himself speaking softly to her.

But Karinna seemed to have no such qualms.

"This is the guy daddy wants to have watch me," she told her mother. "He kicked the crap—"

"Karinna," Jack warned.

"Sorry, the bejesus out of Harvey last night. You should have seen him run. I thought he was gonna cry like a little girl when Angel tore into him."

Angel smiled at Marjorie. "She's exaggerating," he said.

"She does that," Marjorie said. Her face twitched, as if she were trying to smile but was not very practiced at it.

"So I gather."

"Hopefully, physical violence will not be a part of your daily duties, Angel," Jack said. "But if it should come to that, I'm glad that you're capable of kicking the 'bejesus' out of trained bodyguards."

"I'll try to avoid it," Angel promised. "And if it becomes necessary, I'll try to make sure they're not on your payroll before I start kicking."

Jack and Karinna both roared with laughter at that. Marjorie made a small sound in the back of her throat that sounded more like a whimper than a laugh. Angel couldn't help wondering what her story was—she seemed so out of place in this family.

As they ate, Angel picking at his food and trying to look like he was enjoying it, he found his gaze drawn to Karinna more and more. He watched her laugh with her father, watched her eyes narrow with concentration as she cut her filet or tried to spear a green bean with her fork. He wasn't watching her because she was lovely. It was because she still reminded him of someone, and though he couldn't quite place who, it was coming closer to the surface of his consciousness.

Then she looked up and away, as if hearing a distant sound, and at the same time her left hand came to her cheek to brush away a loose curl of copper hair that hung there, and he knew.

He remembered.

He had never known her name, or anything really about her. She lived in Tirgu Bals, a small town in Rumania, in the year 1898. He was there, too, although he still went by the name of Angelus then. He was there with Darla, his love, the beautiful blond vampire who had turned him into one as well. They lived with Heinrich Joseph Nest, the Master, roaming the wooded countryside, feeding when they were hungry. In that year the American Century had not yet begun. Europe was still the focal point of the arts and sciences, and vampire culture was the same as the rest of the culture in that respect. The next century the Master would move to the United States, as would the attention of the world. He would make the mistake of moving to Sunnydale, and Buffy Summers would slay him.

But for now, he was in Rumania, which many considered the homeland of vampires. Angelus and Darla and many others stayed there with him. The hunting was good.

Angelus saw the woman one night, hurrying

along a cobbled street. She carried a basket in one hand, hiked up her flowing skirts with the other, and she looked back over her shoulder with every few steps. Probably, he thought, someone had told her that it wasn't safe to be out after dark, but she'd had some errand and had risked it anyway. And now she regretted it.

Angelus liked the curve of her throat and the way her form flowed under her cloak. But he had just fed, moments before he saw her—blood still ran down his chin. As he watched the girl, he dabbed at the blood with his thumb, licked it clean. If he'd been a little hungrier . . .

But he wasn't, and he let her go.

The next night his life was changed forever. Darla brought him a beautiful Gypsy girl. He was immediately enchanted by her, and the kill, when he finally took her, was like no other he could remember.

But he was observed, and he was cursed by her tribe's elders. As a result of the curse, his soul was restored to him, and with it, an immense load of guilt for all the crimes he had committed as a vampire—and not a small amount for his roguish ways before being turned, for that matter. He determined to make up for his past crimes by trying to help people.

So the next time he was in Tirgu Bals, and he saw the same lovely redheaded woman, he felt a momentary swelling of joy that he had not killed her before. She was just locking a bakery's door, after a long day's work. The scent of fresh bread had wafted into the road as she came out. From a doorway across the street, he could see the weariness in her, in the slump of her shoulders and the set of her mouth. But there was something else, and as she started to walk home through the gathering night, he could see that, too, a spring in her step and a tilt of her head that indicated a strong, confident woman making her way in a hard world. Angelus watched her, pleased that she still lived in the world, that there was something wonderful in the world that he had not destroyed.

But as he watched, he saw another form, also keeping an eye on her. And more than that, moving toward her. Angelus recognized the form as it passed the shadowed doorway where he stood— Tirbol, another of the Master's acolytes. Tirbol had been a vampire for almost two hundred years by that point; he was powerful and respected.

Angelus knew that Tirbol was planing to feed. Only a few days had passed since the curse had taken effect, restoring his soul and all the pain that came with it, and the idea that he could perhaps atone for his sins was not fully formed yet. But he knew he couldn't just stand here and watch as Tirbol corrupted the one thing of beauty he'd seen recently.

He ran. Tirbol was faster, though, and caught up

with the woman before Angelus could reach them. She had turned down a narrow lane. Angelus saw Tirbol make the same turn, and a moment later a shrill scream echoed down the street. Angelus pushed himself, running even faster than he had before. He had to remind himself that, even though he now had a soul, he was still a vampire with a vampire's strength and speed.

He came around the corner and saw them. Tirbol had the terrified woman bent in his arms, and his mouth was lowering to her exposed neck.

"Stop!" Angelus called.

Tirbol looked at him. A thin smile played across his lips.

"Angelus," he said. "We haven't seen much of you lately."

"I've been busy," Angelus said, fighting to maintain his composure. This was all new ground for him, and seeing Tirbol about to feed turned his stomach.

"Too busy for family?"

"I don't have any family," Angelus replied.

Tirbol nodded his head toward the woman in his arms. "Hungry?" he asked. "I can share."

"Leave her alone."

Tirbol laughed. "Unlikely," he said. "She's mine."

"You'll have to kill me first," Angelus said, advancing on them.

"As you wish." Tirbol slammed the woman up

against the stone wall of a nearby house. She fell to the ground, sobbing, petrified with fright. "You stay there," he told her. "I'll be right with you." Then he turned to face Angelus.

Angelus made the first move, charging Tirbol with his arms outstretched. Tirbol caught one wrist in his powerful grip and turned with it, using Angelus's own momentum to hurl him to the lane. Before Angelus could rise, Tirbol had spun again and unleashed a series of kicks.

Angelus swallowed the new, and yet familiar sensation of pain and rose to his feet. He lunged at Tirbol again, this time getting the older vampire's right arm in his grasp. He climbed the arm, finally finding a hold on Tirbol's throat. Tirbol punched and clawed at him, but Angelus ignored the pain. His plan was to snap Tirbol's neck and then find something to stake him with.

He felt Tirbol's head turning in his grip. This would work, he suddenly realized. He would beat one of the most powerful vampires he'd ever encountered, and in so doing, he'd save the life of a beautiful young woman with everything to live for. It was a small thing, he knew, but it was one step on the road he wanted to travel for the rest of his life.

And then Tirbol's clutching hand found his eyes. The pain was indescribable, and Angelus's grip loosened. Tirbol lurched backward, driving Angelus into the stone wall. Then he turned and slammed

Angelus in the chin with both fists locked together. Angelus's head snapped back, and he slumped to the ground. Tirbol kicked him in the head and ribs a dozen times.

Angelus's eyes closed as he writhed on the ground, unable to rise. When he was able to open them again, he saw Tirbol, bent over his prey. She had ceased her crying. Blood trickled from two puncture wounds in her milky throat and smeared Tirbol's chin.

The older vampire dropped her still form, gave Angelus a small salute, and disappeared into the night.

He had tried to save her, but he had failed. His first rescue attempt was a disaster. He dragged himself over to her, looked at her, felt for a pulse. He was too late.

He hadn't been able to help her, but he decided he'd spend the rest of his time on Earth trying to rid the planet of vampires, of those who would prey upon the weak. He'd help those in need.

He wouldn't fail again.

"Angel?"

It was Jack Willits. Angel realized the man had been talking, but he'd been lost in thought—and probably staring at Jack's teenage daughter. Karinna was looking at him quizzically.

"Sorry," Angel said. "I was just . . . thinking."

"I was asking if you were ready to start tonight," Jack said. "With Karinna, I mean."

"Sure," Angel said quickly. "I was expecting to."

"Good, that's good. We should cover some ground rules, then."

"Oh, this is the part where we talk about me like I'm not here," Karinna said. "My favorite."

"She likes to go dancing," Jack said, ignoring her. "But I don't want her to go places where alcohol is served, fake ID or no."

"I understand."

"She needs to be home by three on weekends. If it's a school night, I want her in by eleven."

"Daddeeee," Karinna whined.

"Twelve. No later."

"Twelve on school nights. Got it."

"No smoking, no drugs, no unchaperoned time with boys."

"Makes sense to me," Angel said, thinking, *am I a bodyguard or a baby-sitter? And shouldn't she be making some of these decisions on her own at this point?* Not that he was in favor of the things Jack wanted her kept away from—Angel just thought these were values that should have been instilled at an early age, instead of activities for her to be prevented from doing by a hired employee.

Not for the first time he had the sense that as a family, the Willitses left something to be desired. Angel's own personal experience with families was pretty minimal—he had killed his own, early in his vampiric days. But he'd seen a lot of them over the centuries, and they generally seemed to relate better than these people did. They interacted almost like three strangers: Jack laying down rules as if by memory, as if he'd done this with a hundred other bodyguards over the seventeen years of Karinna's life; Karinna ignoring the whole list, determined to do whatever she wanted to do, no matter what; Marjorie, eyes downcast, staring at her plate as she cut each bite into ever tinier pieces, which she then forked into her mouth and chewed a certain number of times, like a food ritual, before swallowing.

Whatever it was that brought people together as families—and he didn't think it was blood, he'd seen it with Buffy and Giles and Willow and Xander, even been part of the clan, for a while—was missing here.

If it had been replaced by anything else, he couldn't see what. Some kind of mutual distrust, maybe.

"Is there any particular danger you think she might be in?" Angel asked. "Anyone with a grudge against you, any threats?"

"No, nothing that I can think of," Jack said. "Of course, when you're in my position in this town—a certain amount of money, some notoriety, our names in the papers, and so on—you can never be too careful. There are some crazy people out there, and some desperate ones. I couldn't live with myself if anything happened to my baby."

Angel seemed to remember him saying something similar the morning he'd brought her back after Doyle's vision. It sounded almost rehearsed, as if he was protesting too much.

"Don't worry," he said. He tried to put on a reassuring smile. "I won't let anything happen to her."

"I'm trusting you, Angel," Jack said. "I wouldn't want that trust to be misplaced."

Before Angel could answer, Marjorie Willits scraped her chair back from the table. She looked away from the others, as if watching the path of something only she could see. When she turned to walk out of the room, Angel thought he could see tears glistening on her cheek.

"Excuse me," she said. "I'm sorry."

She hurried out the door. When she was gone, Jack said, "You'll have to forgive Marjorie. She's not been well recently."

"Not a problem," Angel said. "I hope she feels better."

"I'm sure she will," Jack assured him.

"Angel, can we get going?" Karinna asked. "There's a new DJ at Hi-Gloss tonight and I want to be there."

Angel nodded. "Sure, I'm ready when you are," he said. "That sound okay, Jack?"

"As long as you're on the job, Angel, I'm happy."

"Is Consuela on tonight, Dad?" Karinna asked.

"I believe she is, yes."

"Good." Karinna left the table, followed her mother out of the room. Angel looked at Jack.

"Consuela does her hair and makeup," Jack explained. "Worked at Monument for decades, and now she's on staff here. I take care of my people, and no one can say I don't."

"I'm sure that's true."

"She'll be twenty or thirty minutes," Jack told him. "I have some paperwork to attend to in my office, I'm afraid. But you're welcome to wait here, or there in the entryway, or in the parlor. Make yourself at home."

"I'll fend for myself," Angel said. "Go ahead, I'll be fine."

Jack put his hand out one more time. "I'm glad you're on the job, Angel. Makes me feel a whole lot better."

"I won't let you down," Angel said. But for a moment he wasn't sure who he was talking to, Jack Willits or a red-haired woman whose name he never knew, who lived and died in a faraway land more than a hundred years before.

CHAPTER EIGHT

Angel turned down an offered cup of coffee and went to wait for Karinna while the kitchen staff cleared the dinner table.

He'd once lived in a home with a roof made of grass and a floor of dirt. Even now he lived in a building in a seedy neighborhood. But he liked where he was. As Cordy said, what it lacked in comfort and style, it made up for in dampness and lack of amenities. It had easy access to the sewers, and that was important when one couldn't go outside in the daytime without experiencing spontaneous combustion. Besides, now he had an established business, and while walk-in traffic wasn't a big part of the clientele, there were a few people who knew where to look for him when they needed help.

Anyway, he hoped the job wouldn't last that long.

There were plenty of other people in Los Angeles who'd be needing his help. Doyle wasn't going to stop getting visions from the Powers That Be just because Angel was currently occupied.

After a while—more like forty-five minutes than the twenty or thirty Jack had estimated—Angel heard an upstairs door close and footfalls descending the staircase. He went into the entryway and saw Karinna coming down. She'd changed from the pants and tank top she'd worn for dinner into a short leather skirt that hugged her hips and thighs, spiderweb-pattern black stockings, a black leather bustier, and a leather collar. She wore tall spike-heeled shoes, and she wavered unsteadily as she walked down the stairs. Her hair was up and perfect, not a strand out of place. Her makeup looked great from where Angel stood, too. The scent of her perfume reached him before she did.

At the sight of her outfit, he found himself hoping she didn't want to go to one of those fetish clubs—there were always vampire wannabes at those places, and they just got on his nerves. But no, he remembered, she'd already said he wanted to see the new DJ at Hi-Gloss, which Angel recalled Cordy saying was one of several hot clubs in a former warehouse district near downtown L.A.

"You look great," he told her when she came toward him. He ushered her out the mansion. As he opened the convertible's passenger door for her,

Karinna looked at Angel with an odd smile. "Are you American, Angel?" she asked.

"Why?"

"Nothing, I guess. It's just, Angel's kind of an odd name, isn't it?"

"My family's from Ireland," he explained. The dodge seemed to work.

He climbed into the car on his side, gunned the engine, and pulled onto the long driveway. "So, Hi-Gloss?"

"That's right."

"Am I dressed appropriately?"

"You're dressed fine for someone who's having dinner with the famous head of a famous movie studio," Karinna answered. "For Hi-Gloss . . . I guess you'll have to do."

The music was, as he figured it would be, deafening, with a pounding beat that never seemed to vary. He couldn't tell when one song ended and the next began, and he couldn't imagine what it was the DJ was doing that earned him his pay, much less any accolades.

But then, he knew people had been saying that about the next generation's music for as long as there had been generations. He could remember a time before rock and roll, before jazz, before big band music—before there was a recording industry at all. He took a long-term view of trends. There was no point in complaining about them, he had decided long ago. They came, they went, something else followed. He had stopped thinking of any kind of music, or art, or literature as his, and just accepted them for what they were.

But that didn't stop this techno beat from hurting his ears.

Karinna had been dancing since they came through the door, allowed in by a ponytailed doorman who either recognized her or recognized that she was the kind of attractive young woman the owners of the club wanted on their dance floor. She hadn't settled in with any single dance partner but instead had been dancing with a number of men and women, and sometimes Angel couldn't tell if she was dancing with anyone at all. He stood near the bar and kept an eye on the dance floor. He'd bought a soft drink, for show, but it sat basically untouched on the bar behind him.

She came toward him, sweat gleaming on her forehead and beneath her collar. "Isn't it great, Angel?" she shouted. "Are you having fun?"

I've had more fun in Hell, he thought, but he called back, "Sure, it's great. You ready to go yet?"

"Are you kidding? I'm just getting warmed up!"

"Oh, good."

"This DJ rocks, doesn't he?"

"I'd have to say, yes, he does."

"Dance with me?"

"I'm working, Karinna. I can't dance."

She tossed him a pouty look. "Spoilsport!" she yelled. "Stick in the mud."

"That's me."

She turned away from him, nearly running into a handsome young guy carrying two tall sparkling glasses of something. She sized him up in an instant and put a hand on his chest.

"Oh, I'm sorry," she said. "I didn't make you spill anything, did I?"

"I don't think so," he replied.

"Well, I'm glad. I shouldn't have run into you though."

"It's okay."

She gestured toward one of the glasses. "Is that for someone? You here with a friend?"

He scanned the crowd quickly, as if to see if his "friend" was witnessing the exchange. Satisfied, he took another look at Karinna. "Yeah, a friend. Kind of a buddy, you know."

"A buddy," Karinna echoed.

"That's right."

"Would your buddy mind if we danced? You know, so I can apologize for almost knocking you over?"

Another quick scan. *He doesn't want to get caught,* Angel realized. *But he wants to do this.*

"I'm sure that—he—would be fine with it."

Karinna touched his hands, caressing his fingers and then plucking the glasses from them. "Here," she said. She turned to Angel, handing him the two cold glasses. "Hold these," she said.

Angel took them, sniffed them, and set them on a nearby table. Fruity, but not alcoholic, which was good. But he wasn't here as a personal servant or drink tender. If anything happened, he'd need his hands free.

Karinna shrugged and led her new friend by the hand, out onto the dance floor.

Call me old-fashioned, Angel thought, *but I think a guy who comes to a place like this with a date should leave with the same date, and should probably even pay some attention to her along the way.*

After a few minutes a young lady passed by. She was searching through the crowd, looking for someone or something. It was hard to make anyone out on the floor—the lighting was blue and indirect, reflected off a series of banked mirrors mounted on the wall almost level with the high ceiling, with occasional sweeps by a brighter spotlight across the writhing mass of dancers. And everyone was uniformly young and fashionable, which meant no one really stood out. Even Karinna's outfit was more or less standard dress for some of the girls.

When the young woman saw the two drinks on the table, condensation creating little pools around them, she smiled and looked around for the person who had been sent in quest of them. When her eyes fell on Angel, he gave a little shrug and cocked his head toward the dance floor.

Karinna was hanging on to the young man, pressing herself against him like a longtime lover. When the young woman saw them, her face fell. Angel felt terrible—that she had seen, that she had in fact been the "friend," that he had been instrumental in her discovery.

She grabbed one of the glasses, giving Angel a second look. He leaned close to her so he could be heard over the music. "Better to find out now than later, right?"

"Guess so," she responded. "So, you busy?"

"Yes, I am."

"Too bad." She shrugged and vanished back into the crowd. He was sure she'd find someone else to ease the hurt before the night was through.

But he felt uncomfortable about Karinna's role in the whole thing. Her behavior didn't seem appropriate for someone her age. He didn't believe that he was bringing eighteenth-century standards to twenty-first-century situations, just wishing that people would practice consideration in all their interactions.

She's better off, he told himself. Hoping, at the same time, that the other young lady made a better choice next time. For a moment he thought he felt sorry for her, but then he realized the ache he felt was something else. She was looking for someone else with whom to make a connection, of whatever kind. But he was past that. He had made his connection, and it was over, and there wouldn't be anyone else like that for him. There couldn't be, or he'd lose his soul again.

He was apart from all these people, as surely as if there had been a window between him and them. He was not one of them and never would be.

He had a feeling the guy who had abandoned this one wouldn't be happy with his decision, either. He'd already seen Karinna dancing with a dozen guys the same way, leaving each one with the impression, he had no doubt, that she was going home with them.

But he remembered one of Jack's rules—no unchaperoned time with boys. And he realized that he couldn't see Karinna anywhere. He'd looked away for a moment, and she had taken advantage of it.

No wonder she can't keep a bodyguard, he thought. *I'm going to be fired, too.*

He pushed his way onto the floor, reminded of the first time he'd gone looking for her, at Sugar Town. At least this club, as dark and gloomy as it was, wasn't as hard on the eyes as that pink monstrosity had been. But it was hard, even for someone whose senses were as keen as Angel's, to find a single person in the mass of movement that was the dance floor.

He stood on tiptoe to see over everyone's heads, hoping to spot her upswept red hair out there. No luck. He made his way to the far side, and tried looking back the way he'd come. Nothing. He sniffed the air, hoping to catch a trace of her perfume, but there were too many scents intermingled, and he couldn't pick hers out.

If she's left the building, he thought, *I'll . . . I don't know what. But she won't like it.*

Then he remembered the mirrors. They had the advantage of height, and a bird's-eye angle on the crowd. He turned and checked in the nearest one. She wasn't in view here, but there were mirrors on every wall, to give the illusion of more space and to reflect the blue lights. He started to work his way around the perimeter of the room, scanning the floor in the mirrors as he went. He could get a good panorama of the club in them, so he knew if she was still in here, he'd spot her.

At the same time he kept checking the door to the rest rooms and the exit, just in case she appeared at either.

He made it all the way back to where he'd started without any sign of her. She wasn't visible in any of the mirrors, she hadn't used any of the doors. She was just gone.

He decided to try outside. Maybe she hadn't gone far. One more look in the mirror—

"Looking for someone?"

He turned and there she was, right by his arm.

"Where have you been?" he demanded.

109

"Dancing," she replied. "Where'd you think I was?"

"I didn't know. I couldn't find you anywhere."

"I don't know what your problem is, Angel. I was right there."

"I don't want you to leave my sight again," Angel said, realizing as he did it that he sounded just like someone's dad. "I thought you were—"

"You're wound way too tight, Angel," Karinna said with a wry smile. "You need to loosen up. You ever had a girlfriend?"

He ignored the question. "Come on," he said, grabbing her arm. "We're going home."

"But, Angel—"

"Home."

She sighed again. Angel felt very much like a parent at that moment. He felt his age.

Every single century of it.

CHAPTER NINE

There are days, Cordelia Chase thought, stretching luxuriously in her bed, *when everything is right in the world. Days when the fates or the gods smile down upon you, when your stars are all in alignment, when your ducks are in a row, whatever that means. On those days the future is spread out before you like a road map to destinations with names like Contentment, Peace, Happiness, with side trips through Fame and Wealth and "I Told You So" to Those Who Ever Doubted You.*

She shook her head, scootched out from under the covers, and planted both feet on the floor.

This was one of those days.

And it felt great!

Monument Pictures was out there waiting for her. A new career, a new life. Stardom. The devotion of millions of fans. She couldn't wait.

111

She jumped into the shower, singing all the way through. Blow-dried her hair, brushed her teeth. Tore through her closet looking for something to wear. Phantom Dennis took a couple of dresses from the closet and floated them around the room on their hangers, but neither one really projected the image she was going for.

A dozen outfits later, she decided it didn't matter all that much since wardrobe would dress her for whatever her part was anyway. She could show up in dirty sweats, and it would be okay with them.

She settled on a simple red dress with crisscrossing straps, and red pumps. A little makeup, a touch-up with the hairbrush. She checked herself in the mirror for about the thousandth time that morning.

Perfection. She left the apartment with a smile on her face.

When she reached the studio gate, she was terrified.

The guard's going to turn me away, she suddenly thought. *He's going to laugh in my face. He's going to have me arrested for impersonating a successful person.*

Her legs turned to water, and she could barely walk up to the little checkpoint.

The guard, a skinny black man in a clean blue uniform, gave her a friendly smile. "Good morning," he said.

"Yes," Cordelia said. "Morning, I mean. And good.

It's just about as good as a morning could be, isn't it?"
She looked up at the blue sky. "I mean, it's got all the
elements, right? Sunshine, sky, birds singing . . . I'm
sure they're singing somewhere, even if the traffic
noises are a little too loud right here, exactly."

"Something I can do for you, ma'am?" he asked.

*This is where he spins me around and kicks me on
my stupid—but shapely—behind,* she thought.

"Well, I don't know," she said. "I'm supposed to
be on a list or something, but I'm thinking I'm probably not there, so—"

"Well, what's your name?" He reached in through
a little window and pulled out a clipboard with a
number of sheets of paper on it. "Let's just have a
look-see."

"A look-see, that's always a good idea, isn't it? And
what an interesting word, don't you think?"

"Your name, ma'am?"

Be there, she thought. *Be there, be there, be there.*
If it wasn't there—and by this point she was more
convinced that it wouldn't be than she had ever been
convinced of anything in her life—she didn't know
how she'd face Angel and Doyle, or anyone, really, for
the rest of her miserable existence on Earth.

"Chase. Cordelia Chase." Her voice sounded very
small and far away.

"Oh, of course, Ms. Chase," he said, breaking into
a big smile. "We've been waiting for you. Welcome
to the lot."

Cordelia looked around to see if there was maybe another Ms. Chase behind her. But there wasn't, she was the only Ms. anything waiting on the walkway to get in. Cars drove past to another gate where another guard met them, but she had not anticipated having a parking place on the lot, hence the walking in.

"Me?"

"Yes, you. It's right here. Cordelia Chase you said, right?"

"That's right. I mean, that's me, I think."

"Well, then, welcome to the lot. Do you know where you're going?"

No clue.

"Umm, I think so, but I guess I could maybe use a refresher."

The guard nodded. "No problem at all," he said. He pointed toward a roadway that led between two huge sound stages. "See that road there? Turn right, then at the first corner, make a left. That'll take you up past some soundstages and the mill. Then you get to some office buildings. The second one is the one you want. It's called the Fairbanks Building. You go on in there, second floor, Room 213. Got it?"

"I think I can manage."

"That's good, that's good. You have yourself a great day, Ms. Chase. I'll see you around."

She liked the sound of that. She liked the sound

of everything: the cars idling at the gate, the voices raised in greeting, the traffic rushing by on the avenue. Now she could hear morning birds. She was on the lot. They were expecting her. They wanted her here.

Life was good.

The soundstages were huge. Their walls loomed huge beside her, like multistory apartment buildings with no windows. The wide doors were open on a couple of them, and she peeked in. Inside, they were like empty warehouses, only warehouses big enough to herd dinosaurs in. They reminded her of airplane hangars, but maybe for zeppelins instead of mere planes.

The feeling of walking on the lot—alone, without a tour guide leading her along in a group—was remarkable. It was like she belonged here. She'd been to auditions in casting offices, and done a few commercials in tiny, cramped studios around town. But the sheer space of all these enormous sound-stages made her think about the enormity of what she was doing. *The movies*.

Everyone on the lot seemed so cheerful. It was not even nine yet, and people were already at work, chatting and laughing as they went about their day.

But then, why not? They were involved in the business of making movies—making dreams. What was there not to be cheerful about?

And now the business would include her.

Cordelia Chase. For a moment she couldn't wait to tell the Scooby Gang about it, but then she thought better of it. *Let them be surprised when they see my name on a movie poster. Or on the cover of* People. They had doubted her prospects in Hollywood, but they'd be eating their words now.

She wondered for a moment what her first picture would be. Action adventure? Maybe a romantic comedy? Something opposite Richard Gere or Tom Cruise, maybe.

Looking ahead, Cordelia saw the office buildings the guard had told her to look for, three-story Mediterranean-style structures with tiled roofs. The second one was the Fairbanks Building, where her nine o'clock appointment was. As she approached it, her feet barely seemed to be touching the ground.

Inside was a large lobby area with a board listing the various offices inside—production offices owned by famous actors and directors, mostly. Who would she be working with? She could hardly stand to wait for the elevator that would take her to the second floor.

When she got off, it was in a quiet, carpeted hallway. Office 213 was to the left, four doors down. There was nothing on the door but the number in gold-plated numerals. She hesitated outside the door, not sure if she should knock or just go in. After a moment she decided to go for it. She turned the knob, pulled the door wide, and entered.

Inside, there was a waist-high counter. Behind it, two clerks, a man and a woman, were working at computer terminals.

The man looked up at Cordelia.

"Help you?" he asked in a pleasant voice.

"Maybe I have the wrong place," Cordelia said. "This is Room 213, Fairbanks Building?"

"That's right. Did you have an appointment?"

"Yes. My name is Cordelia Chase."

The man flipped through a stack of file folders. "Okay, gotcha right here." He rose from his chair, approached the counter with his hand out. Cordelia took it and gave it a shake. "Welcome to Monument Pictures, Ms. Chase. I'm sure you'll have a terrific experience working here."

Cordelia felt her heart falling. *This doesn't look like a star's office,* she thought. *Or much of anything I'm interested in.* "Just what is it I'm supposed to be doing?" she asked.

The man looked back at the file in his hands. "Says here you're the new tour guide for lot tours. It's a great job—I started there, too, and look where I am today!"

Great, Cordelia thought. *Maybe someday I, too, can be a Human Resources clerk.*

"Hey," Doyle said. "Your boss is in the trades."

Angel looked up from his desk, where he was still going over some of the magazines Cordy had

117

brought from the library. He'd slept for most of the day, since dropping Karinna off at her house, knowing that he'd be out with her again tonight. Now it was early evening. "Since when do you read the trades?"

"Cordy got me in the habit. You learn all kinds of interesting things. Look here—'Chix Flix Sell Nix Tix.' You don't get that kind of reporting from the *New York Times*, I'll tell you that."

"So what's new with Jack Willits?"

"Did you know what kind of trouble he was in?"

"Besides having to live with Karinna, you mean? No."

"According to this, Monument Pictures was bleeding cash. Heads were gonna roll, and Jack's was gonna be first. But it looks like he saved the day—he's signed Blake Alten to do a picture this year."

"Blake Alten's that actor who . . ." Angel searched. He knew he'd heard the name.

"The one who can open any movie, no matter how bad the script is. Biggest action star in the world today, they're saying. He usually earns twenty-five million for a movie, but he's agreed to do this one for nine because he loves the script so much. He's gonna make Monument Pictures profitable again all by himself. Looks like Jack Willits's lucky day."

"Again, not counting having that terror Karinna for a daughter."

"Yeah, not counting that."

"So in the course of a single day, Monument goes from losing money to being the hottest studio in the business. And Jack saves the day, and his own neck. I guess he's a happy man today."

The front door swung open. "I'm glad someone's happy," Cordelia railed. "But if I hear the words 'Monument Pictures' again today, I'm going to scream."

Angel and Doyle looked at her, Angel surprised by the frustration and anger that showed on her face. "First day didn't go so well?" he asked.

"You have no idea," she said indignantly. "Your friend Jack Willits tricked me."

"Tricked you? How?"

"Didn't you hear him say that I was going to be a star? Or at the very least, an actress?"

Angel thought a moment. "Actually, no. I seem to remember him offering you a job. But I don't think any details were discussed."

"You think I imagined it? Well, okay, maybe I did. But even so, I didn't think he was offering me a job guiding tours on the lot!"

"Tours?" Doyle said, suppressing a laugh. "You? Don't tour guides have to be cheerful and answer obnoxious tourists' questions with a smile?"

"You think this is funny, Doyle?" Cordelia said. Her hands unconsciously balled into fists.

Doyle held out his hands. "No, nothing funny about it, Cordy."

"I had to lead four tours today," she said. "My feet are killing me. I thought the exhaust fumes from those trams would suffocate me. Smell me—I still stink from it." Doyle leaned in and took a big whiff, but Cordelia waved him away and went on with her rant. "First I had to sit through hours of pointless training, including watching a video so boring I thought my brain was going to ice over. Then I had to point out the house from *My Hero* and the fort from *Wagons West* to people from seventeen countries and twenty different states, and I had to take pictures of people in front of it with forty different cameras. Do you know how hard it is to understand all those different accents?"

"Faith and begorra, I wouldn'a have a clue," Doyle said, pouring on the brogue.

"I'm not even talking to you," Cordelia snapped.

"Hey, I'm not the one who got you—well, actually, a paying job. That's not so bad. And if you get stock options, you got in just in time."

"Yeah, yeah, Blake Alten, blah blah blah, heard all about it a hundred times."

"Maybe you'll get to meet him," Angel offered.

"That's the only saving grace I can find," Cordelia replied. "As long as I'm on the lot, maybe I'll meet casting directors or producers who can give me actual work."

"There you go," Doyle put in. "That's lookin' at the bright side."

"And that's so what I'm known for," Cordelia said miserably.

"The Willits family is driving us all a little crazy, I'm afraid," Angel said, trying to change the subject. "I had to put up with Karinna last night. Have you heard of Hi-Gloss?"

"Heard of it? I've been turned away twice. She got in? *You* got in?"

"I got in because I was with her, I think. Maybe they knew she'd dance with every guy in the place and let them all think they were taking her home."

"Well, of course. That's the way to have a good time, right?"

"Is that how it works these days?"

"I guess you haven't been a teenage girl recently, Angel. Or ever, come to think of it. But yes, that's pretty much how it goes. You never know which one will end up being the right one, so why not test them all until you find him?"

"That's . . . one way to look at it, I suppose," Angel said.

"If you want to look at it through her eyes, that's the only way."

"Maybe I was too hard on her," Angel said. "It just seemed a little dishonest to me. Or at least, disingenuous."

"And then there was the part where she ditched you," Doyle added.

"She ditched you?"

"Just for a minute," Angel said.

Cordelia snorted. "Some bodyguard."

"I got her home alive, didn't I?" Angel shot back.

Cordelia took a long look at Angel, sitting behind his desk. "A little defensive, are we?" she asked. "What's up with you, Angel? You seem to be taking this case a little personally."

Angel shook his head. "It isn't like that," he argued. "She's just a kid."

"Down, boy," Cordelia chided. "I didn't mean romantically."

"But maybe Cordy has a point, Angel," Doyle said.

"Not you, too," Angel responded.

"Just that, I don't know, maybe you are taking this one too much to heart," Doyle explained.

Angel thought about the young lady in Rumania, the one Karinna reminded him of. The one he hadn't been able to save.

"Is that bad?" he asked.

"It could be, that's all I'm sayin'," Doyle offered. "You know what happens when an angel flies too close to the ground."

Kate Lockley knew that a lot of detective work was about knowing the right people and asking the right questions. The drawback was, when the job was about catching criminals, the "right people" were often not the kind that she might have wanted to socialize with, if she'd had her choice.

And the neighborhoods they hung out in weren't exactly high-end, either.

The caller had asked to meet her on a street corner outside a liquor store. She knew him only as Chuey. He'd been an informant for a couple of years, after she cut him a break on a small-time burglary charge in order to get him to turn over the fence who was moving large volumes of stolen merchandise. He didn't call her often, and he hated it when she came to him. But when he did give her something, more often than not it turned out to be valuable. So she grabbed a young detective named Weston—mostly to watch the car when she was away from it—got into her car, and drove into central L.A. She parked between a pawnshop and a bar that opened at six in the morning, and was pulling in the serious drinkers by seven. It was now eight at night, and Kate knew the place would be silent except for the sounds of liquid pouring, muttered conversations and despair.

She told Weston to wait in the car. "He doesn't like strangers," she explained. "I'll be back in a few."

Weston nodded his assent. He'd brought along coffee in a paper cup, and he was sipping from it when she left him.

Chuey was talking on the pay phone that hung from the wall outside the liquor store. He was short, just over five feet, but he was a constant bundle of energy. Even as he talked on the phone,

one hand was tapping on the leg of his jeans while
the other tugged at his baseball cap, his foot was
moving as if keeping a beat, and his head swiveled
this way and that as he kept an eye on everything
that happened on the street. He saw her
approach, gave a sign with his eyes. She didn't go
any nearer, and after a moment he replaced the
receiver on the hook. He came toward her,
already talking as he did. He didn't slow as he
reached her, but she turned and walked in the same
direction he was.

"Let's walk," he said.

"Anywhere in particular?"

"Around the block. We'll be done by then."

He was moving at a fast clip, and she found herself taking long strides to keep up with him.
"What've you got for me, Chuey? I'm pretty busy
these days."

"I know, huh? Those bank robbers. That's what
I'm talking about."

"You've got something on these tunnel rats? Spill
it, Chuey. They're bad news."

"I know, man, you don't have to tell me."

"So what do you have?"

Something seemed wrong about the whole thing,
to Kate. Chuey was strictly small time. The bank
robbers, on the other hand, were major felons. They
used sophisticated weapons, they planned their
crimes carefully, they took large amounts of easy-to-

move cash rather than electronics and junk jewelry like Chuey. These people ran in different circles, and she didn't see where Chuey would have come into contact with them.

But she was willing to listen. That's what cops did. That's how crimes were solved.

"Listen, man, I don't want to get jammed up over this or nothing, you know?"

"Have I ever lied to you, Chuey?" Kate asked, carefully not answering his question.

"Okay, let's just say this guy I know, he was at this place. This night spot, but not exactly one that has an ad in the Yellow Pages, you know?"

"A private party, a card game, something like that?" She stepped around a guy sleeping against the wall, legs wrapped in a thin plaid blanket, bottle in a paper bag near his head. She had to take a second look to be sure he was breathing.

"Yeah, something like that, close enough," Chuey agreed. "So this guy was talking to these people there, and one of them said there was this gas station, you know, one that was closed or something. And he used to go there to get in out of the cold, you know, drink some wine, catch some sleep."

"Okay," Kate said, trying to follow along. "An abandoned gas station he used as a squat sometimes."

"Yeah, that's right. Only a couple of nights ago

this dude said he tried to go there, he raised some dough for a bottle and he took it there, and when he tried to go in through these boards they got over the back door, a guy stuck a gun in his face and told him to beat it."

"A gun?"

"That's what the dude said. He was so scared he dropped the bottle and ran away."

"And this connects to my bank robbers how, Chuey?"

Chuey stopped and faced Kate, in a rare moment of stillness. From a second-story window she could hear the indistinct mutterings of a TV game show. Someone who wanted to be a millionaire was answering easy questions in front of the world, and down here on the street Chuey was just trying to get by.

"This guy, he said when the other dude, the one with the gun, stuck his head out through the boards, he could see inside a little bit. There was some kind of light on in there, like a lantern or something, you know? And in the light from the lantern, he saw like a bunch of shovels."

"Shovels, Chuey? Is he sure?"

"If you talked to this dude like—like my friend did, you'd know he was straight when he saw this. Even if he was drinking, that gun would have scared him straight, man. So if he says he saw shovels, I believe him."

"Okay, Chuey. I believe him, too. Where's this gas station?"

"That's the thing, man," Chuey said. "He didn't say exactly."

"He didn't? Then what good does this do me?"

"I don't think he's a guy who pays a lot of attention to street signs, you know what I mean?" Chuey asked. He started walking again, without warning, and Kate hurried to keep up. "He don't have a car, he don't drive anywhere."

"Where does he usually hang out?"

"He never goes north of the ten," Chuey said, naming one of the major east-west freeways in the city. "I'd look around Avalon, maybe, someplace like that. Avalon and Vernon, or Slauson, maybe, okay?"

"I'll check it out, Chuey, thanks."

"Hey, these bank guys, they're bad news, right?"

"Yes, Chuey, they are."

"So something like this gotta be worth a little something, ain't it? Not for me, but for my friend, you know?"

She dug a couple of twenties out of her pocket that she'd had ready for this moment, and slipped them into his waiting hand.

"The city of Los Angeles thanks you," she said.

"The city's welcome," Chuey said with a smile. "*Adios*, man."

He crossed the street swiftly and disappeared

around a corner. Kate kept going, back to the corner with the liquor store, then around and back to her car. The bar was still there. A neon drinking glass sputtered in the night, but otherwise there was no sign of life. Kate climbed into her car, nodded to Weston, and drove away.

CHAPTER TEN

Tony Chen moved briskly through his shop, dusting the bottles with an ostrich-feather duster. The shop was simply called "Chen's." It fronted onto an alley instead of a street, off North Main, just at the edge of L.A.'s Chinatown district. A block away a trickle of water ran down the cement canal that was called the Los Angeles River

The shop had been in the family since his grandparents had come to California from the mainland. His parents had worked it for their whole lives, and now it was his turn. If one knew what it was, and where, one could find it, but it wasn't the kind of place that was advertised in the Yellow Pages, or the backs of bus stop benches. Much of his stock was, after all, illegal in the U.S.—things like powdered rhino horn, tiger claws, and the like. And then there were the items that weren't quite what they were represented as: the dragon's teeth that were really shipped to him by an alligator farm outside New Iberia, Louisiana, for instance.

Chen's was a magic shop, but not the kind that sold parlor tricks and illusions. When he was feeling philosophical, Tony liked to think he was selling dreams. When he was in a more prosaic mood, he considered himself to be selling power.

He was on his way behind the counter to put the duster away when the door opened with a tinkle of chimes. He turned around, laying the duster on top of the counter. A man had come in, European, tall and white-haired, his face as lined as a roadmap. Piercing blue eyes drew Tony's gaze.

"Help you find something?" he asked.

"I am in need of the eyelash of a two-headed ewe," the man said. His tone betrayed no sense that the request was at all strange.

"An interesting curiosity," Tony replied.

"Your level of interest could not be of less importance to me. Do you have it or not?" the man demanded.

"Could be," Tony offered. "Let me look." He turned to an array of tiny jars stacked on shelves behind the counter. As he did so, he let his thoughts drift toward the stranger's. He had picked up a trick or two in his time, and this man's mind was something he wanted a closer look at. Ewe's lashes were a pretty specialized item.

Reading most minds, at least on the most superficial level, was not particularly difficult for someone practiced at it. People tended to keep their dominant thoughts at the front of their minds, and for most people, the dominant thoughts were nearly all they had. They wanted money, material things, women, fame, power.

This man was different. It was as if he had better control over the workings of his own brain. Tony had to dig for a while—a process he visualized as probing, as if with a dentist's tool. But finally, just as he closed his hands on a bottle of two-headed ewe's lashes, a particular image came into his head with a suddenness and clarity that he felt like a spike of pain behind his eyes.

He couldn't contain the word.

"Balor," he muttered. He put the bottle down on the countertop.

"Looking around where you're not wanted?" the man asked.

"No, I—" Tony started. But it was too late. The man moved forward more quickly than Tony would have believed, and caught Tony's wrist in his bony fingers.

"All right, then," the man said angrily. "You might as well look more closely." His blue eyes bored into Tony's. Tony tried to throw up a mental defense, but he felt the man's thoughts push past it as if it were the merest gauze curtain.

131

And then he was out of his shop, on a rocky windswept plain. Leaning against one of the rocks, his single eye closed in slumber, was Balor. Tony had never seen Balor, even in a drawing—his tradition was Asian, and he hadn't studied much Celtic magic—but he knew at a glance who it was, probably because this man had implanted the image in his mind.

And even though he knew that it was only a projected mental image, he also knew the damage that it could do. He needed to fight back, and fast.

He closed his own eyes and summoned up a dozen giants of his own, huge warriors carrying longbows. They brought arrows to their bowstrings, lifted them to shoulder-height, drew back the strings, and held them there. If Balor so much as shuddered or blinked, he'd be skewered.

Tony looked at Balor with terrible fascination. The god was as tall as a three-story building. He had a wild mane of flaming red hair and a thick growth of beard around his chin. His arms, the size of massive trees, were crossed over a vast belly. Gigantic legs were spread before him as he slept.

In the center of his forehead there was one eyelid, covering an eye the size of the gong that stood inside Tony's maternal grandmother's Chinese restaurant.

Suddenly Balor let out a snort, like a peal of thunder.

The archers tensed.

The god came awake instantly, as if forewarned of the danger. The eyelid snapped open and Balor's single, horrible eye was exposed.

The archers released their arrows.

Balor whipped his head from right to left, across his entire field of view.

Where his gaze traveled, the arrows burst into flames, mid-flight. Before they reached Balor, they had disintegrated. Puffs of smoke bounced harmlessly off his skin.

Then he pushed his mass to a standing position, hands at his sides. His mouth opened in a ferocious growl, and he focused his gaze at Tony's warriors.

One by one they burst into flames and vanished.

Then Tony saw a tiny figure on the rock-strewn plane. He recognized it as himself.

The small mental image of Tony tried to run, tried to hide behind the boulders. But Balor sniffed the air, finding his scent, and strode forward on legs that pounded the earth, shaking it with every step.

The small Tony trembled, his back pressed against the rock. Then Balor's face appeared above the rock. His mouth was twisted into something resembling a smile. His red-veined eye rolled in its socket, finally settling on Tony. Tony screamed—

In the shop Tony went limp and fell to the floor behind the counter. Mordractus looked at him there. The shopkeeper still breathed, but Mor-

ANGEL

dractus knew he would never come out of the coma.
In his mind's eye he would be in that spot, waiting
for the force of Balor's gaze to land upon him, until
the day he died.

Mordractus took the bottle of ewe's lash and went
outside, to where Currie waited with a car. He'd
have been willing to pay for it, but this way was so
much cleaner.

In the Willits household that night's hair and
makeup routine was much like the night before's.
Karinna went upstairs to where Consuela was waiting
for her. Inside a closed room she was attended to for
about half an hour. When she emerged, she was a different woman, more grown up, more sophisticated,
more lovely. The air was thick with her usual perfume.

At least on the outside. Angel was never sure how
the outside, in Karinna's case, matched up with the
inside. Her exterior could be carefully thought out,
artfully arranged, done to perfection. But inside she
was a spoiled brat used to having things her way, a
little rich girl who ran roughshod over her parents
and their employees, a tease and a flirt.

Tonight she wore wide-legged, hip-hugging black
pants, and a short top that left a large chunk of
midriff exposed and barely closed over her chest.
Her hair was left down instead of pulled up. Angel
thought it made her look younger. Closer to her real
age.

When they were in the GTX, headed for Sunset and a Hollywood club, she playfully punched his shoulder. "You were telling me about your girlfriend, before," she said.

"No, I wasn't."

"But you have one, right? I mean, you must. Look at you. Unless you're—"

"No, I'm not," Angel assured her. "And no, I don't. Not right now, anyway."

"What happened?" Karinna wanted to know. "Was it a tragic love story?"

"What happened, Karinna, is none of your business," he said. "If I want to talk about it, I will. Don't hold your breath."

"Man of mystery," she said. "You always like to keep people guessing, don't you?"

"Maybe I just don't like to share every single thought that flits through my head."

"Ouch! Tender mood tonight? What's wrong?"

"If I wanted to talk about it," Angel said, "I'd talk about it."

"Sorreeee," she said. From the corner of his eye he could see her slump against her door and fold in on herself. The top was up tonight, so she wasn't huddled against the wind. He'd hurt her feelings.

What is with me? he wondered. *There's no need to snap at the girl.* But even as he asked himself the question, he knew the answer lay in the things Doyle and Cordy had been saying earlier. Maybe he was taking this whole thing too personally. Maybe he'd let Karinna get under his skin, somehow. The connection to the woman in Rumania? When he thought back to her, he could still smell, in his mind, the yeasty odor of the bread that wafted from her bakery door, and the coppery tang of her blood after Tirbol had killed her.

And what was it Doyle had said? "What happens when an angel flies too close to the ground?" Angel could only come up with one answer that made any sense.

The angel crashes.

He shook his head. None of this would help with Karinna. He had to focus, had to figure out what the threat against her was and how to deal with it. Someone was out to get her, for some reason. Between Doyle's vision and Jack's concerns, he was sure of that, even though, so far, he'd only been a baby-sitter. He just had to know who, and why, and he could neutralize the threat, leave Karinna and Jack to their millions, and move on.

The Belvedere GTX had no rearview mirror— not usually a problem, since mirrors and vampires weren't exactly the best of friends. But on some occasions, he recognized that it would come in handy. This was one of those. He had the vague sense that they had been followed since leaving Bel Air, but all he had to back that up was the way head-lights shone through his rear window, and what little he could see by craning his head around and looking back.

All he could see back there were two round headlights. Left him little to go on. He decided he'd take a few side streets, try some evasive maneuvers, and maybe if there was someone back there, they'd have to show their hand.

He made a sudden right off of Sunset at Ogden, went down two blocks, and made another right. Then he went up one block and made a quick left.

"Hey, what are you doing?" Karinna asked him. "This isn't the way to the Wet Sprocket!"

"Just hang on a minute," he said, spinning the wheel to pull a U-turn. Now he was heading north on Orange Grove. Another left put him on Fountain, and he shot across Fairfax on a yellow light. No one came through behind him. He breathed a sigh of relief and headed back toward Sunset.

"Just playing it safe," he said. "That's what we bodyguards do."

"I think you bodyguards are all whack jobs," Karinna suggested.

"That may be, but—"

He never even saw it coming.

The car blasted out of nowhere, no headlights on, and slammed into the GTX. There was a sound like an explosion. The Plymouth went into a skid and stopped ninety degrees from the way it had been headed.

The engine had died upon impact. Angel was

reaching for the key to restart it when he saw a van turn sideways in the street ahead. Five men jumped from it, and four more were coming from the car, a big Lincoln, that had slammed into them. They were all dressed in black, and Angel saw chains, knives, even a couple of handguns.

This was no simple traffic accident.

"Karinna, listen," he hissed. "I'll stall these guys. You drive like a crazy woman. If they had any more vehicles here, they'd be unloading, too, so there are only the two. I'll keep them from chasing you, but you've got to go straight home and wait for me there. It's the only place I'll know you're safe."

"Angel, I'm s-scared," Karinna said, her voice breaking.

"I know. I'll be okay, and you will too if you get out of here. As soon as I'm out of the car, slide over and just go. I'll come by later and check on you, okay?"

"Okay," she agreed.

He shoved open his door and jumped from the car, landing in the middle of the street. There was glass on the road, from the Lincoln. The GTX had come through the whole thing remarkably well, he noted. Good old Detroit engineering from the days when they built cars to last.

There were nine men on the street, coming toward him from every angle. They were quiet, a couple of them issuing one-word commands to the rest but otherwise not talking, not laughing, not taunting him. They had the air of professionals, doing a job. That would make this easier and harder, Angel knew. Harder, because they'd be good at it.

And easier, because they weren't innocents. He had no qualms about hurting people who hurt others for a living.

"We're not here for you," one of them said. He was tall, with steely gray eyes and black hair slicked close to his scalp. "You could go. Take your car. We'll take the girl."

"No deal," Angel said.

"Didn't think so," the guy said. "Thought I'd offer, though."

"Appreciate it."

"Kill him," the guy instructed calmly. One of the guns was raised, held in a massive fist by a short dark-skinned man with a bald head and a goatee. Angel heard the gun cock, and he went to work.

Letting the change wash over him, he threw himself into the air, tumbling twice, heels over head, and landed behind the short stocky man. The man swung around, trying to keep the gun trained on Angel. But Angel was already moving in. He threw a fist at the man's goateed chin and felt it connect with bone-crushing force. At the same time he swept his other arm down into the wrist of the man's gun hand. The man let out a soft grunt. The pistol clattered to the street. Angel kicked it and it skidded into the next block, disappearing under a parked car.

There was another gun in play—Angel could smell the powder, the oil. He leaped again, turning in the air, until he could see it. A tall man, basket-ball-player tall, held a .38. It looked tiny in the man's long hand.

There were still knives and chains to contend with, but Angel knew that guns carried the potential to injure innocent bystanders, even people blocks away. And Karinna hadn't left the scene yet—in the seconds since he'd left the GTX, its powerful engine had been started, but she hadn't pulled away. The guns had to be taken out of action first, even though they couldn't hurt him.

But the gunman could fire before Angel could possibly cover the distance to him. So he tried a chain reaction tactic—he grabbed the nearest guy, an overweight bruiser carrying a length of bicycle chain, and lifted him over his head. He hurled the guy at another one, who fell into a third. This one stumbled into the gunman, who threw his arms out to his sides to maintain his balance. When he was thus occupied, Angel charged over the bodies of the fallen and dived headfirst into the gunman's solar plexus. The guy gave a "whoof" and went down in the street.

By this time Angel heard distant sirens approaching. The attackers seemed oblivious to the oncoming police presence, though. They had Angel—and his car, with Karinna inside—surrounded, and they appeared intent on finishing what they had started.

Angel's goal had to be to keep the girl safe and get her out of there. A black man, as wide and solid as a tank, was yanking on one of the GTX's locked doors. Angel leaped to his side, drove a fist into his kidney.

The guy looked at him and smiled.

Angel threw another punch, then a left-right-left combination.

This time the guy winced.

"Are you human?" Angel asked. He hadn't smelled demon.

"What they tell me," the guy said. He punched at Angel. His fist had the power of a pile driver. Angel went down in the street, then picked himself up again. A mortal man could have been killed by such a blow.

Angel approached the guy more cautiously this time. The other men were standing around them in a semicircle, anticipating the battle to come.

"Gold's Gym?" Angel asked.

"San Quentin," the man replied. He moved in a slow circle around Angel as they spoke. Angel, too, was moving, turning in small steps, never off-balance for more than a second.

"Paid off."

"Thanks."

"The rest of these guys, they're just along for the ride?"

141

"Pretty much," the man said.

"But you're the real deal."

"You're the real something yourself," the guy said. "Nice teeth."

Angel knew Karinna was inside the car, engine running. He spoke softly. "Vampire," he admitted, hoping it would throw his opponent's concentration. Still turning. Watching the man's eyes. He'd know when the guy was going to make his move by his eyes. But he had to keep himself from being distracted by the way his fists flexed and opened. His arms were the size of tree trunks.

"No way."

"Way."

"That's freaky, man. That's why you got the forehead and stuff?"

"That's it."

"So I could stake you or something? Cross, maybe?"

"Stories," Angel said. Why give anything away?

"You drink blood, though?" Still circling.

Angel smiled. "All the time. Little hungry now, in fact."

The guy moved then, and Angel saw it in his eyes a half-second before he lunged. Angel stepped to his left, so the guy charged to his right. Angel brought his right arm high into the air, bringing it down as the shorter man stumbled past him, thrown off-balance by the fact that Angel was not where he had been. His elbow slammed into the back of the guy's head, driving him toward the ground. Stepping back into the man, Angel brought his right knee up and it caught the man's chin.

The guy fell back a couple of steps, his eyes glassy. The blows had had some impact this time. He still stood, but his legs wobbled, his solidity seemed less certain. Blood showed at the corners of his mouth.

And still, he came for more.

This time his fists found Angel's solar plexus. He hammered, landing blow after punishing blow. Angel blocked with both hands, but the man was fast.

Finally Angel closed on the man, trying to grab his flailing fists in his hands. When he was close enough he drove his head into the guy's face. He felt cartilage tear, and the man reeled back, blood spraying from his nose. Angel followed, pressing his advantage. He landed a couple of jabs against the guy's chin, then a left hook into his temple.

The guy's eyes crossed and his legs went out from under him. When he hit the street, Angel was sure the impact would cause earthquakes.

A glance at the car showed that Karinna was still sitting inside, fingers white on the wheel, eyes wide. Angel pounded on the hood. "Go!" he yelled. "Get out of here!"

She blinked a couple of times, as if just waking

up, and cranked the key. The engine was already on, though, so it made a grinding noise. When she put it in reverse and hit the gas, it bucked, clipping the legs of a guy approaching it from behind. He fell away, and the car roared up Fountain.

Angel turned back to the business at hand.

CHAPTER ELEVEN

With Karinna escaped and their strongman down, the fight seemed to have gone out of them. Some of them headed for their cars, others backed away from Angel. Three came at him at once, knives flashing, but they were easy.

One blade ripped into his side, and he flinched, but the wound would heal almost immediately. He backhanded that knifeman across the mouth, and the guy fell down. Angel caught the wrist of the second and wrenched it, pulling the man's arm from its socket. The knife clattered on the street. The third guy was already retreating when Angel lashed out with a kick, sending him spinning into the window of a tailor's shop. Glass rained onto the sidewalk and an alarm started to whoop.

They all ran for their vehicles.

"Not leaving already, are you?" he asked. "I'm just getting warmed up."

A couple of them lifted the stocky black man up and helped him into the van. One of those guys met Angel's gaze. "We're done," he said. "You're on your own."

Whatever that means, Angel thought. *It's not like these guys are doing me a favor by jumping me.*

Is it?

But he couldn't imagine any way in which it could be. He stood on the corner and watched as they piled back into their vehicles and drove away—at reasonable speeds, and not in the direction Karinna had gone. The sirens were closer, would be here within moments, but Angel couldn't see any advantage to making his attackers wait for the police. Sure, they could be booked for assault, but Jack Willits wouldn't want his daughter's name associated with something like that, and Angel tried to keep his activities to himself as much as possible.

He turned the corner onto Fairfax and went south, away from the flashing red and blue lights he saw approaching. As he walked he transformed again, back into his human form.

So what was that all about? he wondered. It had seemed planned, premeditated. They'd been followed, they'd been rammed. Somebody trying to get to Karinna. But for what? Kidnapping and ransom? Her family certainly had the money, and everyone in L.A. knew it.

146

CLOSE TO THE GROUND

*Or were they trying to kill her? Why? What
could a seventeen-year-old girl have done that
would get hired professionals after her?*

No, the kidnapping theory seemed more likely.
Or something else that Angel hadn't hit on yet.
Revenge of some kind. If they'd wanted to kill her
they could have done a drive-by, strafing the
Plymouth with automatic weapons. Knives and
chains weren't killing weapons, not for serious play-
ers. They were for maiming, causing injury.

They didn't want her dead, but they wanted her
hurt.

Angel knew he had to get a cab, get back to Bel
Air. He didn't know if she was even safe inside the
walls of that security-conscious community, or
inside her own alarmed house. He wanted to make
sure she survived the night.

But he'd been walking away from the main
streets, just wandering as he mulled over the attack
and its possible ramifications. He wasn't sure where
he was now—a dark and quiet neighborhood of
closed shops and silent upstairs apartments.

He was stopped on a corner, looking for street
signs, when the car pulled up beside him. It was a
huge black Ford Excursion with dark tinted windows.

Not again, Angel thought. He was still tired from
the last battle—it had taken a lot out of him, and he
was distracted from thinking about Karinna and

wondering why groups of armed men were after her—and even when the vehicle's doors opened and four people came out (but they weren't people, he knew, not really), he had to force himself to focus on them.

When he did, he saw that they really weren't men at all.

They were demons. Four of them. They looked strong, they looked fierce, and they looked dangerous. The smell of them, earthy, like freshly turned loam, struck his senses.

Or like graveyard dirt, he thought.

There was one who stood seven feet tall, with long powerful arms that ended in hands the size of small houses. The backs of its hands were horned, five ridges of bone that looked knife-edge sharp. Its skin was sky blue, and its long tangled hair was the color of summer wheat.

Another was shorter, barely five feet tall, and the same measurement wide, like a beach ball with stocky legs. It had white hair growing in tufts all over its body. The overall effect was comical— except for the four rows of spiked teeth glistening inside its huge mouth.

The next was as gaunt as an ancient man, stick thin, with dull yellow eyes sunken into its skull and a dour expression on its face. It wore a tall hat and an old-fashioned suitcoat and baggy slacks, and in long slender fingers it held a staff, as tall as it was, with a hook in one end. This demon was very still—Angel had to watch it for a moment to be sure it was alive—but its long fingers moved and twitched around its staff, independently of the rest of it, like the legs of many spiders.

The last looked female, though Angel knew that was no more likely than the possibility that the rest were male. You just couldn't tell with demons like this—form followed function. The arguably female one looked, for all intents and purposes, like one of the many L.A. beautiful people. Under other circumstances Angel would have thought she was a young starlet. Her luxurious hair was long and as black as the deepest night. Her pale face held eyes of a startling cobalt blue and crimson lips parted in an open-mouthed smile. She wore a tunic of a diaphanous gold fabric, and beneath it Angel could see a shape that would make a centerfold weep. She appeared to be one of the most beautiful women he had ever seen.

The illusion held until her skin started to ripple and bulge. He watched in shocked fascination as—whatever it was, beneath her flesh—moved inside her. It took Angel a moment to realize what he was seeing, and even then he didn't believe it. He'd heard of it—it was called a Maelabog demon, he was pretty sure—but he'd always believed it to be a myth.

Now he was convinced. Her skeleton—its skeleton, he reminded himself—was revolving, slowly turning around beneath it skin. It was meant to frighten enemies, and Angel had to admit that it was effective.

Recognizing the Maelabog clued him in to what the one with the staff was, as well. A demon called Mr. Crook, star of stories told by Irish peasants to frighten their children in centuries gone by.

If these two were Gaelic, chances were the others were as well. But Angel, in his Irish days, had not been as well acquainted with the demonic world as he was now. He had not paid close enough attention to the stories, tales of Faerie, of the *Sidhe*, of the Otherworld.

One thing he did know, though. They weren't here on a social visit.

"Look, it's been a really long night," he told them. "I'm not up for whatever it is you've got in mind."

Mr. Crook slowly tilted his head down. His eye-balls moved independently of each other, and he fixed one on Angel. "Your name is Angelus," he said. His voice rasped like a door that hasn't been opened in a hundred years.

"Used to be."

"You will accompany us," Mr. Crook said.

"I know you're probably not much on conversation," Angel said. "But there are rules, you see. Give and take. I say something, then you say something that relates to what I said. If you just ignore me, it makes me feel like you don't value what I have to say. And that's just plain rude."

"You will accompany us," Mr. Crook rasped again.

Angel waved a hand at them. "Okay, now you're starting to make me angry," he said. "I'm just going to walk away before I really get peeved."

The short round one clacked its teeth together like a mad castanet player. The tall one shuffled forward a couple of steps, toward Angel. Even the Maelabog stopped turning, almost back to the beginning stage, which gave it an odd protrusion in the left side of its face and a sunken look in the right. Its pelvis, too, was slightly out of line, and there was nothing beautiful about it now.

"You will—" Mr. Crook started.

"I know," Angel said. "And thanks for the invite, really. Very kind. But I'll pass."

Even as the tall blue-skinned one reached for him, Angel knew they weren't going to just let him go, though. One didn't gather four Gaelic demons and set them on someone if the plan was to let him walk away. He counted himself lucky that he was still standing—had they wanted to, they could have killed him the moment they saw him.

Angel vamped out and dodged the blue one's long reach—dodged straight into Mr. Crook's staff, swung at him with unexpected strength and speed. It slammed into Angel's temple, and he saw a flash of bright light, then the world started to dim.

As he struggled to maintain his balance, the blue one caught him with a backhanded punch. The horny knobs ripped Angel's skin, and he cried out in pain. He grabbed one of the demon's hands and yanked, pulling the tall creature off-balance. It fell to the sidewalk, and Angel kicked it twice in the head.

But the staff hit him again, this time in the throat. Angel gagged and stumbled, and it came again, jammed into his stomach.

He fell to his knees. Shaking his head to clear it, he looked up just in time to see the beach ball plowing into him. Its rotund body was amazingly firm— more of a medicine ball effect than beach ball, after all. Its arms could barely reach past its bulk, but the impact of it knocked Angel back to the ground.

When he tried to regain his footing, the Maelabog was there, holding something that glittered in its hands. Its skeleton was back to normal now, and Angel once again had the sense that he was in the presence of intoxicating beauty. He looked at her—it—through blurring eyes, and then realized that what it held was a rope.

More specifically, a kind of lasso. The Maelabog twirled it once and threw it around Angel, then pulled it tight. His arms were pinned to his sides.

It wasn't much of a rope. Breaking it should be a piece of cake. He flexed.

It held.

He tried to reach it, but his arms were held down tightly. Much more tightly than if it were just the rope. Angel caught a whiff of something strange on the air. Ozone, and a coppery tang, almost like blood.

The taste of magic.

Enchanted, then.

He stopped struggling, knowing it was pointless.

Four demons from Gaelic legend, armed with an enchanted rope. And they'd caught Angel when his guard was down, when he was focused on Karinna instead of his own security. When he was tired from a big fight, and worried about the girl.

Someone had gone to great lengths to capture him.

He guessed he'd learn who it was, and why.

Not that I have any choice . . .

CHAPTER TWELVE

"Welcome to my home, Angelus," a voice said.

Angel opened his eyes.

When he'd been taken into the SUV, he'd been hit with some kind of slumber spell. He had no idea how much time had passed between then and now, and there was no window in this room to the outside, no clue as to whether it was day or night.

"Call me Angel."

In point of fact, there wasn't much in this room at all, now that he looked around. It was vast and cavernous, but largely empty. The floor was smooth gray stone. The walls were rough gray stone. The ceiling was high—either really high, beyond the light cast by torches mounted in iron sconces at intervals around the room, or not quite as high but painted black.

Besides the sconces, Angel could see a wooden

cabinet of some kind on a far wall. Next to that was an opening in the rock, and through the opening was the beginning of a flight of stairs leading up and away.

Which was where Angel wanted to be. Except he was standing against the rock wall, arms extended far out to his sides and slightly higher than his head, held there by iron manacles. Angel guessed that these were also enchanted, as he was unable to break free of them.

Standing before Angel, at a distance of about six yards, was a man.

"Old habits are hard to break," he said.

Angel studied the man. He seemed to be in his seventies, maybe late seventies. He was old and lined and looked battle-weary. Wispy white hair covered some of his head, but patches of smooth pink skin showed through, as if his scalp were younger than the rest of him somehow. His bright blue eyes held an elfin twinkle, like a smile lived there that didn't reach his mouth, which was set and somber. He wore a simple white cotton tunic and slacks, with white hemp sandals on his feet.

"I don't know you," Angel replied.

"Nor I you," the man said. "But I've seen you. I've heard of you, time and again over the years."

"You have the advantage, then."

The man took several steps forward. "Forgive me," he said politely. "My name is Mordractus. I, like you, am from Eire."

The name was familiar, but Angel wasn't going to give him the satisfaction of revealing that. "You don't sound Irish."

"Nor do you. The price of living a rootless life, I imagine. I have stayed close to the Auld Sod, lately, but I traveled extensively in my younger days. These past years I've remained largely isolated, though. I'm afraid my accent, like so many these days, comes more from television than anything else."

"Whatever," Angel said, in no mood to stroll down memory lane with this guy. "Mind telling me why you're holding me prisoner here?"

"You might recognize this house if you saw the outside of it," the man said, as if Angel hadn't even spoken.

"I doubt it. I don't go in for those open-house tours."

"It belonged to a man named Pennington. Arthur Pennington. He went by 'The Magnificent Pennington.' "

That did sound familiar, but Angel couldn't place it. He'd have shrugged, but his arms were somewhat occupied at the moment. *And going numb,* he thought. *How long is he going to keep me here?*

And what does he have in mind for me after that?

"I don't know who that is," Angel admitted.

"He was a student of mine once, many years ago. In the twenties and thirties—the nineteen twenties, that is," he specified with a chuckle, "when you're our ages you have to specify these things—he was a very famous magician here in Hollywood. He could have been one of the greats—had the skill of Crowley, he did. But he chose to be well known and loved, like a trained chimp instead of a great magician. He appeared in movies, where his 'magic' was nothing but camera trickery, and into the early days of television. You may have seen him on the *Ed Sullivan* show or someplace like that."

"I think maybe that's it."

"A tragic waste. And now he's dead, more's the pity."

"And you're not."

"Exactly my point," Mordractus said. He turned away from Angel and started walking across the room, toward the exit. "With what I taught him, he could have extended his life almost indefinitely. As I have. But he squandered his gift, wasted his years, and when he wanted to put it to use again, late in life— when he built this room, in fact, beneath his Hollywood mansion—it was too late. A gift like ours has to be used. It's like a language, or a muscle. If it isn't used it atrophies and becomes no use to anyone."

"Fascinating," Angel said. "You ever planning to answer my question?"

"I'm getting to it," Mordractus snapped. He stopped, looked at Angel over his shoulder. "Patience, young Angelus. We have plenty of time together."

"Before what?" Angel demanded.

Mordractus continued his march across the room without answering. When he reached the far wall, instead of going through the doorway he opened the wooden cabinet and took a small pail from a lower shelf. Sticking out of the pail was a wooden handle. He closed the cabinet door and turned back toward the room, and Angel.

"I have lived for a little over five hundred years," Mordractus explained. "I've enjoyed my time. I'm not ready to give it up."

"You don't look a day over three-fifty," Angel told him. "What's got you worried now?"

The magician walked to the center of the room, stopped, and looked around as if getting his bearings. When he seemed satisfied that he was in the exact middle of the space, he knelt on the floor and grasped the handle that extended from his pail. "I'm dying," he said simply.

He drew a brush from the pail. On the end of it was a white substance, like paint but not as wet. Angel couldn't be certain what it was. Mordractus seemed to read his uncertainty.

"Paste," he said. "Made from the ashes of cremated murderers."

"Lovely."

Mordractus began to paint a circle around himself on the gray stone floor, with a diameter of about three feet.

"I'm dying," he said again. "But I'm not ready to

die. My spells won't extend my life any further, I'm afraid. And to make matters worse, I've put something in motion that is taking a lot out of me. Sapping my strength, my life force. If I die before I finish it, the results won't be pleasant for me."

"Sorry to hear that," Angel said. "I'm sure there's a lesson here. Look before you leap, or something like that."

"So for the last year, I've been looking far and wide for some alternative. Something that would allow me to live on. My forces have roamed the world searching for the answer."

"I've got the answer," Angel said. "Let me go and I'll bite you."

Mordractus finished his circle, carefully joining the ends with his brush. "Not that way," he said. "Vampires have no soul. I don't want to be without a soul."

"Why not?"

"A soul is more than a conscience, although I understand from stories I've heard that you view it largely that way. A soul is your being, your very self. Without it, you become someone else—no, some *thing* else. What is the point, I have to ask myself, of keeping myself alive if I am not really keeping my *self* alive? And then, there's the practical consideration. I do magic, you see." He waved the brush toward Angel as if to demonstrate. Then he turned back to the floor and started painting a long straight line on it, outside the circle. "Complicated magic," he continued. "You would probably call it black magic, though I might have a quarrel with your definition.

"And much of this magic requires the magician to have a soul. I summon demons from the darkest pits of Hell, and from the Otherworld. The magician's soul functions as a sort of tag, you see—they know who summoned them, and they obey, because they can read the soul. Without one, the results could be disastrous."

"So you need your soul," Angel said. "What does this have to do with me?"

"Don't be coy, Angel. It doesn't become you. You are a vampire, I know that. You're immortal. And yet, you have a soul."

"Suppose you're right?"

"That makes you unique, at least in my experience. I had to see you, to study you."

"Here I am. Pinned like a butterfly to this wall, and I gotta tell you, I've been more comfortable."

"Yes, well, my apologies for that," Mordractus said. "You're very strong. I need to be sure you won't be a problem for me."

"What if I make a promise and cross my heart?"

"I don't think I can trust you, given the circumstances."

"And they are? The circumstances?"

"That which makes you unique is exactly what I

need," Mordractus said. He reached some predetermined end point in the line he was making, drew a sharp corner, and started a new one. "You are immortal but have a soul. That is exactly the situation I'm after. Therefore, I am going to transfer your life essence—that which makes you immortal—to me."

"Mind if I ask how you're going to do this?"

"It's a tricky ritual, but not impossible," Mordractus replied. "I will raise a demon—Orias, if you want specifics—and he will transfer your life force into me."

"Leaving me mortal?" Angel asked.

"Leaving you, I am afraid, dead," Mordractus said. "The soul, according to our belief, resides in the head. To move your life force into me, Orias will have to first tear off your head. He will then grind it into a special potion, which he will give me to drink of. When I have done that, I will become immortal. You, on the other hand, will not survive the first part."

"Glad to hear I can be a help to you," Angel said sarcastically. "I don't suppose I get any say in this."

"I didn't expect you to willingly embrace it," Mordractus said. "Otherwise I would have just approached you rather than going to considerable bother to trap you. I've been having you watched, recording your every move, keeping track of you day and night. Waiting for the right moment."

"Well, I am glad that it was a bother. I'd have pre-ferred that it was more trouble than it was worth, and you'd just stayed home. But it was you, I guess, behind the attack on Karinna? What was that, to wear me out? Slow me down?"

"The entire Karinna situation was meant to lure you in," Mordractus explained. He had reached the end of another line and was continuing it back toward the others. He was painting a five-pointed star. Each line passed the central circle without intersecting it, or each other, but they contained the circle within the star's center. "To make you focus all your attention on her, without thought of your own safety. There was an attack on you, weeks ago."

Angel remembered. The four guys who had come out of nowhere and been easily beaten back. "Right."

"They made a pathetic attempt. I'm embarrassed even to admit that they worked for me. And after that I was afraid that you would be on your guard. I needed you distracted, putting someone else's prob-lems above your own. I needed you to be thinking about someone. I chose Karinna Willits because I believed that she would put you in mind of someone else, someone you tried to save but couldn't. I hoped that you would be extra involved in trying to keep this one safe. It seems to have worked."

The girl in Rumania. How could he know about that? Angel had forgotten it himself, until seeing

Karinna had reminded him of her. He asked Mordractus.

"Careful research," the magician explained. "Once I knew who you were, it was not terribly difficult to retrace some of your past movements, find those who knew you when. In the old days you were quite well known, and you are well remembered to this day. I tracked down some of your friends, and some who are not so much your friends. Tirbol sends his regards, by the way."

"He's alive?"

"And doing quite well, apparently. All this . . . unrest in Eastern Europe. Victims have been quite easy to come by, and no one asks questions when one more corpse turns up. He seems to be thriving."

"Remind me to make a trip out there."

"I would, Angelus, but instead I remind you that you won't live to see another sunrise."

"What time is it now?" Angel asked.

"No harm in telling you," Mordractus said. He rose from his painting. It seemed to be done—a pentagram, drawn around a circle on the floor. Angel recognized preparations for a black magic summoning. "You slept through the night. It's probably about ten in the morning now, though I can't be sure. I can't wear a watch in here—nothing machine made, while I'm preparing the circles." He waved a hand at his own clothes. "This is all sewn by hand, by three virgin sisters."

"They roll cigars for you, too?"

"I'm afraid that a sense of humor isn't one of my strong suits, Angelus. You may very well be funny. I wouldn't know."

"I thought you watched TV. Don't you get sitcoms over there? *Seinfeld? Friends?*"

"I'm sure I do, but I don't watch them. At any rate, as I was saying, it's morning. The ceremony will take place tonight. By tomorrow you'll be an empty vessel and I will be immortal. I would thank you for the gift, but you are not giving it willingly, are you?"

"You got that right."

"No matter. I have always taken what I need—I pride myself on it, in fact."

"I just bet you do."

Mordractus began to paint another circle, a bigger one, all around the outside of the pentagram. The diameter of this one was probably twelve feet. "I have a bit more painting to do," he said. He touched his lower back. "Hard, at my age, all this bending over. Then I need some time to prepare myself, purify myself, for the ritual ahead. You will spend the day here, and when I am ready for you, I'll have you brought to your position in the circle."

"Don't feel like you have to explain yourself to me," Angel said.

"But I do. I want you to know that your sacrifice is not in vain. You are helping me to accomplish a great task. When I am through with you, when my youth and vigor are restored, I will be able, come the equinox, to finish what I have started these long months ago. I will be able, finally, to summon Balor from the Otherworld."

"Balor?" Angel asked. This name he knew. Ancient King of the Fomorians and god of Death. If this guy could really summon Balor to modern-day Earth, it would be a catastrophe like nothing the planet had ever faced.

"You know of him?"

"Heard the name. I know who he is supposed to be, in the legends."

"More than just legends," Mordractus said. "Like all legends, this one has a basis in truth. Balor is there, and he will be here. When he is here, he will belong to me. He will be mine to command."

"I hope you're sure about that. If the stories are anywhere near true—"

"They are true," Mordractus said. As soon as his first was done, he began a new circle, inside the first, the lines about eighteen inches apart. He worked calmly and with intense focus, looking up now and again at Angel as he carried on his conversation. He reminded Angel of a construction worker, matter-of-factly building one more house in a long series of them. "I assure you. His evil eye, that causes mass destruction. His huge size. His ill temper. Balor will stand at my side and ensure my power for all time."

"Sounds like you've got this all worked out," Angel said.

"Believe me, I have given it a great deal of thought."

"Then you won't mind my expressing my opinion about it?"

"Your opinion would be entirely meaningless, Angelus. I have considered every eventuality. Nonetheless, I have to say that I am curious, so go ahead." He finished this inner circle and then began to paint names in certain sections of the pentagram. The words were in English and Hebrew letters, and interspersed among them, in a pattern that looked random but certainly wasn't, were symbols of the Zodiac and other signs that Angel didn't know.

"I think you're nuttier than a fruitcake," Angel said. "A few bricks shy of a load. A few fries short of a Happy Meal. Out there where the buses don't run. If you were twice as smart, you'd be a half-wit."

"Pointless verbal insults, Angelus? I'm surprised at you."

"I'd express my feelings physically, but you've got me chained to the wall." Angel rattled the manacles. "Remember? Enchanted manacles, I'm sure."

"Indeed," Mordractus said. His final touches with the paint were to draw two small, partial circles, near the farthest point of the star. These he left unfinished, though. "And there you'll stay, until tonight. So remain comfortable. You aren't getting out of there until I am ready for you to come out."

He tossed a final look Angel's way, then carried the pail and brush back to the cabinet and put them away. Without another word, he slipped through the doorway and padded upstairs.

In the silence Angel tested the manacles again. No good. He couldn't budge them.

He was here to stay.

CHAPTER THIRTEEN

Doyle looked at his watch. Then he looked at the clock on Angel's computer. Or was it Cordy's? Seemed like she was the one who'd gone down to Staples and come back with a trunkload of office supplies when she'd gotten it in her head that Angel should have a real business. And it sat at "her" desk in the outer office.

Whoever the machine belonged to, the point was that both timepieces agreed that it was 11:30 in the morning and Angel hadn't come home all night. And Doyle was worried.

I mean, he told himself, *there's always the possibility that he met someone and had a pleasant night with same, and is having some trouble dragging himself away.*

But this is Angel, he reminded himself. *So no, that's certainly not what happened.* The vampire was more of a brooder than a mover, Doyle knew. Women seemed to find him attractive, but it all seemed to slide right past him.

So where can he be? Outside the sun was high and bright. Angel wouldn't exactly be wandering the streets—he'd be a crispy critter out there now, so Doyle hoped he was at least holed up someplace dark.

All kinds of horrible images presented themselves to Doyle when he thought about it. Angel bursting into flames, exposed when the sun rose over Southern California. Angel staked and dusted, the way he and Cordy always feared he'd end up—the way they knew they might have to finish him themselves, if he ever lost his soul and turned evil again.

Maybe that's what had happened—he'd gone bad, and either couldn't remember his way home or was afraid to come back, afraid that his best friends would have to kill him.

Or afraid that he'd kill them.

Either way, it was bad news.

Doyle reached for the phone, dialed information, and asked for the number of Monument Studios. When he got the main switchboard, he asked for the studio tours department. After a minute's wait, listening to some annoying soft pop on the hold music, a woman's voice came on the line.

"Monument Tours," she said. "Can I help you?"

"Yeah," Doyle replied. "I need to talk to Cordelia Chase."

"I'm sorry, Ms. Chase is working right now. Is this a personal call?"

"Personal?" Doyle asked. "Course not. It's a . . . an emergency. A work-related emergency. Highly work-related."

"So you're on the lot, then? Give me your extension and I'll page her."

"Never mind," Doyle said. "I'll find her myself." He hung up.

No help there.

But he had to do something. This sitting around, waiting, not knowing . . . he couldn't take much more of it. Francis Doyle—the first name was a state secret, more closely kept than the recipe for a nuclear weapon or Coca-Cola, although Angel and Cordy had found out at the same time they learned that he had been married once, to a human woman—owed a lot to Angel. He'd been—was "assigned" the right word?—to Angel by the Powers That Be, to help lead the vampire from his lonely life in the shadows to a point where he was actually getting to know humans again, mixing with them instead of just saving them and keeping score. But over the time they'd been together, Angel had done a lot for him as well. Showed him reserves of courage he didn't know he'd had. Taught him that he had worth in the world. Introduced him to

Cordelia, who was just about everything a man—well, half of one, anyway, say a man/demon—could want in a woman. Except for the part where she hated demons.

He owed Angel some mighty debts, though, that was for sure. And he wasn't paying anything back sitting in a chair.

Cordelia piloted the tram down a narrow roadway between two soaring soundstages. The thing had two cars, and she had to make sure that both of them made every turn. She had found out on her first day behind the wheel that if you made a sharp left, the rear car could snag on the corner and an obnoxious percentage of the "guests" wanted their ticket money back. Then there were the ones who complained of motion sickness after riding with her, just because she kept turning the wheel in whatever direction she was telling them to look, and then correcting it when she noticed an oncoming wall or vehicle. It was enough to give a girl some kind of complex.

While doing this, she had to keep up a running patter, explaining to the guests what they were looking at, how it was significant to Monument Pictures history, and she had to work in plugs for current Monument releases while she was at it. Which was hard to do, since Monument's current crop was all duds and losers, as far as she was concerned.

"On your right," she said, for the seventh time this week, "you'll see Stage Seventeen. This classic stage has been the setting for many great movies. Remember *Hill Seventeen,* the classic war movie? The hill was really a mound of dirt piled up in a corner of Stage Seventeen. Imagine sweeping up that mess when they were finished."

The laughter from the guests was just as canned as the line had been. It was a totally scripted "off-the-cuff" one-liner, as were most of the groaners she had to deliver.

But you're on the lot, she reminded herself. She had to remind herself of that several times a day to keep from running over herself with the tram.

The idea of quitting came to mind nearly as often as self-squishing did. But, while Cordelia had been called many things in her time, "quitter" was never one of them. Not when she was fighting alongside the Scooby Gang against all kinds of icky dead things, or even when she was leading the pep squad in cheering for a team to whom victory was a totally alien concept. No way was she going to quit now.

"Also, the town square in the movie *Fridays with Dad* was totally created on this big stage, which is not only the largest on our lot, but the fourth largest in all of Hollywood. This was because the town square on our back lot, which we saw a little while ago, was in use as the town square in the gangster film *Election Day*, which was shooting at the same time in 1958."

"Miss!" one of the guests shouted from in back.

Great, Cordelia thought. *Another obscure question*. They were constantly asking about movies she had never seen or couldn't remember. Who really cared about a bunch of movies made long before anyone she knew was alive? But Olivia Mulroy was on the tram. Olivia was her trainer and supervisor. She was watching for any slip-ups—Cordelia had been on a kind of probationary status ever since the tram-meets-corner incident—so Cordelia knew she had to be on her best behavior.

"Yes, sir?" she asked.

"Wasn't *Camp Kidsworth* shot on one of the big soundstages here, too?" a man asked. Cordelia caught a glimpse of him in her rearview. He wore a powder blue baseball cap with a gas station logo on it, and his nose looked big enough to apply for statehood.

Who would care where that fiasco was filmed? she wondered. *Every kid actor who hadn't been able to make a success of a TV series was in it, and it had still done no business at all*.

But she knew she couldn't say that, and she also knew she had no clue what the real answer was. She glanced at Olivia. The woman reminded Cordelia of a vulture—she had a long, sharp beak that shadowed a thin-lipped, down-turned mouth. Her eyes were beady and narrow and always seemed to be watching Cordelia like a scavenger waiting for something to die. Her black hair was slicked tightly to her head and held back with a rubber band.

"Stage Fifteen," Olivia whispered.

"*Camp Kidsworth,*" Cordelia said with a chuckle. "Wasn't that a classic. Just the cutest movie. And filmed, of course, on Stage Fifteen, just behind us on the left, now."

She eased the tram into a slow right turn. The tour was almost over—another block of sound-stages, then across the main road and back into the parking area in front of the tour office. All the sights had been covered, and she just had to keep the masses entertained for a couple more minutes. Then they'd get back into their cars and drive back to wherever they came from, and until the next group got under way the lot would belong only to those who had a reason to be here and a Monument Pictures ID card to give them access.

She was dreaming of the few serene moments between tours when she felt Olivia's talons digging into her arm.

"Ow," she said.

"Blake Alten," Olivia hissed into her ear.

"What about him?" Cordelia asked.

"Right there!"

Cordelia looked forward, and there, in fact, was Blake Alten. The biggest action star in the world.

He had appeared in three of the top-ten all-time global box office champs. Big names in the States couldn't necessarily open a picture in Japan, or India, or France, or a hundred other countries around the planet. But Blake Alten's could. And he was crossing the street, twenty yards ahead of Cordelia's tram.

"He's the best," Olivia whispered. "Always has a few minutes to chat up the fans, get pictures taken, whatever. Catch up to him and you'll give these guests the memory of a lifetime."

"Okay," Cordelia agreed. She pushed down on the accelerator, and the tram lurched forward at its top speed, which was still only about ten miles per hour.

"But don't run into him," Olivia warned.

"Thanks for the tip." Then, into the microphone, Cordelia announced, "Ladies and gentlemen, we have a special treat for you today. Our tour is almost over, but we have a very special guest on the lot today who I think you'll recognize. You may have heard in the last day or so that Blake Alten has agreed to do a movie for Monument Pictures. That's Mr. Alten dead ahead, and we'll see if he can't stop and visit for a moment. He's well known for his generosity with his many fans."

Behind her the tourists let out a gasp, almost as one, and then the air was full of whispers and questions and noise, all of which Cordelia tried to ignore. She concentrated on piloting the slow-moving tram, making a right turn instead of crossing the street to go back to the tour office, in order to follow the actor. He didn't seem to hear the tram drawing up behind him, so Cordelia pulled to his right, and came up even with him.

"Mr. Alten," she said. "We have some of your fans here, and—Mr. Alten?"

He continued to walk, eyes staring somewhere ahead of him, not even registering her presence. It was almost like he was a Blake Alten robot instead of the real, human Blake Alten. "Mr. Alten?" she tried again. "Blake?"

No response. He kept walking.

"Give it up," Olivia said quietly.

Cordelia applied the brakes. "Mr. Alten has a lot on his mind," she told the guests. "So we'll just let him get to his meeting or whatever without disturbing him."

When he had gone on ahead, she made a left, across the road. They were a block up from the tour office, and she would just need to cross over to the next street and double back. Blake Alten had only cost them a minute. And a big dose of embarrassment.

Twenty minutes later, after a short break, Cordelia went to meet her next tour group. After purchasing their tickets, they sat in an auditorium and watched a short film about the history of Monument Pictures, loaded with clips from the studio's classic films. Then the guide came in to meet them, and to lay out the ground rules for the tour.

She slipped into the auditorium while the lights were still out and the film was wrapping up. When the last clip was finishing and a big THE END was flashing onto the screen, she stepped to the front of the room, where a podium stood just in front of the screen. The last moments of the film flickered over her face, and she held her pasted-on smile until the lights came up.

"Welcome to Monument Pictures!" she shouted out with all the exuberance of the cheerleader she had once been. "We're so glad you're here!"

As if.

"My name is Cordelia Chase, and I'll be your guide today," she went on. "We'll be together for the next two hours or so, as I give you a real behind-the-scenes look at Hollywood moviemaking. We'll see everything: the back lot, the soundstages, the recording studios, special-effects labs, our studio museum and gift shop."

As she gave her well-rehearsed intro, she scanned the crowd. Another capacity group of thirty-five. There was a family from Japan, another from some Middle Eastern country, several from the United States, a few single people sitting by themselves, and—

Doyle?

Sure enough. He was hunched over in the third row, toward the aisle, conspicuously looking inconspicuous. He also looked uncomfortable. Behind him, a boy of about five was buzzing a toy plastic airplane around Doyle's head, which explained the uncomfortable part but didn't really explain what he was doing here.

He made eye contact with her and gave his head a little nod toward the exit. She responded with a tightening of her lips and a tiny shake of her head. She couldn't speak to him. Olivia was standing in the back room, eyeing her like she was halfway across a wide desert with no water for days. She'd already been chewed out once today for getting a personal phone call, and just now it occurred to her that the caller was probably also Doyle. Having failed to reach her that way, he'd come all the way out to the Valley and shelled out the thirty bucks for a tour.

It must really be important, she thought. *Getting Doyle to lay down thirty dollars for anything that doesn't involve referees is a major life challenge.*

Seeing him there shook her well-established routine monologue. "Just a . . . a couple of, uh, ground rules, before I take your—I mean, before we go out to the tram for the tour," she stammered. "First, no, uh, no photos unless I specifically say that you can take pictures. Remember, this is a working movie studio, and some of the things you will see might be

things that we don't want to end up on the Internet
or anything. Also, please keep your voices at a con-
versational level at all times. I'll be able to hear if
you have a question, and we want everybody to be
able to hear me. Hands, feet, and heads should stay
inside the tram at all times, and if anyone is standing, the tram won't be going anywhere. You have to
be sitting down at all times." She glanced at Doyle
again. He gave a little shrug. "If we're all ready to
go, please follow me."

She headed for the exit door. Olivia opened it and
held it for the guests to pass through, then followed.
She was coming along again. Cordelia led the way to
the tram, peeking over her shoulder now and again
to keep tabs on Doyle. He was stuck several people
back, though, and ended up in the second car.

She felt his eyes on her as she started the tram.
She wanted to just stop it and pull him aside. But
Olivia would have her for dinner if she tried anything like that. If she'd been giving the tour unsu-
pervised she'd have done it as soon as the tram was
out of sight of the tour office.

So it went through the tour's first several stops.
She took the group onto Stage 9, which was where
the sitcom *Danny's Kitchen* was filmed. They
walked around on the sets, sat in the restaurant's
chairs, examined prop salt shakers and ketchup bottles. From there, a quick trip through editing,
where there were actually some people working on

a new medium-budget cop flick. Each time they stopped, Doyle closed in on her, but each time Olivia moved in, too, as if she sensed blood on the air. Cordy waved him off both times, once pointedly asking out loud if he had a question. He hemmed and hawed and backed away.

After editing, she drove the tram onto the back lot. They drove up New York Street and down Chicago Street, circled around the Town Square, and then took the left that led into the Jungle—really a motley assortment of trees, real and fake, a couple of big fake boulders, and a pond where a waterfall could be started by turning a valve. Past the Jungle was Western Town, a collection of old frame facades that had been built back here in the fifties. They were still used occasionally. Cordelia stopped the tram on the dusty street and told her guests they were free to wander around Western Town for five minutes.

Doyle stepped out of the sunlight and passed through the doorway of a general store. Cordelia gave Olivia a minute to get involved in answering a detailed question about the two Roy Rogers features that had been filmed here, and then she followed Doyle through the door.

He turned around when he heard her come in.

"What are you doing here?" she demanded. "Do you have any idea how fragile my job is here? I know it's not much of a job, but being fired from a job that's not even worthy of your talents is much more demeaning than being fired from one that's way over your head, and I won't have it."

"Angel's missin'," he said simply.

"So if you think you're—what?"

"He didn't come home this mornin'."

"So . . . maybe he's with somebody?"

"Try to keep in mind who we're talkin' about."

"Right, sorry. You try his cell phone?"

"Of course. No answer."

"Did you try calling the Willits house? He left the number, right?"

"Tried it. I talked to Karinna. She came home by herself last night. In his car. With a big dent in it. Someone rammed 'em. Angel was last seen fightin' off about a dozen guys, while Karinna escaped in the convertible. He said he'd meet her there, but he never showed up."

"Oh," Cordelia said. The possible meaning of this started to sink in. "Oh."

"I don't even know where to begin lookin', but I got a bad feelin' about it all."

"So do I, Doyle," Cordelia agreed. "But there's really not anything I can do about it now. That woman, Olivia, is watching me like a hawk. I'm about this close"—she held her fingers up, very close together—"to losing this job. A couple of carsick tourists hurling in the tram and they think you're worthless. So I feel really bad for Angel, I mean, I'm scared, you know?

But I don't think I can help. Can't you just, you know, have a vision or something and find him?"

"You know it doesn't work that way, Cordy."

"I guess so. But really, what's the point of the whole vision thing if you can't use it for your own purposes once in a while? I think the Powers That Be really didn't think this thing out all the way."

"I'll tell 'em that next time they ask my opinion."

"When was the last time they did that? Ask your opinion about something."

"Never."

"Oh."

"So what you're sayin' is, your job's more important than Angel."

"No. I mean, what I'm saying is—yes, I guess that's what I am saying. But I don't mean it the way it sounds." She thought about it—about what Angel had done for her, since she made the big jump from little Sunnydale, where she knew everybody, to sprawling Los Angeles, where she had to admit that she was only a tiny fish in a big, big ocean. And she realized there was a lot more to life than pointing out imaginary sites to a bunch of short attention span tourists who'd be here one day, at Disneyland the next, and go home thinking they'd seen California. "What I mean is . . . well, never mind what I mean. In fact, never mind the whole thing. Let's go."

"Go?" Doyle asked.

"You think I'm going to leave something this

important up to you? If Angel's missing, we need to find him. You're going to need my help for something like that."

"Okay, then," Doyle said. "Let's go."

They stepped back out into the sunlight. The tourists were still wandering around the Western buildings, snapping pictures of each other in front of the saloon and through the barred windows of the jail. Cordelia climbed into the driver's seat of the tram and started it. Doyle jumped onto the bench seat behind her.

"Great time to tell me this," Cordelia said. "We're as far from the exit as we could possibly be and still be on the lot."

"Hey, I ain't the one who didn't want to talk," Doyle reminded her.

Cordelia put the tram in gear and started down the Western street, back toward the Jungle and civilization. Behind her, she could hear Olivia screaming. A couple of the other guests came running.

"Where are you going?" one of them asked, panting. "We're all back that way!"

"You'll see more if you walk back," Cordelia told him. "This is an emergency."

"You're fired, Chase!" Olivia shouted.

"You can't fire me, I quit!" Cordelia snapped back.

After a couple of minutes they could no longer hear the yelling.

By the time the tram pulled up to the tour office, security had been alerted. Cordelia figured Olivia must have either had her cell phone with her, or gone into one of the office buildings that stood between the Town Square and the Jungle. There were six burly officers in short-sleeved blue uniform shirts, striped pants, and gun belts, waiting for them with angry expressions on their face.

Behind the guards, Don Davis, the tour manager, stood, also with an unpleasant scowl. The rest of the tour department was standing at the windows inside, watching the show.

Cordelia pulled the tram to a stop. "I know, I know," she said. "We're going."

"You most certainly are," Don told her. "We don't take kindly to joy riding here at Monument Pictures."

Cordelia shot a grimace at Doyle. "I can assure you, there was very little joy involved," she said. "But I quit, about thirty seconds before Olivia fired me. There are more important things I need to be doing with my life than entertaining the rubes who come here."

So much for not being a quitter, she thought. *But then, flexibility is a virtue, too. Adaptability to changing circumstances. Quitting isn't always the worst thing to do.*

"You're just lucky I'm not charging you with grand theft, Ms. Chase," Don proclaimed. "You may leave. But you're not welcome to return to Monument Pictures, ever."

Cordelia locked eyes with Doyle and smiled. "Ahh, show biz," she said. "There's nothing like it."

CHAPTER FOURTEEN

No one on the street knew anything.

Doyle could hardly believe it. Criminals, for all their talk about Codes of Silence and Honor Among Thieves, were the least discreet people out there. They bragged about everything, no matter how lame their accomplishments. Most of them were too stupid to keep their mouths shut, but shared the slightest thought that popped into their tiny brains.

And yet, there was no word on Angel anywhere.

Which meant that whatever had happened to his friend, it didn't involve the criminal community. Which meant Doyle was even more scared. Angel up against a bunch of crooks would be a situation Angel could handle.

If it wasn't the criminal underworld that had done something to Angel, then it was the *other* underworld. The one from which the demons came. And

Angel, Doyle knew, was tough enough to take care of himself, even in that company—so if this was a problem that he hadn't been able to deal with, then what could Doyle do against it?

He stood on the corner of Hollywood and Highland. The day had turned into a real scorcher and the sidewalk radiated heat into the evening, but despite that there was a constant stream of traffic— tourists in short pants, street people in layers, wearing what they could and carrying the rest, hustlers, punks, gangsters. All of them trying to get by or get over, one way or another. Doyle knew the streets well enough to blend in, to keep out of the way of the square citizens and pick out the ones who might know something and be willing to share.

And yet, nothing. He hoped Cordy was having better luck back at the office.

Cordelia was having no luck.

She had agreed to wait at the office while Doyle went out hunting, on the off chance that Angel might call. The sitting around and listening to the thundering silence from the telephone was getting to her, though. A few minutes before, it had occurred to her to try calling Detective Lockley, with whom Angel had developed something resembling a working relationship.

And again, no luck.

"I'm sorry," the officer who answered the phone

told her, "but Detective Lockley is out on a case. Would you like to leave a message for her?"

And that would be what? Cordelia wondered. *Tell her I'm concerned about her friend Angel because daylight has come and gone. I know he's not officially a missing person until forty-eight hours have passed, but does the same rule apply to vampires?*

"No, thanks," she told the voice on the other end of the line. "I'll catch her later, I guess." She hung up, then lifted the receiver and punched out one more number. One more thing had been bothering her all afternoon.

She'd met Mike Dailey when he was cameraman doing a commercial shoot she was on. He had asked her out a couple of times, and she had been putting him off so far because she had already done commercials. If he'd worked on a series, or features, maybe. But he seemed to know everything that happened in town. He was as tapped in as the trades were, and he was a better source because he'd talk to her.

He answered on the third ring, and after she rushed through the initial pleasantries, she got down to the point of her call. "I saw Blake Alten on the Monument lot today," she said. "Is there a substance abuse problem or something, there? Because he was practically sleepwalking. I almost—he was almost run over by one of those trams. And he didn't even seem to notice."

"Alten's been getting progressively weirder for the last week or so," Dailey said. "From all reports, anyway. He hasn't been seen in public much. Dinner at Morton's a couple of nights ago, but he sat by himself. People kept asking him about the Monument deal, but he blew everybody off. Didn't hear that he drank to excess or anything, just that he seemed to be spaced-out, noncommunicative. Somebody said maybe he had a cold or something."

"It didn't seem like a cold to me. More like, lights on, but nobody home."

"Well, this is the movies you're talking about, Cord. Nobody said he had to be a mental giant. Just good-looking."

"He was that," she admitted.

"You could ask his girlfriend, Sherrie Dupree," Dailey went on. "Except that, suddenly, she seems to be his ex-girlfriend. Word is he hasn't spoken to her in days. She's not happy about it."

Somehow I don't see Sherrie Dupree taking my calls, she thought. She made a few vague promises about going out with Dailey, then hung up.

She found it interesting that others had noticed Alten's odd behavior recently. But she didn't know what it meant. And in terms of getting closer to figuring out where Angel was, she was no better off than she had been. She hoped Doyle was having better luck.

* * *

Kate Lockley drove. Special Agent Glenn New-berry sat uncomfortably in the passenger seat. He had wanted to drive, but she had insisted on taking her car, and she didn't let FBI agents drive her car. Or anyone else, she told him. She was very protective of some things, like her car.

And her cases. She let Newberry come along because at least this way she could keep an eye on him. She'd know what he knew, and if the price was that he would also know what she did, that was a price she could pay. She didn't really mind sharing information, she just didn't want to be kept in the dark.

They parked a block from the corner of Avalon and Slauson, where Kate had located an abandoned gas station that might have been the one Chuey had told her about.

His story made a certain amount of sense. Gas stations, she knew, had large underground storage tanks where the gasoline was kept. Once the stations were abandoned—but before they were razed to make room for a new corner mall, which was usually defined as progress in L.A.—the tanks were empty. An underground tank like that could provide the perfect staging area for a tunnel job, giving the robbery crew a bit of a head start and someplace safe to dump the loads of dirt they pulled from their tunnel.

Kate couldn't imagine having spent such a hot

day digging. The morning had started cool, but the mercury had edged up into the nineties by midafternoon. Finally now, at ten-thirty, with the sun long gone, it started to slack off. A faint breeze whispered down the oddly quiet street. She wiped sweat from her forehead as they looked at the gas station from across the street.

She glanced at Newberry, who seemed cool and composed in his dark suit. *Ice in their veins,* she thought. *A physical requirement for the Feebs.*

"So that's it?" he asked.

"That's the gas station my informant told me about. Whether there's anything to his story or not, I don't know yet. That's what we're here to find out."

"We're not going to do it from here, are we?"

"That's not what I had in mind, no."

They waited for an ancient lime green Ford Fairlane to lumber down the street, and then crossed at a fast walk. The street was wide and they didn't especially want to be spotted, if there was a lookout posted.

There was no movement from the gas station that they could see, though. A tall chain-link fence surrounded the corner property, but even from the street they could see a place where the gate had been padlocked shut, only now the lock hung, broken, and the gate was open a couple of inches. Kate caught Special Agent Newberry's eye to be sure he saw it, too, and he nodded. Her hand went to her weapon. He drew his from a small holster on his belt and ticked his head at the gate.

Wordless, Kate pushed the gate open far enough to slip through. She went first, and Newberry had to shove it a little wider to accommodate his bulk. He came up behind her and off to the side, trying not to present a single target in case there was anyone inside drawing a bead on them. Kate drew her own weapon now.

Straight ahead, at what would have been the entrance to the service bay on the side away from the pumps, was the boarded-up entrance that Chuey's friend had mentioned. The boards had clearly been disturbed.

Kate remembered him saying that his friend— probably Chuey himself, she knew, but one had to leave informants their dignity—had encountered a man with a gun when he'd tried to go through those boards. She had no illusions about what would happen if they were made as cops.

Newberry, ever the gentleman, let her go first.

Up close, she could see that a flat piece of plywood, about four feet wide, was simply laid over the other boards. This was the doorway, then—they slid this out of the way to go in and out, then placed it over the opening. There were several small nails driven into it, probably where they tacked it into place if they were going to be gone for a while. But none of the nails were driven home now. It was just loose.

Newberry stood to one side, his weapon pointed past Kate at the opening. She touched the plywood with her left hand—her right held her weapon— closed her fingers around its edge, and tugged it back an inch. The inside was dark. She pulled it wider, trying to let some of the light from a nearby streetlamp inside. There was nothing from within, no sound, no motion. Wider.

Now a single shaft of light stretched from ceiling to floor. Kate blew out a breath she hadn't known she was holding. The service bay seemed empty. She pushed the plywood the rest of the way over, drew a flashlight from a pocket, and shined it inside.

Newberry came in with her, playing a light of his own across the bay. His beam came to rest on a shovel with a broken handle abandoned in a corner.

"Looks like the place," he said.

"Could be," she agreed softly. She inched closer to a well where mechanics once stood to work on the undersides of cars, shone her light inside.

And found the beginning of the tunnel.

"This is it," she said quietly, looking at the black, gaping mouth. "They dug from that bay into the storage tank, then across to—somewhere. Some bank."

"This isn't a big neighborhood for banks," Newberry said.

"Even the poor are allowed to have bank accounts, and some of them do," Kate said, knowing as she did that this was no time to argue sociology with the agent. "I'll go back out, find whatever bank is nearby, and call for backup. You stay here and keep an eye on this end. I'll have the backup meet us at both places as soon as I know where I'll be."

"You go find the bank," Newberry agreed. "I'll call for backup, though. Keeping in mind that this is a Federal operation."

Kate opened her mouth to say something, then shut it again. It wasn't worth arguing. The Feds would know that they couldn't bring this crew down on L.A. streets without bringing in the LAPD as well.

"See you later," she said. She left him alone in the gas station and went back into the street, looking in every direction for a building that wasn't a run-down apartment or a vacant lot or a corner market.

Backup, Special Agent Newberry thought. *For an operation like this? Any agent who couldn't bring in punks like these didn't deserve to carry the shield.* He climbed down into the bay and entered the tunnel.

The city of Los Angeles contains incredible diversity, and nowhere is that more evident than in the range of wealth to be found there, from incredibly rich to heartbreakingly poor.

In one of the poorest neighborhoods of all, there was a corner building, made of brick painted white across the sides and top, left natural underneath the tall, iron-barred windows. A neon OPEN sign glowed in a lower corner, but the place looked anything but welcoming. Another sign, higher up on the window, said something in Korean and LOTUS SPA—KOREAN MINERAL BATHS in English.

Just what Doyle was looking for.

The streets were a fine place to seek information about what L.A.'s criminal element was up to. But the races of demons had their own hangouts, and the Lotus Spa was one of them. He tugged open the barred door and went inside. The waiting room was empty, but a young Korean man stood behind the cheap pressboard counter.

Soon, the desk clerk, said something to him in Korean. Doyle didn't speak a word of it, and Soon, if he spoke any English at all, would never admit to it. Doyle tried a couple of lines of Ano-Movic—as a group, these demons were highly assimilated into human culture, which made their language a natural bridge between the two worlds. Doyle thought he remembered Soon responding to Ano-Movic in the past.

"Hi, Soon," he said. "I'm looking for Angel. You heard anything about him today?"

Soon responded with a swift barrage in Korean. Again, Doyle didn't catch any of it, but he understood the intent. Suppressing a groan, he reached into his pocket and drew out a twenty-dollar bill, which he smoothed flat and placed on the counter.

"Anything at all?" he asked.

"About Angel?" Soon replied in fluent Ano-Movic, scraping the bill smoothly into his palm. "Not a word."

"But something else? What do you mean?"

"I might have heard a couple of guys talking while they were taking some steam," Soon said.

"Talking about what?" Doyle demanded, growing angry at Soon's obfuscation. "Damn it, Angel's been missing all day. He's never done you any harm. If you know anything, I want to hear it now."

Soon put up his hands defensively. "Don't make threats. If you want cooperation, that is not the way to go about it."

"Spare me the philosophy," Doyle grunted, dragging another bill from his pocket. "This is it. I'm broke after this, so you can't squeeze any more outta me." He dropped the bill onto the counter.

It vanished into Soon's palm. "A couple of sensitives," he said. "They were tense. One of them was griping about the level of mystical activity flowing down this way from the hills. Put him on edge. He compared it to being in a dentist's chair having his teeth drilled for twelve hours straight—said he wished it would go away, but it just kept building."

"That's fine, but what's it got to do with Angel?"

"I don't know if it has anything to do with Angel. You asked if I had heard anything out of the ordinary. You know this place, lot of things most people

195

would consider out of the ordinary walk through these doors. But that's the only thing I've heard today that sounded especially strange."

"What hills? What do you think is causing this?"

"Hollywood Hills, the guy said. I heard there used to be some strange stuff going on up there, long time before I was born, though. Some movie star magician lived up there, used to practice his craft. But it hasn't exactly been a hotbed of magical activity, last few decades. Too much nouveau riche, day traders, and brat actors buying up property. No respect for tradition."

"You remember his name?" Doyle asked. "This magician?"

Soon thought a moment, until Doyle became convinced he was fishing for another payoff. But there was nothing left to give. He was ready to turn and go when Soon slapped his own forehead a couple of times. "It's there but it won't come out," he said. "Pembroke. Pemberton. Something like that."

"I'll look it up," Doyle said. "Thanks for your help, Soon."

"I never saw you," Soon replied, followed by a couple of staccato bursts in Korean. Doyle slipped out through the barred door.

And ran straight into the arms of a demon named Koffliss.

"Doyle, buddy," Koffliss said when he saw who he had bumped into. Koffliss stood almost seven feet tall, as broad as a doorway and as muscular as a weightlifter. Three short purple horns protruded from his orange-skinned forehead, and patches of the same color purple spotted the back of his bald head and down his thick neck. He smiled a toothy grin with absolutely no genuine humor in it. "Been looking for you."

"I been looking for you, too," Doyle bluffed, thinking, *just what I do not need. Tell me again why I gamble?* "All over town. I thought sure you said you were gonna be at that Sports Bar on Sunset, waited there all night."

"Well, I'm here now," Koffliss said.

"So you are," Doyle agreed. "Damndest thing. I had your dough, not ten minutes ago—you were right about those Padres, I'll never bet on them again—but I was lookin' for some information, real important, you know. And that guy Soon squeezed me for every dime. So I'm a little financially embarrassed at this exact moment. I'll, uh, liquidate some assets and come find you when I have more coin in my pockets. Where you gonna be, say, three hours from now?"

"I'm thinking I'll stick close to you," Koffliss told him, giving his arm a crushing squeeze. "Protect my investment, right?"

"That'd be great, really," Doyle said. "But these people I have to go see about, you know, liquidatin' those assets? Humans. You don't exactly pass, if you

197

know what I mean. They might get a little freaked, and then where'd we be?"

"Yeah, but—"

"Listen, you got a pager, bud? 'Cause I can just beep you when I got the dough, we'll set up a place to meet, how's that?"

Koffliss considered this proposal for a moment. "You got anything to write with?"

Doyle patted his pockets. "Fresh out. Just tell me the number. I got a real head for numbers."

Koffliss recited a number to which Doyle didn't even bother to listen.

"I don't wanna keep you," he told the big orange demon. "Go on in, get a rubdown. I'll be in touch soon."

"You better be," Koffliss warned.

"You can count on me, bud," Doyle said. By the time Koffliss was inside the spa, Doyle was a block away.

Some demons, he thought as he hurried away, *are just too dumb to be allowed to exist in civilized society.*

"The Magnificent Pennington," Cordelia read off the computer screen.

"That's gotta be it," Doyle agreed. He sat in one of the guest chairs, watching Cordy search online.

" 'Arthur Pennington took Hollywood by storm in 1939, turning a background shrouded in mystery into a calling card into the homes of the rich and famous,' " she read. " 'Rumors abounded about his early days, some saying that he had been a stage magician in Kansas City, others that he had performed primarily at high society children's parties in Philadelphia, before moving to Hollywood in the mid-twenties. Pennington himself never revealed anything about his early life, apparently preferring to let the rumor mills run rampant and imbue him with the stuff of legend. Persistent stories had him traveling and studying extensively in Europe, even at the times that he was supposedly in various parts of the U.S. making his name as a prestidigitator of only moderate talent. Whatever his background, when he suddenly hit in Hollywood, it was in a big way. He performed in several hit motion pictures, including the *Big Broadcast* series, before being offered a star turn in his own Saturday afternoon serial. . . .' That's really it. The rest just tells about the movies he was in, then a TV show in the fifties, and then he died."

"Does it say where he lived?" Doyle asked.

"No, not this article."

"Can you cross-reference him or something? Isn't that what the Internet is supposed to be good for?"

"I thought it was good for making sure everyone knew the same set of bad jokes," Cordelia said. "And I know a site with some good skin care advice. Maybe if we had Willow here—she was great with his online stuff."

"I don't know who Willow is," Doyle said, "but she ain't here and we don't have time to find her. Keep lookin'. We gotta find out where this Pennington guy is. If he's come back to life or somethin', it might explain where Angel is."

"I'm looking," Cordelia said. "Give me a break. I mean, I took a computer class in high school, but it wasn't my life or anything. You think I'm some kind of closet geek?"

Doyle turned his head away, hiding a smile. "No," he said softly. "I don't think that."

CHAPTER FIFTEEN

Angel had, finally, dozed.

It had taken awhile. Hanging there by his wrists wasn't exactly conducive to a good night's sleep. The pain was excruciating—pain in his arms, his shoulders, his back, his legs. But he had let his mind drift, eventually reaching a place where the pain was pushed aside and his thoughts floated free. Images came to him, unbidden, rushing as swiftly as a roaring river. Doyle and Cordelia and Kate Lockley, his best friends in Los Angeles, and the City of Angels herself, sprawling across the hills and flats of the Los Angeles basin. At night the city's glow lit the sky, and looking down from a high point, a turnoff on Mulholland Drive, say, or Coldwater Canyon, it looked like the sky turned upside down, glittering stars as far as the eye could see.

Then L.A. faded away and Sunnydale replaced it.

The town was far smaller, but its residents were precious. The beautiful face of Buffy Summers, the Slayer, and still the only girl Angel had ever truly loved, came to him. In his mind he heard her voice, but couldn't quite make out her words. Then she was gone, and her friends were there, the ones she called the Scooby Gang. Willow, Xander, Giles, the werewolf Oz.

And still his mind floated, as if untethered to any reality. Friends and enemies mixed together in a blur of mental pictures. Spike and Dru, Darla, Heinrich Josef Nest, Angel's father, mother, and sister. The landscape changed and changed again, from Southern California's coastline to Manhattan's jumbled skyline to the dark and eerie forests of eastern Europe to the rolling green hills of Ireland.

A sound brought Angel back to consciousness— and to the pain.

Mordractus had returned.

He looked ancient.

He was dressed, once again, in raw white linens, a knee-length tunic and trousers. This was not the same outfit, though, or since he had been here before he had inscribed bizarre symbols on his clothes in a purplish ink. This time he wore slippers of what looked like soft white leather, and a cap of the same covered his skull. A few strands of wispy white hair issued from beneath the cap.

His face was a map of lines and crevices. Even his

blue eyes looked cloudy now, half-hidden behind folds of skin. Liver spots mottled his hands and bony wrists. He looked to Angel as if his age had doubled in the hours since Angel had seen him—and though he had no way of knowing how many hours had passed, he was sure it hadn't been decades.

The noise that had awakened Angel was caused by Mordractus scraping the plain wooden table across the floor. The old magician dragged it to a certain spot, near the circles he had painted earlier. He stepped back from it, looked at it, carefully eyeing its position in the room. Then he returned to it and shoved it a couple of inches to the left. Once again, he stood back, then pulled it forward ever so slightly.

When he seemed at last satisfied, Angel spoke up. "I think it'd look better by the window," he said. "Oh, that's right. You don't have a window."

Mordractus scowled at him. "Keep telling your jokes as long as you can," he said. "Not much time left now. It's midnight, Angelus. You know what that means."

"I'm worried," Angel said. "See me shaking? Oh, wait, that's you, trembling with age. You sure you'll live long enough for this?"

"Don't you worry about me, Angelus," Mordractus said. "You've your own skin to fear for."

"I'm a worrier," Angel said. "It's what I do. What happens to you if you don't bring Balor through on time?"

"Let's just say that, should I end up in the Otherworld myself at some point thereafter, there would be many who would be glad to see me come. And they wouldn't be my friends."

He padded across the stone floor, carefully avoiding walking across any of the lines he'd previously painted, and went back to his rough wooden cabinet. From this, he withdrew several items wrapped in black fabric. He carried them back to the wooden table, where he carefully undraped each one in turn and set them in a line on a bolt of rich purple silk which had been spread on the tabletop. As he unwrapped them and set them out, he muttered words that Angel couldn't understand. From the tones he used, though, the rising and falling of the words, they sounded like prayers in some language that was old when the world was young. When he was finished, he took the lengths of black cloth back to the cabinet and put them inside.

Angel had encountered many aspects of the supernatural in his long life, and though his experience with the rituals of black magic was limited to hearsay, he recognized the objects that had been so carefully placed on the table.

A long wooden stick, carefully sanded and polished and oiled: the Rod. A knife, sharp-edged and gleaming, with a handle of chipped black rock: the Dagger. A goblet, of hand-blown glass: the Cup.

Mordractus returned to the table, which Angel

had come to recognize was to fulfill the function of an altar, bearing two fat candles of a grayish-pink substance. They looked unclean, and Angel was not eager to smell them when they burned. Mordractus stood these on the ends of his altar and went back once again to the cabinet.

"You know, candles are on sale at Wal-Mart," Angel said. "You could replace those old things for a song."

Mordractus gave no indication that he had heard. He went about his business, totally focused on what he was doing. Angel knew that concentration was mandatory in these rites, was, in fact, largely responsible for the success or failure of the ritual. It was said that the "magic" was often nothing more than the magician's mental power, focused so powerfully that he was causing his own intended result through sheer will.

From the cabinet Mordractus—by now continually speaking—brought a brazier and an earthen jar. He set it down near one of the points of his five-pointed star and poured what looked like an assortment of herbs from the jar into the dish. He returned the jar to the cabinet and brought out several long wooden matches. He struck one against the floor and dropped it into the brazier. A ball of flame burst up from it, then lowered to a soft crackle. The herbs smoked, releasing a sharp tang of incense into the room. That was where his brain was to be pureed, Angel figured. Mordractus took another match, struck it on the underside of his altar, and touched it to both candles. They spat and caught fire, casting a flickering light into the room.

Finally Mordractus brought three small books from the cabinet's depths. They were bound in pale brown leather and looked very very old. As he carried these to the altar, he looked at Angel for the first time since his preparations had begun.

"Going to have time for pleasure reading?" Angel prodded.

"I have never summoned the demon Orias," Mordractus replied. "The phrasing, the invocation, is quite different from the rituals I have used to contact Balor. I will have to read sections from my grimoires, rather than reciting from memory. In a perfect world I would have taken the time to memorize it all, but as we both know time is the one resource I'm short on."

"What about common sense?" Angel asked.

"You're hardly in a position to judge, my young friend."

"I don't know about that. It looks to me like you're messing with forces you don't know that well, in a desperate, last-ditch attempt to save yourself. What's the old saying—scared money never wins?"

"This is not a game of chance, Angelus," Mordractus snapped. "This is something I've prepared for my whole life. I know what I'm doing."

"I'd like to think so, since my brain is the one you're planning to make soup out of. But I have my doubts."

Mordractus waved a gnarled hand at him. "You're simply trying to shake my confidence. Well, I can tell you it won't work. I'm nearly ready to begin, so take a last breath of the world, vampire. Enjoy it while you can." He walked around the outside of the room with a large metal snuffer which he used to extinguish the torches mounted on the walls.

When he was done, the snuffer went inside the cabinet. The only light in the room came from the flaming brazier and the two greasy-smelling candles on the altar.

Mordractus hurried across the room, his feet shuffling on the stone floor with a sound like sand-paper on blocks. He went to the altar and picked up the Dagger, jamming it into his belt. Then he came over and stood before Angel. He fixed his cloudy gaze on the vampire.

If I could break these irons . . . Angel thought. But he knew it was useless. Mordractus's magic had its effective moments; the rope with which he'd been captured and the manacles that held him still were testament to that.

"Are you ready, Angelus?" Mordractus asked.

"What if I say no?"

"No matter. It's only out of courtesy that I ask at all. I bear you no ill will, you know. You have cost me much recently, but that was all out of your own desire to stay alive—"

"I'm not alive," Angel interrupted.

"Undead, then. Whatever you call it, it's a motivation that I must respect. No, this is simply a matter of need. You have something, I need it, I will take it."

"Nothing personal."

"Exactly."

"You're insane."

"There is no need for insults, Angelus. I've already told you, your verbal barbs find no target in me."

"Can't blame a guy for trying."

"I suppose not." Mordractus raised the long bony fingers of both hands and gestured toward Angel. The vampire felt the manacles fall away from his arms, and tried to bring his limbs back under his control. He couldn't. Even without the iron there, his arms were useless.

Mordractus walked backward, continuing his bizarre hand motions. Angel felt himself drawn across the floor, away from the wall toward the center of the room. Toward the pentagram. His legs wouldn't respond, either. There was no escape from Mordractus's holding spell.

Angel hated the sensation. Control was important to him. Control was all he had, really. When he had no control, he was the rogue vampire Angelus, scouring the countryside for victims to drain of

208

blood. Once his soul was restored to him, control was also restored, the ability to make his own decisions, to choose good for its own sake.

And now, he had no control.

Mordractus moved him into one of the incomplete circles he had painted. When Angel was centered inside its two-foot diameter, Mordractus took the Dagger from his belt, leaned over, and completed the circle by scratching its last segment on the floor with the knife's point.

"I heartily suggest that you remain within the circle at all times," Mordractus said. "You may think, what do I have to lose—I won't survive this invocation anyway. But I assure you, there are far worse things than death in this universe, and from this point on, for any man to leave the circle would be to risk those exact things. Understood?"

"I hear you," Angel said.

"Good." He went to his own circle, next to which he had placed the altar. He removed the Cup and the Rod and the books, his grimoires, and placed them all within his circle. Then he stepped inside and closed his own circle, as he had Angel's, with the point of the Dagger.

He faced the circle at the center of the star, and began to speak in a loud voice.

"I invoke and conjure thee, O Spirit Orias, and, fortified by the power of the Supreme Majesty, I strongly command thee by Baramelamensis, Baldachiensis,

Paumachie, Aplolresedes, and the most potent princes Genio, Liachide, Ministers of the Tartean Seat, chief princes of the seat of Apologia in the ninth region, I abjure thee by the names of Lucifuge Rofocale, Satanachia, Agalaiarept, Fleurety, Sargatanas, and Nebiros; do thou forthwith appear and shew thyself unto me, here before this circle, in a fair and human shape without any deformity or horror; do thou come forthwith, from whatever part of the world, and make rational answers to my questions. Come presently, come visibly, come affably, manifest that which I desire. I command thee, Orias, arise, arise, arise!"

Angel had no idea if Mordractus knew what he was doing, but he spoke with authority, his voice ringing firmly in the vast cavernous space. He knew enough about the ways of the world—the things that most people denied—not to write off Mordractus as a fraud without seeing him at work. But no demon showed itself, so Angel began to relax. Maybe the magician was too weak already. He was breathing pretty heavily over there, trying to get his wind back for a second round.

Angel was heartened by the man's lack of success. *I will get out of this,* he thought. He started to look forward to spending a day in his own bed.

And then he heard it, distant but clear. A bell rang, a bell so true and pure that it could never have been forged on Earth. It rang again, closer. And one more time. Angel felt the hairs on the back of his neck rise.

The ringing stopped, but the room was suddenly cold as a wind whipped in from nowhere. Angel could see his breath, and Mordractus's. The candles guttered and went out, simultaneously. The only light in the room was from the brazier, and that fire burned only faintly.

Mordractus had composed himself, and started in again. This time he held one of his small leather books in his hand and read from it.

" 'I invoke, conjure, and command thee, O Spirit Orias, to appear and shew thyself visibly before this circle, without deformity or guile; by the name Hagios, by the Seal of Adonai, by Jetros, Athenoros, Paracletus; by the three Secret Names Agla, On, Tetragrammaton; by the dreadful Day of Judgment; by this name Primeatum; do thou make faithful answers unto all my demands, and perform all my desires, so far as thine office shall permit. Come therefore peaceably and affably, come visibly and without delay, manifest that which I desire, speak with a clear and intelligible voice that I may under-stand thee.' "

The room's temperature dipped still more. Angel felt himself shivering against the cold. A bell began to ring again, too, but this time it was louder and deeper, as if he were standing inside something the size of the Liberty Bell or larger, turning from a ringing tone into a deafening roar.

And in the center of the circle, bound by the lines

211

of the star, a glow began to appear. There was no shape to it, no form, no solidity.

"Shew thyself!" Mordractus commanded. "Be disobedient and I will curse and deprive thee of thine office, thy joy and thy place! I will bind thee in the depths of the bottomless pit, there to remain until the Day of the Last Judgment!"

The amorphous glowing mass began to coalesce into a real shape, though not one that Angel had ever seen before. The shape spilled over the boundaries of the small center circle Mordractus had painted for him, but was still clearly constrained by it. As Angel watched, it became more clear, almost like he'd been looking through a camera's viewfinder as someone turned the focus knob.

Standing before them was a lion mounted on the back of a powerful black stallion. The lion had a serpent's tail, and in his right hand, which was more human than feline, he clutched two huge, hissing snakes. Somehow Angel knew, looking at the thing, that no single part of it was the demon Mordractus had summoned. When it spoke, the sound seemed to come from the lion's mouth, but the lion was no more Orias than the snakes were.

"Why hast thou summoned me?" it demanded.

"I wouldst have thee perform a transformation for me," Mordractus replied. He still held his grimoire in his hand, and he flipped through pages as he spoke.

He's stalling, Angel realized. *He didn't expect*

Orias to come so quickly, or to respond so positively, or something. Now he's got to find the right phrases to use to command it.

As he came to this understanding, he also realized that he could move again—that Mordractus, in giving all of his concentration to the demon, had been unable to keep holding him.

He could move—but he couldn't leave the circle.

Or could he?

Mordractus had warned that no man could leave the circle without risking eternal torment of some kind. But Angel was no man. Angel was a demon himself.

He took the chance.

CHAPTER SIXTEEN

There were banks in L.A., and then there were banks.

Downtown, Santa Monica, Beverly Hills—these places had august financial institutions worth billions. Branches of nationwide banking chains set up in such locations. Much of the business done at these centers of finance was in large movements of currency—buying, selling, trading, investing. All on paper—or, more accurately in the modern age, on computer. No actual pieces of paper changed hands, just bits of information, moving from one account to another. The meaning was in what it could buy, in terms of other bits of information.

As Kate Lockley stood on the dark sidewalk outside Western Standard Savings and Loan, she thought about that kind of bank. The kind where the bankers wore thousand-dollar suits and six-hundred-dollar shoes and carried briefcases from Gucci or Mark Cross, and the clients came in similarly attired, and sometimes they went out for tennis or drinks together at the end of the day.

The people who banked at Western Standard couldn't take bits of information and buy groceries for the table. The people who banked here deposited paychecks and welfare checks and Social Security checks, or they just cashed them outright. The purpose of a bank, in this neighborhood, was to be a dispenser of cash to those who needed it, when they could manage to keep their accounts out of the red.

Western Standard was no billion-dollar business. But it was a business that went through a lot of cash in the course of a day.

And it was just a block from the gas station at the corner of Avalon and Slauson. It didn't face onto either of those streets; it was on Fifty-eighth, sandwiched between a dry cleaners and a discount jewelers.

This was where the crew was tunneling toward, she could feel it in her bones.

Kate glanced at her watch. It was a little after midnight. The neighborhood was deserted. No one walked these streets so late except those no one would want to meet here anyway. She was a cop, her gun was close at hand, and even she was a little nervous.

Okay, a lot nervous. But that had more to do, she

knew, with the fact that she was standing outside a bank that even now might have a crew of robbers with automatic weapons emptying the vault into big cloth mailbags or heavy army surplus duffels.

On the other hand, she thought, *the crew could be halfway there, digging underneath the street and dreaming of cool drinks and warm beds.* Just because she had found the target didn't mean they were there yet.

She blew out her breath, realizing that she was probably tensed up for nothing. They were in time to stop this. She'd get some backup down here, they'd get the bank open, and they'd be waiting inside the vault whenever the crew came through the wall. The robbers would be so surprised they'd drop their shovels and give up.

That's how it would happen. In her dreams.

Police work just didn't come that easy. Not in the job description.

Speaking of backup, she thought—*where are they?*

It had been fifteen minutes since she'd left Glenn Newberry back at the gas station, telling him to call in. She hadn't heard a peep from her radio, hadn't heard a siren, hadn't seen a squad car or one of those American boxes the FBI liked to think would blend in.

She was alone on a dark street in a tough neighborhood with a bunch of killers possibly cornered inside a bank. She wanted (Angel) a SWAT team down here, at the very least. She wanted to see cops with guns, cops in body armor, cops with flashing lights and roadblocks and yellow crime-scene tape.

Angel? Where did that come from?

Sure, he was probably working somewhere in the city. Working nights didn't seem to phase him a bit. He was probably doing some pro bono job for a client who couldn't afford to pay him what he was worth, and wouldn't even if he could, and he'd probably let the client get away with it.

Angel was a tough guy; she'd seen that. But he let his clients walk all over him. Almost as if he wasn't in it for the money, but for some other, less definable, motive.

PIs didn't do it for those motives, though.

Cops did. Cops believed in those vague ideals like justice, protecting the innocent, fighting crime. *The only cops who are in it for the money were—well, there are some crooked cops,* she figured, *but mostly if they're in it for the money, they're on the other side.*

Or they're a PI. In a city like L.A. a private investigator could get in good with a couple of movie stars and be set for life, keeping their little mistakes and indiscretions out of the papers. For every Philip Marlowe or Sam Spade in the city there was a joker with a license and a gun on somebody's payroll getting rich for doing a publicist's work.

But Angel didn't fit into any of those categories, as far as she could see.

Kate shook her head. She was letting herself get distracted. Not a good idea. She had to act as if she were on a stakeout. As if the darkened windows of the bank could erupt in gunfire at any moment.

And still no backup, she noted. She made a call on her portable.

"Detective Lockley," she identified herself to the dispatcher. "I'm in front of 378 Fifty-eighth Street, the Western Standard Savings and Loan. I have reason to believe that our bank robbers are tunneling inside this bank, and I need some backup down here right away."

"I'll take care of it, Detective," the dispatcher promised.

She'd have to give Special Agent Newberry a piece of her mind when she saw him. She wondered if he had even called for the Federal backup he'd mentioned. She didn't like the idea of him waiting at the end of the tunnel alone—if the crew came out that way, they were likely to be edgy and scared, and when they saw Newberry—who a five-year-old could pick out as a G-man from a hundred yards—they'd shoot him on sight.

He stepped from the circle.

And Orias whipped around to face him, serpentine tail whipping through the air, snakes in its fist hissing and snapping. The demon opened its lion mouth and a jet of flame blasted from it directly at Angel.

Angel dodged. He jumped, hit the ground, and

rolled. The flame scorched the stone floor but missed him.

"Thou art mine!" the demon's voice roared.

"Not yet," Angel replied. He was on his feet again, running around, putting Mordractus, still presumably safe within his circle, between himself and the fire-spitting demon.

To leave the circle, according to Mordractus, was worse than suicide. But to stay in it was certainly suicide as well—this monster would snap his head off and make soup from his brains, so what did he really have to lose?

"If I release thee, give to thee the gift of this one," Mordractus shouted to the demon, "Thou shalt returneth to thy circle forthwith!"

"Agreed!" roared Orias.

"You really think you can take a demon's word like that, Mordractus?" Angel asked. "You let it out of the circle, it might run rampant through the city. How will you rein it in?"

Mordractus's face was fraught with uncertainty. The magician gave it a moment's thought, then made up his mind.

"Take him!" he called. *Again, nothing to lose,* Angel thought. If the demon doesn't get me, then Mordractus is finished anyway.

The demon stirred as the invisible bonds that held it to the circle fell away. There was an undeniable smile on the horse's face.

Angel vamped out. It was fine to pass as human, but in vampire form he was stronger and faster, and he knew he'd need all the power he could muster.

His first impulse was to escape, to head through the doorway and up the stairs. But he knew if he did that, the thing would only follow. Then what he had warned Mordractus of would surely come true— unleashed on L.A., the demon would cause untold carnage. It wouldn't be as bad as if Mordractus succeeded in bringing Balor back to life. But it wouldn't be pretty.

So he stayed where he was and let the demon come to him.

When it did, it lunged suddenly, snake heads spitting and biting the air in his direction. Angel leaped into space, somersaulting over the demon and landing behind it. The thing spun around, tracking him. But before it could get its bearings, Angel moved in, kicking twice at the stallion's face. The lion roared and spat flame again.

Angel kept moving. He dodged fire, charged, hitting and kicking, dodged again. He tried to attack each of the thing's joined bodies, horse, lion, and snakes. Each of them, in turn, tried to get at him.

So far, he was staying out of trouble, but he didn't seem to be having any adverse impact on the thing. He wasn't sure it could be beaten. This wasn't like the demons he usually went up against, the kind some experts referred to as subterrestrials. Those demons had existed on Earth long before humans rose to prominence, and though they were outnumbered now, they still made their homes here, or nearby, beneath the attention of the mortal community.

But this demon, Orias—he lived somewhere far different. Some called it the Otherworld, some called it Hell, some had still other names for it.

Angel had spent time there.

He was in no hurry to go back. And he could understand why this thing, once it was released here on Earth, would not be anxious to return, either.

As he sparred with it, a plan occurred to him. The thing, as he'd suspected, seemed to be all one entity, in the form of three. But they remained joined at all times. The fist never let go of the snakes. The lion kept the horse between its knees at all times. If he could separate the components, he might be able to beat it.

And beating it would be crucial. It was strong, a ferocious opponent. But he knew it was nothing compared to the might of Balor. If Mordractus could succeed in summoning the God of Death to the earthly plane, it wouldn't matter that he'd have had to kill Angel to do it. Everyone else Angel had ever cared for would be at Mordractus's mercies, too.

The horse wheeled on him and lashed out with powerful hind legs. He heard the wind whisper past his scalp as the slashing hooves just missed him. He dodged, but instead of moving away from the thing, he dived closer, beneath the horse. It bucked, trying to come down on him, but he kept clear of its hooves.

And then he reached out and grabbed one of the snakes. When he had it firmly in his grasp, he tugged and jumped away.

The lion did not let go. Instead, it whipped the snake back over its head, drawing Angel close to it, and snagged him with its other arm.

It opened its mouth wide. Angel felt its hot, fetid breath on his face.

That, he thought, *was a big mistake.*

The hot day had finally turned cold.

They always did in Southern California. No matter how hard the sun pounded the city, the heat radiated back out into space. The Pacific kept the climate temperate, not too hot and not too cold. At night, after the sun went down and the earth released the heat it had stored up, the mercury dropped fast. Sometimes it was still boiling at ten, but by midnight a jacket was required.

Kate didn't have a jacket. She'd been standing outside this bank for twenty minutes, and she felt every degree slip away. Now she wrapped her arms around herself and marched briskly up and down the block across from the bank, trying to keep warm. She kept to the shadows between the widely spaced streetlamps, the nearest of which that worked was on the far end of the block. She didn't think they'd have a lookout on the street, but there was no way to be sure, and she wanted to avoid being spotted if she could help it.

Backup was on the way, though, and as soon as they were here she'd be able to call in the bank manager to get the door opened. Another hour and they'd have this wrapped up. She'd sleep in her own apartment tonight.

She—*is that a light?* she wondered. There had been a momentary glint in one of the bank's windows. Or had there? Had it simply been the reflection of a car passing on the cross street, or the light of a distant airplane, or her imagination?

No way to tell from here, Kate knew. She looked up and down the street, scanning carefully with her trained eyes, mentally dividing the street into sections and checking each section one after the other. There was no one watching. There were no occupied cars.

She crossed.

Western Standard Savings and Loan was in a storefront that had been made by combining two existing storefronts into one. There was a single doorway, but she could see where the other doorway had once been, the door removed and glassed over. All the windows were tinted against the bright L.A. sun. To see inside, she had to push her face against the glass, shield her eyes with her hands.

In the distance she heard sirens. Her backup, at last. She breathed a sigh of relief.

And saw the light again.

It was definitely coming from inside. Someone was in there, and there could only be one reason. She reached for her weapon, keeping her gaze focused on where the light had been. Wouldn't do to lose sight of them now.

Behind her she heard a car squealing around the corner. Finally the LAPD had her back. She unholstered her automatic, stepped back from the bank door, braced herself.

A car door opened, a gun cocked.

"Drop it, Officer!" she heard.

Oops.

The lion head sniffed Angel.

The lion's eyes narrowed, peered at him.

"You're not human," the lion said. "You have the stink of Hell on you."

"Very perceptive," Angel agreed. With his free hand he tapped his ridged forehead, his protruding fangs. "Not human."

The lion released him. "What is this, some kind of scam?"

Angel straightened his clothing. "What happened to the 'thees' and 'thous'?" he asked.

"That's for the benefit of that clown," the lion said, waving a furry hand at Mordractus. "He's still working from texts that are hundreds of years old. He thinks he has to use that kind of language or I won't get it."

"Don't believe him," Mordractus warned Angel. "Orias is a born liar. He's able to see inside your mind, to tell you what you want to hear. He can speak in a thousand tongues, but everything he says is a lie unless he's commanded to speak the truth."

Angel turned to the magician. "Yeah, and you've got my best interests at heart, right?"

"At least I'm human," Mordractus said. He looked even older now, the strain of performing the ceremony having sapped the years from him.

"Like that means anything to me," Angel said. "So what's the deal? He can only hurt humans?"

"I can hurt whoever I wish to," Orias said. "I prefer humans."

"He can't take you back with him, which is what he wants," Mordractus argued. "He comes here when commanded, to fulfill a specific function. But left to his own devices, he wants someone to toy with, to ease the boredom of eternity in the Otherworld. Apparently you don't do for that purpose."

"Maybe because I've been there and come back," Angel suggested.

"That might be it," Mordractus agreed.

"If I wanted you, Angel, you'd be mine," Orias insisted.

"I'm having my doubts," Angel said. "But let's see something. . . ." He leaned forward and snatched the grimoire from Mordractus's quaking hand.

225

"No!" the magician shouted. "I need—"

He lunged for the book. Angel swept it away from him, and Mordractus lost his balance. His left foot slid across the painted circle.

Orias attacked. With a pounding of hooves and a ferocious roar, the demon swept down upon the ancient magician. The lion grasped his scrawny arm in its free hand.

"At last!" it yelled triumphantly.

"Noooo!" Mordractus wailed. "Angelus, help me, for the love of God!"

"I think you've given up that right," Angel said.

The demon dragged Mordractus back to its circle. All the way the magician begged and pleaded with it, and with Angel to save him.

He flipped through the grimoire. "I'm looking, Mordractus. Really. I guess I'm just not finding the right spot."

From nowhere, or from everywhere, another strong wind blew in, fluttering the pages of the old book. The glow from Orias dimmed and then went out, and the room was plunged back into darkness. Only the dim glow of coals in the brazier provided illumination. The wind died to nothing.

In the far distance Angel could hear a bell ring three times.

Then all was silent.

He went to the cabinet, rummaged in the dark until he could find Mordractus's stash of matches.

With them he lit some candles, and with a candle lit a couple of the torches on the wall.

By the light of the torches, he studied the grimoire. It was in Latin, but he remembered enough of that language to get by. At last he found the spell that would bring closure to this invocation, that would seal the opening so that Orias couldn't return.

He read the incantation, performed the spell as best he could.

When he was finished, he headed for the stairs, and home.

CHAPTER SEVENTEEN

Angel made it halfway up the dark staircase when the door at the top opened, letting in a shaft of light. A moment later the shaft was partially blocked by a silhouette.

"Everything okay, boss?" the silhouette asked.

"Hunky dory," Angel replied.

"You're not—hey!" the guy shouted.

"You're right," Angel said. "I'm not."

The guy started down the stairs. Angel charged up at a crouching run and met him, throwing his head to the side and driving his shoulder into the guy's gut. With an "Ooof!" the guy folded around him. Angel straightened and rolled the guy over his back. He tumbled down the stairs with a howl, thumping and bumping all the way down.

Great, Angel thought. *Don't know how many are up there, but now they know I'm coming.*

He stopped just inside the door and glanced around the corner. The doorway was off a kitchen. To his right there was an open pantry, and then a big kitchen, full of avocado-green appliances and ceramic tile, but empty. On the far wall was a door that opened to the dark outdoors.

To his left, though, was a short hallway. And from the hallway he could hear voices, raised in alarm and coming his way.

He chose the right.

He dashed across the tile floor, past a center island cluttered with papers and, well, clutter, and a sink piled high with dirty dishes. The door was locked, but with a thumb-lock in the center of the knob. He turned it, pulled open the door, and ran outside. The night air was scented with pine and woodsmoke.

"There he goes!" he heard from inside. Someone had spotted the door closing. Angel sped for the shelter of the trees.

He figured he could take them. He had before, except for the four demons who had finally brought him down. And even then, if they hadn't had that enchanted rope, he thought he had a good chance against them.

But they might still have the rope. And who knew what other weapons? Better to be cautious, try to find out how many he was dealing with, and how they were equipped. Or just make his escape and not worry about them. With Mordractus gone, chances were they'd have no beef with him.

Loyalty seldom extended beyond the grave.

He had just reached the treeline when the kitchen door flew open. Two men were outlined in the doorway, looking out. After a moment they went back inside.

Angel thought they might have given up. Maybe someone had already realized that Mordractus was missing, that they were without an employer.

But no, as long as there was no body they'd be uncertain. They'd think he was still out there somewhere, and they'd think Angel would know where to find him.

Well, that much is true, at least. Go to the Otherworld and look for the one screaming in torment.

Leaving wasn't going to cut it, Angel realized. They knew where he lived. They had found him before, they'd do it again. Or they'd find Cordy, or Doyle. Angel was going to have to stay until he could convince Mordractus's troops that their boss was history.

He'd have to find a way to talk to them.

He was about to step from the trees when the kitchen door opened again. Powerful beams of light pierced the dark night. One of the beams fell on him. There was a shout, and then the bark of gunfire.

Bullets *thwicked* into the tree immediately before him. He dived to the ground, hit, rolled behind some brush.

The beams played across the ground. More voices came to the door. Now that he'd been spotted, they'd blanket the area. They'd find him. Guns weren't necessarily a big problem—the bullets would hurt, but not kill. But guns weren't the only weapons they had.

He pushed himself to his hands and knees, and then to his feet, running in a zigzag pattern farther into the trees, away from the house. Moonlight splashed through the pines, and centuries of living in the dark had given Angel amazing night vision, but still it was dark enough to make running difficult and silence impossible. More bullets whizzed through the air behind him.

"You don't want to do this," Kate said. She didn't turn around—there were still armed robbers somewhere in front of her, in the bank. And she still had her gun in her hand, trained in that direction.

The bank door opened. A tall, goateed man in dark clothing stepped out, pointing a MAC-10 at her. He wasn't looking directly at her, though, but past her—presumably at whoever had just climbed from a car behind her and pointed a gun at her back.

"Waste her, man," he said.

"No time," the man behind her said. "Listen!"

She knew what he meant even before the gunman did. Sirens. They were closer now—less than a block away. In seconds the street would be full of police cars.

"Let's go," the goateed guy said.

"We're not getting out of here," the man behind her responded. "They're right on top of us. But if we had a hostage—a cop . . ."

A smile split the goatee's face. His head nodded. "Good thinking," he said. He beckoned Kate inside the bank with his weapon. "Come on in, Officer. Hand me that automatic. You're going to be staying with us for a while."

Kate knew that one of the worst things a cop could do was to surrender her weapon. And one of the other worst things was to allow herself to be taken hostage. A lot of cops tried to substitute themselves for civilian hostages, but it almost never turned out to be a good idea.

But playing hero almost never turned out to be a good idea, either. And with a MAC-10 pointed at her belly and who knew what pointed at her back, for her to make any kind of move would be playing hero. Within seconds after trying it, she'd be a dead hero.

As a hostage, they'd have a reason to keep her alive.

She handed over her weapon.

Doing so went against every lesson she'd ever learned—her father, also a cop, would have words for her later, if she survived. Her stomach was in knots. When the goateed guy took it from her hand, she felt like her soul had just been bared to the world, like she was totally exposed.

He just smiled and tucked it into the waistband of his black jeans.

As she walked past him into the bank, he shoved the MAC-10's barrel against her ribs. "Don't try anything stupid," he warned.

"Don't worry," Kate replied.

The guy from the car followed them in. Kate glanced over her shoulder and saw him for the first time as he closed the door, dimming the flashing lights that were even now rolling toward the bank. He was shorter than Goatee, with long dark hair pulled into a ponytail at the back. He also wore dark clothes, only they were covered with dirt. Part of the digging crew, she figured. Goatee must have been a digger as well, but he had been inside cleaning out the vault for who knew how long, and had probably had a chance to dust himself off.

"How're they gonna know we've got her?" he asked.

Goatee thought about this for a moment. Then he smiled again—a snaggle-toothed grin that Kate would grow to despise. "You got a radio?" he asked.

"Yes," she said.

"Tell them where you are. They come in, you die. Simple as that."

Simple, Kate thought. *Maybe to you.*

The magician's house had been built on the side of a hill overlooking Hollywood. There was a lot of land around it—houses up here were large and expensive, and built farther apart than most of those on the flats. Angel darted from tree to tree, trying to keep some cover between himself and the guys with guns and lights. His path took him down the slope, and it wasn't until the city's lights vanished that he realized he'd dropped into a side canyon, and was no longer on the hillside itself. The tall, straight pines were left behind; down here he was sheltered by live oaks with spreading branches, and tall grasses clutched at his ankles.

There were no more sounds of pursuit, at least that he could hear. That didn't mean they weren't out there. Angel believed in optimism, but when his life was on the line, he believed a healthy dose of caution was warranted. They probably were still out there, he knew, but they were probably being more careful.

Which made them more deadly.

Angel moved back toward the house, on an angle, keeping the slope of the canyon between him and where he believed it to be. With a little luck he could come up behind most of his pursuers, who'd be focusing their attentions on where he had been instead of where he was now. Hiding was fine for the short term, but it wasn't going to do him any good in the long run.

When he thought he was beyond the house, he began to climb. He pulled his way up the canyon's short steep wall, holding on to the branches of small trees, gripping fistfuls of grass, until he could bring his head above the rim.

Twenty feet away three armed men stood looking straight at him.

He was exposed in a patch of clear moonlight. They had certainly seen him, and within seconds weapons were raised toward him.

He offered a smile. "We've got to talk," he said.

Without a word one of the men fired. Instead of the sharp report of a firearm, though, he heard the *thwip* of a crossbow. A wooden bolt slammed into his chest.

He fell.

At the bottom of the canyon wall, he landed in a bed of thick, sharp-bladed grass. Sticks and rocks poked and prodded. Every part of him hurt.

But that meant he was alive, or at least, still undead. The wooden bolt had missed his heart. He found an end, grabbed it, yanked the bolt from his chest. The pain was excruciating.

Angel found himself wanting to pass out, but he knew he couldn't afford the luxury. The guy with the crossbow was still at the top of the canyon somewhere, and he knew his prey was down below, and injured.

Something about this plan wasn't working.

And there was no more time left to make a new one.

He could hear them massing above him. He rolled over a couple of times, through the snagging grasses, to find the shelter of overhanging oak branches. Rolling was noisy, though. They'd have him pinpointed by now. The next bolt might not miss.

Angel's mind worked rapidly, running through the possibilities. None of them looked promising.

When there are no good options, he thought, *take the direct route.*

Mustering all the strength he could, he leaped into the branches of the oak. The tree shuddered violently, and the noise drew fire from above. Bullets and bolts blasted through the thick growth.

Angel kept going. Reaching the top level of the branches, he bounced once on a broad one, like a diver on the springboard, and jumped for the rim.

He caught the air, did a somersault over the heads of the shooters, and came down behind them. Landing on his feet, he kicked out toward the nearest man, catching the small of his back. The man staggered and then went over the edge, reaching out to one of his colleagues. They both disappeared into the canyon with startled screams.

"I know how they feel," Angel said.

The third man, the one with the crossbow, was still standing. He pointed it at Angel.

"Your time is up, vampire."

"Listen to me," Angel said. "Your boss is gone. There's no reason for this fight." Even as he spoke, though, he was moving, sidestepping to the cross-bow wielder's right. The man tracked him with the weapon, but the farther Angel went, the farther from his body the man had to hold the bow. Finally, to keep his balance, he had to take a step to his right.

Which was when Angel attacked.

The man was off-balance for a moment. Angel dived in low and fast. A bolt whistled over his head, vanishing into the dark canyon.

He hit the man in the legs, and they both went down in a tangle of limbs. A booted foot struck Angel's brow, breaking the skin. Angel caught the foot and twisted, wrenching the leg as hard as he could. The bowman shrieked in pain. Angel dragged himself up the man's body, finally getting a bead on his face. He was about to take a swing for the man's jaw when a wooden bolt, clutched in the man's fist, drove into his right tricep.

Angel fell to the side, clawing at the bolt with his left hand and pulling it free.

The bowman got to his feet and took a couple of quick steps backward, putting himself out of Angel's immediate range. He shoved another bolt into place and aimed the weapon at Angel's heart.

When the hand landed on his shoulder, the bowman started and nearly screamed.

"We'll take over now," Mr. Crook said.

The bowman nodded and drifted away. Angel stood, facing the four demons from the other night. Gaunt Mr. Crook, holding his long staff. The short round one, shaped like a giant ball with stumpy legs and arms and dozens of teeth. The tall, powerful blue-skinned one with the ridges of cutting bone on the backs of his hands. And the Maelabog, skeleton rotating beneath its lovely skin.

"You guys again," Angel said.

"And you," Mr. Crook replied.

"Got your magic rope?"

"Will we need it?" Mr. Crook asked with that claws-on-blackboard voice. He seemed to be the designated spokesman for the group.

"Only way you took me last time."

"Last time you were tired and distracted. Now you're twice as tired, and you're hurt—much more badly than we think you are willing to show."

"I've felt better," Angel agreed.

"And worse, we're sure. But we don't have to let you feel bad ever again. We can end your pain right now."

"Appreciate that, really," Angel said. "But I'll pass."

"Do not be so hasty. Consider our offer."

"You know, Mr. Crook, I just can't believe that you really are looking out for me. I keep thinking you have some agenda of your own here."

"You must learn to trust."

"People keep telling me that. I'll work on it—take a self-improvement seminar or something."

The longer he kept them talking—well, kept Mr. Crook talking, anyway—the better he was feeling. Angel healed quickly from any wound that didn't dust him. Crossbow-guy had come close to that a time or two, but so far, Angel was still solid.

He wanted to keep it that way.

"You know Mordractus is gone, right?" he asked. "He was taken to the Otherworld by the demon that he summoned."

"We felt something," Mr. Crook rasped. "It disturbed Maelabog quite a bit. A hollowness, she said, an emptiness in her soul. She was quite fond of the human."

"She looks all broken up," Angel said.

"You mock," Mr. Crook said. "You are a demon yourself. You have declared war on your own kind. How self-loathing must you be?"

"I don't think of myself as a demon," Angel said. "I was human. I made a mistake. I became a vampire. That's my biology now. But biology isn't destiny. My roots are in the human world, and that's the world I embrace."

"A facile rationalization," Mr. Crook argued.

"Mordractus had you watched. We have seen his tapes, his notes. You do not seem comfortable in either world to us."

"I can't believe I'm standing here debating philosophy with you," Angel said. "Can't we just fight or something?"

"Exactly the kind of simplistic response we would expect from you."

"That's the kind of argument you get from someone who has no argument."

Mr. Crook sighed, a noise like an old iron gate swinging in a strong wind. "Very well," he said. He gestured toward Angel with his staff.

The blue demon and the round demon attacked as one, from opposite sides.

Angel kicked at the beach ball, careful to avoid its gnashing teeth. The big blue one came in close, arms swinging, and one of those spurs of bone caught Angel's right cheek, slicing it open. Angel batted the hand away and shot a left jab into the blue demon's gut. The thing doubled over.

Angel moved away from it, caught the beach ball's short, useless arm. Teeth snapped and slavered at him. Angel tugged on the arm, pulling the demon off balance. Angel kept the pressure on, kept pulling, and the demon literally began to roll. Angel jumped high into the air, over the rolling demon, and landed behind it. With a mighty push he rolled the demon into its blue partner.

There was a moment when it looked as if the blue-skinned demon would maintain its balance. But the force of the rolling round demon was too much, and they both went down, over the canyon's rim. After a moment they landed with a huge crash of branches.

Angel hoped they squashed the human soldiers down there.

But he returned his attention to Mr. Crook and the Maelabog. They were still here, still threats. And he couldn't take all night with them—there were more humans out there, undoubtedly more crossbows and stakes. They had known, after all, that their prey was a vampire.

Mr. Crook, though, wasn't even looking at Angel. He was standing next to the Maelabog, whose skin rippled alarmingly, with his head bent toward her. He appeared to be listening to something that Angel couldn't hear. He could only make out the faint sounds of her bones shifting beneath her skin, and he hoped that the memory of that wouldn't persist in his dreams after this long night was through.

If indeed he survived the night to dream again.

Finally Mr. Crook raised his head. "She says you're right," Mr. Crook said. "Mordractus is gone. He has been taken to the Otherworld."

"She's in touch with him?" Angel asked. "Good long-distance provider."

"You mock. She is in touch, as you put it, with the

Otherworld. Not with Mordractus himself. He is in no position to be communicative."

"I guess not."

"Our battle is ended," Mr. Crook announced. "We have no further dispute with you."

"The fact that I just threw two of you off the side of a mountain doesn't bother you?"

"We were here to do a job for Mordractus," Mr. Crook said. "Mordractus is no longer in need of our services."

"Demons for hire, is that it? Now that there's no more paychecks coming, you don't have any interest in the outcome."

"That would be the way that you would understand it."

"What about Mordractus's human troops?"

"We cannot speak for them," Mr. Crook said. "But we will communicate their employer's fate to them."

"I hope they feel the same way about it that you do."

"They were paid employees."

"That's what I thought," Angel said. "Mordractus was nuts, but at least he believed in something. The rest of you are just in it for the money." He rubbed his arm where the bolt had pierced it. "That's more insulting than Mordractus trying to cook my brains."

"We will not argue this point with you," Mr. Crook said. "We differ in our beliefs."

"Agree to disagree," Angel said. "Good enough for me."

He turned away from the demons and headed toward the front of the house. The driveway, he hoped, was there, and maybe there would be a car he could take. Showing the demons his back made him nervous, but he took them at their word. They were hired help, nothing more, in the final calculation.

He had just reached the drive when a car came bouncing up the path toward him. Caught in its headlights, he froze, not sure if there was another fight coming.

He hoped not. He was beat. But he'd take what came.

The car slowed, pulled up to him, and the front passenger door opened. Angel braced for anything.

"That's a good look for you," Cordelia said, climbing from the vehicle. "Sticks, leaves, twigs. Nature boy. Very now. And the cuts all over your face just add the right kind of drama, I think. You've really put it together well."

Doyle stepped out from behind the wheel.

"Looks like you were right, Cordy," he said. "He's obviously in need of our help. Looks like he's surrounded."

"A couple of comedians," Angel said. "Just what I need." He opened the back door, folded himself into the seat. "One of you want to drive this thing?" he asked. "I just want to get some sleep."

Cordelia got back into the passenger seat. She flipped down the visor, pulled off the mirror mounted there, and handed it to Angel. "Take a look at—oh, wait," she said. "Never mind. You'll have to take my word for it. You look ridiculous."

Leave it to Cordy to put everything into perspective. It was all about how he looked. Angel started to laugh.

By the time the car was turned around and heading down the hill, they were all roaring.

CHAPTER EIGHTEEN

Doyle pulled off the bumpy drive and onto a paved road, leaving Mordractus's rented home behind.

Angel sprawled in the backseat and closed his eyes.

"So you wanna tell us what that was all about?" Doyle asked. "We were worried about you, I don't mind sayin'."

"I appreciate it, Doyle," Angel replied.

"I quit my job to help find you," Cordelia said.

"I appreciate that, too, Cordy."

"You'd better. Because it seems like the last time you gave me a paycheck for working at Angel Investigations was never."

"I'll pay you something out of what I get from Jack Willits."

"Are you still working for him?"

Angel thought for a moment. "I guess that depends on whether or not Karinna is still alive."

"I haven't heard anything different in the news," Cordelia said.

"You don't listen to the news," Doyle pointed out.

"Well, it would have been in the trades. And people would have been talking about it on the lot."

Doyle pointed at her. "Score one for you."

"Head for Bel Air," Angel said. "My car's at the Willits house, and I want to check in on Karinna. And turn on the news, why don't you? Let's just see if there is anything going on."

"Such as what?" Cordelia said. "You look like the guy who won the fight. Barely, I'll grant you. But at least you're standing up. Or you were when we found you."

"I think I won," Angel said. "Mordractus is gone."

"More who?"

"That's right, you don't know any of this. Mordractus was an aging Irish magician who wanted to make soup out of my brain in order to summon the ancient one-eyed God of Death."

"Look, Angel, if you don't want to tell us, just say so," Cordelia complained. "You don't have to make up ridiculous stories."

"Sorry," Angel said. "Guess I'll just keep it to myself."

Doyle fiddled with the car radio, finally bringing in a news station. ". . . market closed up today another ninety points," a male newscaster's voice said. "More business news in a moment, but let's go back to that breaking situation downtown."

"Gee, I wonder how my stocks would be doing if I had any stocks," Cordelia said.

"Quiet," Angel hissed.

"Excuse me."

". . . robbers holding police detective Kate Lockley hostage for almost two hours at this point. They have issued demands, which the police department has refused to make public. An official spokesperson said only that the demands are being negotiated and every effort is being made to ensure the safety of Detective Lockley."

"Kate?" Angel said, struggling to sit up.

"That's what he said," Doyle agreed.

"Downtown," Angel said. "Fast. Forget about Bel Air."

"Angel, I'm sure the place is swarmin' with law," Doyle said. "Swat teams, hostage negotiators, you name it. No way you're gonna be able to do anything down there."

"Just drive, Doyle."

"Drivin' here, boss," Doyle said. They all lapsed into silence and listened to the news reports.

Kate Lockley was Angel's friend in the Los Angeles Police Department—which wasn't necessarily saying a lot, as cops and private investigators didn't really buddy up to each other as often in real life as they did on TV. But she'd always played straight with him. She had no idea, of course, that he was really a vampire, and he was hoping to keep it that way. People had a tendency to react in a negative fashion to that particular news bulletin.

But he liked her and he respected her abilities, and he wanted to keep her liking him. So the vampire thing would stay buried in the back of the closet, as far as he was concerned.

And now she was a hostage to killers. He didn't know how it could have happened, but he knew it was trouble. The bank robbers knew she was a cop—the radio had been broadcasting that fact, along with her name and police record. That could only mean trouble, and he had to help.

Once off the surface streets, Doyle took the Hollywood Freeway south to the 110. This late at night the freeway was remarkably smooth sailing, and Doyle made good time.

Until just south of the Santa Monica freeway.

There, a reality about Los Angeles freeway driving reared its ugly head. The reality is, there's no such thing as a time of day or night when there's no traffic. Traffic in the Southland could jam up at any time, for any reason, or none.

Doyle saw brake lights ahead and slowed the car. A moment later the brake lights came to a halt. He slowed further.

"Come on," Angel said impatiently.

"One of those things," Doyle said. "Mystery traffic."

"Is there another way? Surface streets?"

"There would have been if we got off at the last exit," Doyle said. "But we didn't, and it's a ways until the next one."

"What's wrong with this city?" Angel asked. "Where are all these people going in the middle of the night?"

"You think you're the only night owl in town?" Cordelia asked. "L.A. isn't even alive until after the sun goes down."

"I thought that was New York."

"New York is the city that never sleeps," Cordelia explained. "L.A. is the city that dozes on the beach and power-naps by the pool. Daytime sleeping. This place was made for your kind, Angel."

A massive truck rumbled on their right, and in front of them an ancient T-bird belched noxious fumes into the air. To their left, a pickup's stereo system screeched deafeningly as the driver, a dread-locked white kid who couldn't have been more than seventeen, bopped and bounced and drummed on the steering wheel.

Angel looked around in frustration.

"Sorry, man," Doyle said. "Nothin' I can do. We're stuck."

"You're stuck," Angel said. He opened the car door. "I'm not."

"Angel!" Cordelia called. "Where are you going?"

"I'll see you back at the office," Angel said.

"You think you're gonna get there faster on foot?"

Doyle called. Then he looked at the interminable line of cars parked on the roadway ahead of him. "Yeah, I guess you will at that."

There were five of them. Six, counting the driver. *But then, I pretty much have to count the driver,* Kate thought. *He is, after all, inside the bank with an automatic weapon in his hands.*

So six. All males, all Caucasian, between twenty-five and thirty-five years old, she figured. They wore work clothes—jeans, sweatshirts, work boots, all in dark colors. They all looked reasonably fit and healthy—*all that digging,* she guessed. *Builds upper-body strength.*

They had taken her into an office deep in the bowels of the bank building. Two of them stayed back there with her—the Goatee, and a young guy with piercing blue eyes and wavy blond hair. *Surfer hair,* she thought. He had a strong jaw and a wide friendly mouth. In other circumstances she'd have found him handsome.

But somehow she just couldn't overlook the Beretta he kept clutched in his fist. His knuckles were white against its steely blue grip, and there was a quiver to his hands. He probably had not anticipated being trapped inside a bank with half of the LAPD surrounding it on the outside.

Most bank robbers failed to consider too carefully the likelihood that they would someday get caught.

But most bank robbers did get caught—it was too high-profile a crime, and too many people came looking, and too many witnesses lived to testify. Kate tried to calm herself with the knowledge that, no matter what happened here, tonight, these guys would not remain free.

Of course, it would be better if she were there to see them locked up. Her dad would appreciate it, too—he had just retired from the force, and she knew he'd like his daughter's career to continue even though his was over. So all in all, dying tonight would be a less-than-optimal end to the workday.

But at the same time she knew that it was out of her hands. She had surrendered her weapon to desperate felons. The police were out there now. The crooks were in here, with her. They were scared. They were surrounded. They'd split up—two in the front part of the bank, watching to make sure the police didn't get too close to the building. Two had gone back to the tunnel opening to make sure no one came in that way. That left two with Kate. Their job, she knew, was to kill her if either of the other pairs gave the word.

In her mind's eye she pictured the scene outside. She'd been part of it often enough that she had a better-than-passing familiarity with it. To the untrained eye it would look like utter chaos. There were police cars everywhere, parked at awkward angles, parked on sidewalks, parked perpendicular to one another. Most of them had their light bars flashing and their headlights on—at least, those with headlights facing the front of the bank. There were also, by now, banks of floodlights on metal stands, powered by portable generators, and those also faced the bank. Behind cars, mailboxes, benches, in doorways and windows—behind anything that offered some degree of protection— there were men and women of the LAPD pointing their weapons at the bank. Some of them wore body armor, heavy Kevlar vests that, on hot nights, functioned like mini saunas. This night, she knew, had finally cooled to the point that the officers wouldn't be sweating off the pounds in them, but they were still uncomfortable.

They stopped bullets, though, which was the important thing.

There would also be a trailer outside, somewhere close by. In the trailer there would be communications equipment, computers, and one or two hostage negotiators. Two, she suspected, because she was LAPD, so Parker Center, L.A.'s main police headquarters, would want one of its own on the scene. But this was a bank robbery in progress, and robbing banks was a Federal offense, so the FBI's hostage negotiator would be there, too.

Goatee had, a few moments ago, released a long string of obscenities into the ear of one of them and slammed the office phone down into its cradle. He sat in a swivel chair behind a desk, which he slammed with the flat of his hand.

"More time," he ranted. "They keep asking for more time."

"All we're askin' for is some cars and stuff," the surfer said. This one leaned against the wall by the doorway, listening for any signals from his buddies. Kate sat on an uncomfortable straight-backed guest chair.

"Was that Riddle, or Hopgood?" Kate asked.

"What are you talking about?" Goatee demanded.

"The negotiator," Kate explained. "Riddle is our guy, LAPD. Hopgood is the FBI's man in Los Angeles. He's good. He's been doing it since the late seventies. I'm just a little partial to Riddle, you know. Home team."

"I guess it was Hopgood," Goatee said, a little more calm. "Called himself an old man."

"That's Hopgood, then. Most patient man to ever walk the Earth, I believe." She was glad she'd steered the conversation in this direction. Part of the negotiator's job was to make the hostage taker think of his hostages as people, not just bargaining chips. Kate hoped that if she could humanize the negotiator, maybe he could do the same for her.

"Why do they need more time to get some stupid cars?" the surfer asked.

"Think about it," Kate said. "You asked for cars that would blend in, right? They can't give you squad cars, and that's all they've got out there. They can't give you your old car back—that's probably already been towed away, stripped down, and dusted for fingerprints. So they have to somehow get their hands on some cars that they can afford to give away, and that they'll probably have to shoot at sooner or later. They can't just grab them off the street or the impound lot—some citizen would complain for sure. So yes, it'll take some time to come up with a couple of spare cars for you. Why not just take one car, anyway?"

"We want to be able to split up, in case we're followed," the surfer told her.

"In case? Of course you'll be followed."

"Better not be," Goatee said with a scowl. "Told them we wanted a clear road and safe passage."

"Think about it from their point of view," Kate said. "You are wanted for murder. Now you've kidnapped a cop. You think they can let you just drive away?"

"They don't, you'll just be one more cop funeral," Goatee replied. "They still play those, what are they, bagpipes, at cop funerals?"

"They will at mine," Kate said. "But if you kill me, I don't think you'll get any music at yours."

Angel ran down the freeway's shoulder. The stink of hundreds of idling cars spitting exhaust into the air smelled to him like L.A. itself: noxious, dirty, poisoned, but ripe with the promise of better times ahead; the traffic would clear, movement would happen, soon they'd be rushing toward their individual futures in the golden city by the sea.

At first only a few people noticed him, a dark shape moving quickly through the dark night. Then the headlight of someone stopped at an odd angle, in the midst of a lane-change, caught him and illuminated him for a split second, and someone called out to him.

As he continued—wondering where the next exit was, and wishing it was closer—more and more seemed to notice he was there. The occasional shout became a constant, and as people sat in unmoving cars or stretched their legs on the freeway, the din moved ahead of him, so that people actually began to look for him coming.

By the time he reached the exit, it was a steady roar. The words were hard to make out, and probably meaningless. It was more a matter of voices raised in recognition of someone stopped in traffic who had finally done something about it. The traffic was going nowhere, so by running he was outpacing it dramatically. These people wouldn't abandon their vehicles; they knew that sooner or later whatever had blocked the roadway would be cleared and they could continue their car trips. But that guy, that one guy in the long black coat, they'd tell their friends and families, that guy didn't put up with it. He ran. He ran and he ran and then he ran some more.

At the front of the pack there was a moving van

on its side. It had jackknifed and overturned, and its contents—all the furniture and possessions of some unlucky family—were spread across the lanes. Movers and motorists and police officers were trying to gather it all up, and had made what looked like a homey sitting area off on the shoulder, with a big easy chair and a floor lamp and a coffee table. They all stopped their work as the roar of the stranded drivers reached them, and looked up, and saw Angel coming toward them. As he passed them they joined in, clapping and applauding as if they were at some kind of interstate sporting event.

Then Angel hit the exit ramp, just beyond where the van had gone over. It was empty and dark, and he left the sounds of his public behind. Within a few moments after reaching the surface streets below the freeway, he couldn't hear anything except the hiss and rumble of regular street traffic.

He kept running.

"You really don't think they'll let us get away?" the surfer asked Kate.

"Of course not," she replied.

"Shut up!" Goatee growled. "She has to say that, man. What are you, some kind of idiot?"

"I ain't no idiot," the surfer said. "I been to school, man. I got a two-year degree."

"Yeah, in being a idiot," Goatee said. "Just don't talk to the lady, okay?"

"But you were—"

"I'm the one talking to the negotiator, right? I'm the one's gotta get our demands met so we can get outta here. I wanna talk to her, I can."

"Sure, okay," the surfer agreed. "Whatever."

"You don't have to listen to me," Kate pressed. "Ask Hopgood. Ask him what your chances are, out there. Half of the cops in L.A. are just itching for an excuse to shoot you. The only hope you have is to go out there with me, and show them your hands. If you go out unarmed and surrender, then not only do you not upset the cops, but the judge is likely to be more lenient on you. Judges are pretty harsh when it comes to cop-killers."

"You said it yourself, cop," Goatee said. "We're already wanted for murder. What've we got to lose?"

"Can it be proven?" she asked. "Did you leave your fingerprints on the bodies, or the bullets? Are you still using the same guns?" A panicked expression flitted across the surfer's face. "Oh, no," Kate said, suddenly filled with dismay at just how clueless these people really were. "You're still using the same guns you shot people with? What were you thinking?"

"Hey," Goatee said. "I don't tell you how to run your business."

"Well, I'd be better than you at yours," Kate insisted. "You always ditch a gun you've killed someone with. It's just common sense. I mean, come on."

"You just shut up," Goatee said. "I don't want to hear any more from you, you understand?"

"Got it," Kate agreed. "But really—"

"Shut up!"

Kate shut up. She'd let them stew in the juices of their own stupidity for a while. Soon the phone would ring again, and Hopgood would go to work on them. Between herself and Hopgood, she was starting to think that maybe she'd live to see morning after all.

The prospect was an attractive one.

But the sounds of a commotion from deeper in the bank brought her reverie to an end. There was shouting, and then there was a sharp report that could only be one thing. A bullet. There was a scream, and then there was a scuffling sound, coming closer.

"What's goin' on?" the surfer called down the hall.

"It's okay!" one of the robbers shouted back. "Just got us a new hostage."

Kate heard the sounds of someone being manhandled down the hall. *A new hostage? Who?* she wondered.

The phone on the desk started to ring.

"That'll be Hopgood," she said. "Wondering about that shot that was fired. Wondering if I'm okay."

"Hopgood can wait," Goatee said.

"Not too long," Kate said. "He thinks I'm dead, there's nothing that'll keep them from storming the place."

Goatee snarled and snatched the phone off the hook. "She's fine!" he said. Then he held the phone out to Kate and ordered, "Tell him!"

"It wasn't me!" Kate shouted. "A shot was fired, but I don't know what at! I'm okay!"

Goatee held the phone to his ear again. "Got that?" he asked. "Good. I'm busy here." He slammed the phone down again.

And from the hallway another of the robbers appeared. This one was heavy, with a big round nose set in the middle of a big round face, and an oddly tiny mouth below it. He tugged on someone's arm, and drew that someone into view in the office doorway.

"Brought you a present," he said. "From the tunnel."

Kate gasped.

Glenn Newberry.

CHAPTER NINETEEN

It wasn't hard to tell where the action was.

There probably hadn't been this many people on the streets at this hour, in this neighborhood, since . . . well, ever, Angel guessed. It was like the block party to end all block parties. Except that the locals, the area's residents, were out on the streets in pajamas with coats or robes pulled over them, or shirtless, or in hastily assembled jeans and T-shirts. The ones in party wear were the police, dozens of them—maybe a hundred, he estimated—in uniforms, some with body armor, some with helmets, a few with SWAT stenciled across the backs of their jackets.

Lights everywhere. Cars everywhere. The press had shown up, and were held back away from the bank by a phalanx of law enforcement. Helicopters circled overhead, their blades pounding out a soundtrack to the scene.

CLOSE TO THE GROUND

Angel moved through the crowd like a shadow, slipping across the police line unnoticed. He looked for a familiar face and finally spotted one—Trevor Lockley, Kate's father. Angel had accompanied Kate to her dad's retirement party, as a favor to her, and had met the man there. He drifted up behind Trevor.

"Hi, Mr. Lockley," he said.

Trevor turned, blinked a couple of times, and then recognition set in.

"Angel," he said. "Kate's inside."

"I heard. What's going on?"

"They're keeping me in the loop," Trevor said, his words clipped with tension. "There's a negotiator talking to them. FBI, not ours. Feds are here, LAPD's here. The place is surrounded, but we can't go in without risking Kate's life. There was a shot fired a couple of minutes ago, but nobody knows who fired it or why. The negotiator heard Kate's voice after the shot, saying that she was okay, so it wasn't that, thank God."

"Glad to hear that."

"Still, I'm worried, I can tell you that."

"I know." Angel touched the man's shoulder. "She's a tough lady."

"She is that," Trevor agreed. "Raised her that way."

"I'm sure you did. Do we know where they tunneled in from?"

"Abandoned filling station around the corner,"

Trevor said. "FBI has the end sealed up, but they can't go in that way. The crooks are probably watching the tunnel as well as the door. If only someone *could* get inside there," Trevor said. "And . . ." He looked around.

Angel was gone.

The ground beneath the city of Los Angeles is honeycombed with tunnels of varying sizes. Sewers, electrical access shafts, remnants of an old subway system and the beginnings of the new one . . . there were thousands of miles of underground passageways, and no one on Earth knew every mile of them.

Angel knew more than most. After getting his bearings, he realized that the bank robbers wouldn't have needed to tunnel half the distance they did if they'd been aware of the sewage layout in the area. The manhole he wanted was right in front of the bank, in fact.

But there were about two hundred cops standing on top of it. Instead, he went around the corner, down the street, and around another corner. A block out of his way, but he could make that time up in a hurry. And there was nobody here; the action was all on the next street over.

He pried the manhole up, started down the rungs cemented into the wall, and scraped the manhole back into place over himself. In the dark he went down.

That was the thing about sewers, they were dark. Most people, if they were willing to put up with the smells, the rats, the occasional underground dweller, still needed to carry a light.

Angel didn't bother with one. The dark had ceased to bother him a long time ago.

When he reached the bottom of the ladder, he put his feet onto solid ground—more or less solid, anyway, but coated with a slick layer of moss and fungus and who knew what else? There were times that Angel wished the whole undead thing involved losing his sense of smell. He paused for a moment, listening.

It was quiet. Choosing the right branch of the tunnel, he crouched and began his trip.

Special Agent Glenn Newberry sat on the floor, his back against the wall, next to Kate's chair. There was blood at the shoulder of his jacket, a dark patch that was spreading quickly.

"You okay?" Kate asked him.

"No," he replied. "Took a hit. I'm feeling a little light-headed."

"This man needs a doctor," she announced.

Goatee glared at her. He was good at that, the glaring thing. "He'll get a doctor when we get our freaking cars."

"What are you even doing here?" she asked Newberry. "I thought you were calling for backup and waiting at the gas station."

He stared glumly at their captors. "I didn't," he said.

"Didn't call, or didn't wait?"

"Didn't either. I went into the tunnel. Didn't know they had you, so I figured I could come up behind them. But they were waiting."

"So now they've got two hostages. Two heads are better than one, I guess."

Special Agent Newberry didn't smile.

"You two lovebirds want to shut up?" Goatee asked. "I don't want to listen to any more cop talk."

"Sorry," Kate said. "I'm sure bank robbers make much more stimulating conversation. And the tunnel digging stories you must be able to tell."

"You'd be surprised," Goatee responded.

"I'm sure."

Approaching a T intersection, Angel heard voices. He froze, waited, then silently pressed himself against the dank wall of the sewer pipe. It was taller here, bigger around, and he was able to stand upright. He walked to one side to avoid the inch or so of water that flowed through.

The voices were male, speaking in hushed tones.

". . . another hour, maybe," one of the men was saying. "No longer than that."

"I was on one in Kansas City, took fourteen hours," the other replied. "Three hostages were killed, two came out of it."

FBI, it sounded like. If they saw Angel in here, it would all be over.

He edged his way to the intersection, risked a glance around the corner. Two men, in blue windbreakers with FBI stenciled on the back in white letters. They carried guns and steel-cased Maglite flashlights.

And they were between Angel and where he needed to go.

They didn't show any indication that they'd be getting out of his way anytime soon.

He turned back. Another couple of blocks out of his way, then. He could come in ahead of where they were. It would just cost him another fifteen minutes or so.

He'd try to cut it to ten.

Every minute counted.

"The one with the goatee," Kate whispered, "works, or worked, for a janitorial service that hired out to banks all over town. At one time or another he must have been inside half the banks in the city."

"The service is bonded, right?" Newberry asked.

"Sure. But that doesn't mean that they can't hire a loser once in a while. Maybe he didn't have a record before. Maybe he didn't get this idea until he'd spent a lot of time in banks. Maybe—"

"Shhh," Newberry silenced her. Goatee was on the phone again.

"That's right," he barked. "Another hostage. An FBI agent named Newberry. He's wounded, but he's okay." He turned to face Newberry, holding the phone out. "Tell Hopgood you're okay."

"I'm hit!" Newberry called. "I'm alive, but bleeding."

"He's okay," Goatee claimed. "For now. But we're getting tired of waiting, I can tell you that." He listened for a moment. "No, that's *not* all right. This has gone on too long. We have two hostages now, and one of them's a Fed. Tell you what, Hoppy Hopgood. We get those cars in front of the bank, and all the cops cleared away, in ten minutes, or we'll give you one of the hostages. In a *bag*."

He hung up the phone with a malicious chuckle.

"You guys want to draw straws, or what?" he asked.

He'd been in sewers the world over, now that he thought about it. Famous ones, like those in Paris, and New York—although he had never seen any of the legendary alligators there—and less famous, and downright disgusting ones, like those in Rome and Prague and New Orleans. L.A.'s were pretty middle of the road—not much to recommend them except the degree of access they afforded, but not as noxious as many others.

Once he was sure the agents couldn't hear him anymore, he broke into a run. It was dangerous, moving so fast in the dark. Even with vision like his, a broken pipe or a loose two-by-four hanging into the passageway would be a major obstacle if he slammed into it headfirst. And he definitely wasn't at his best right now—the events of the past couple of days had left him nearly exhausted. Every muscle ached, including some he didn't know he had.

But he didn't think he had time to move any slower. There had been too many delays already.

This time, when he came out into the main pipeline, he was about a hundred feet beyond where the two FBI agents had been. If they shined their lights down the shaft, they'd probably be able to see him. He had to hope they were too involved in their war stories to bother.

He stayed as close to the pipeline's wall as he could and hoped for the best.

Another fifty feet ahead there was another intersection, this one a four-way. Angel knew he wanted to go right. This would lead into the section that the bank robbers had tunneled into. If they'd had charts of the sewer system they could have saved themselves about twenty-five feet of tunneling—a good week's work, he figured, with picks and shovels. He was surprised they'd never had a cave-in, at least, one that did enough damage to make the news.

But then, he figured, if they'd been geniuses, they'd probably have had jobs instead of going into the bank business through the back door. That was the thing about criminals—comic books and pulp novels notwithstanding, they were very rarely the smartest guys in the class.

He approached the intersection cautiously. They'd have guards posted in the tunnel some-where, he guessed. They would have to assume that the police would send a team up the tunnel to block them in from that side. And the police would have to assume that the bad guys would have figured this out, so they wouldn't send the team after all.

Instead, they'd do as the FBI had done, and post some agents inside the sewer system, blocking each of the possible egresses.

Except the roundabout route Angel had taken.

At the intersection Angel stopped, listened closely. He heard the steady drip of water, the gentle *splosh* of drops falling into the flow. He heard a faint rumble from the streets above.

He heard something that might have been a person breathing.

He hazarded a peek to his right.

They were at the end of this stretch of sewer. Two men, standing in the sewer, automatic rifles in their hands. Not Feds. They were clever—they'd taken a position in the sewer itself, outside the tunnel they'd carved. If anyone followed their tunnel from the gas station to here, these guys would have the drop on them because they'd come from an unexpected direction.

Except now there was someone coming up on them from behind. And Angel was even more unexpected.

Unless they heard him coming.

He had to cover fifty feet without making a sound. It was quiet down here, quiet enough for him to hear one of them drawing breath. If they heard him, they'd turn, see him, fire. He'd survive.

Kate might not.

Angel was out of alternatives. Sitting around hoping that Kate survived this was not an option. So action was called for, and action meant taking out these two gunmen as quickly and quietly as possible. One shot fired, one voice raised in alarm, and this whole plan would backfire, big time.

And these were men who would kill—who had killed—for money. There was nothing lower than that. Angel felt no compunction about taking them down hard.

He moved.

Swiftly, silently, keeping his feet from the flow and against the dry concrete of the pipe's curve, he dashed the fifty feet. The men heard nothing. They kept watching their tunnel, even when Angel drew up behind them. They held semiautomatic rifles, pointed into the tunnel, and they squatted about two-and-a-half feet apart, at the opening.

Feeling a bit like a character from a Three Stooges routine, Angel spread his hands wide.

When he brought them together the right side of one's face was in his right hand, the other guy's left side in his left. He drove them together like a man trying to crack two coconuts.

The thud seemed loud to him, but the two men slumped, unconscious. Angel snagged their weapons before they clattered to the floor—that would have echoed up and down the tunnel—and placed them gingerly in the couple of inches of sewage flow. Even if they worked after that, and even if these guys came to, they'd have a hard time finding their guns and a harder time working up the courage to try them.

He wiped his hands on one guy's jacket and kept going.

The tunnel led from the gas station into this neck of the sewer. Forty feet or so up the sewer, they'd started digging again, just a short jog this time, into the bank. Angel made his way to this secondary tunnel, shaking his head once again at crooks who'd rather dig for days than check out a sewage system plan. He glanced inside the tunnel, and saw, after a ten-foot stretch, where they'd breached the bank's wall.

There was a light on inside.

He stepped into the tunnel. It was empty, and he couldn't hear anything from inside. Probably the two men he'd already encountered were the only guards for this side. Probably there was nobody else between him and wherever Kate was being held.

Probably, probably, probably.

He listened for a long moment, and then headed for the bank wall.

When he reached it, he stopped, listened again. They'd broken through high on the wall in a hallway of the bank's basement. Old, dusty filing cabinets lined one side of the hall. There was no sign of anyone here, though. No sound. He let himself through the hole in the wall, lowered himself to the floor.

He was inside.

Listening again, he heard the faint mumble of voices. He followed the sound, and the voices grew more distinct as he went. The noise led him to a staircase. There were lights up there, as well.

That's where Kate was.

And more armed men. No telling how many, from here.

He ascended silently.

At the top he found himself in another short hallway. Right led to the bank's main lobby, where tellers served the public.

Left led to bank offices.

The voices came from the left. They were quiet; he still couldn't make out what was being said. He didn't really care. He wasn't here to eavesdrop.

He remembered something announcers said on those sports programs Doyle watched. "He came to play," they said. "This team came to play." To which

Angel's response was, yeah, why else would they have come?

When he voiced this, Doyle told him he was too literal.

Today, Angel didn't come to play.

He came to work.

There was an open door down the hall. The soft voices came from in there. Light spilled from the doorway.

Another voice sounded over the first, and Angel recognized Kate's. She was still alive, then. And he knew where she was.

Now he just needed to be able to get to her without anyone shooting her.

He was about to make for the doorway when a phone rang.

Goatee snatched it up.

"Yeah?" he demanded. He listened. "Okay, then. That's better. We'll have a look. You better not be messing with me."

He gestured toward Kate and Glenn Newberry.

"Bring them," he said to the surfer guy. "Hoppy says the cars are outside, and the cops have pulled back."

The surfer helped Newberry to his feet. The agent was unsteady, and Kate rose, helped him maintain his balance. Goatee led the way, and they left the office.

✹   ✹   ✹

Angel pressed himself against wall, just inside the staircase doorway. When the phone rang, the front of the bank went dark. His first thought was that the robbers had turned off the lights, but then he realized that it wasn't bright enough out there for regular bank lights to be on. That was when he knew that all the lights the police had been shining on the bank's façade had been turned off, probably in answer to the robbers' demands.

He could barely see into the hallway from where he stood, just a tiny sliver of space through the doorway. But it was enough to let him see Kate pass by, with the barrel of a MAC-10 jammed against the base of her skull. One move, one whisper from him, and she'd be dead.

He couldn't take that chance. He let them pass by. Two armed men, two hostages. The second one, in a suit, looked to Angel like an FBI man.

They went into the bank lobby.

"What's going on out here?" he heard one of the men ask.

"All the cops are out of sight," someone answered. "They took all those lights away. They're still out there somewhere, but they've moved back to where we can't see 'em from here. They left those two cars there, doors open, motors running."

"Cool. That's what we wanted."

"What about the hostages?"

"When we know we're clear, then we'll worry about them."

Angel knew what that meant. No way could they let law-enforcement officers survive to provide clues, and ultimately to testify against them at trial. Once they knew they weren't being pursued, Kate and the other guy were dead.

Angel slipped around the corner and moved to where he could get a view of the darkened bank lobby.

There were four robbers, all armed. All peering through the big windows at the street outside. Looking for the police, who had done a good job of pulling back, it seemed.

Right outside the door were two nondescript cars. If they took Kate and the agent into those, Angel would never see her alive again.

Goatee touched the surfer guy on the arm. "Get those guys outta the tunnel," he said. "We gotta move fast when we go out."

The surfer nodded once and started back toward the hallway.

Angel felt himself change, felt his vampire self take over. Fully transformed, Angel charged.

He took two steps into the room and then leapt into the air. Somersaulting twice in midair, he landed between Kate and the nearest crook.

"Surprise," he said. He drove a hard right jab into the crook's jaw. There was a loud crack, and the guy's eyes crossed. Angel followed with a snap-kick to the guy's stomach. Wind blew out of him and he folded.

Angel spun to the next closest robber, who was already raising his weapon toward Angel. He swatted the gun barrel to one side, grabbed the crook's collar with his other hand, and yanked the guy forward. Angel's upraised knee collided with the man's face. Two down.

Kate had turned on a third bank robber and kicked the gun from his hands. Now they both circled each other, looking for an opening. The FBI agent and the fourth criminal struggled for possession of the fourth guy's MAC-10, teeth clenched, breathing hard.

Angel turned his attention back to Kate's guy, who made his play, lunging for her throat. She parried the attack and slammed the flat of her hand against his nose. He staggered, dropped to the floor.

The fourth guy, still wrestling with the Fed, must have realized that he was greatly outnumbered. He didn't stop, didn't let up, but the look on his face was turning to one of panic.

But as Angel watched him, a movement reflected in the big, dark windows caught his attention.

Behind Kate, where Angel wouldn't have been able to see him except in the glass, the first guy he'd dropped had rolled onto his stomach and was raising his gun, taking aim at Kate.

His hand tightened on the trigger.

Angel plowed into Kate, driving her back six feet. A blast of gunfire sprayed the air where she'd been standing, tearing up the wall. Angel covered the space in less than a second, kicked the gun from the guy's hands, dragged him to his feet.

He head-butted the guy with his bony forehead. When he felt the man go limp in his hands, he let go.

As he turned to face the room, he reverted to his human state, hoping Kate hadn't noticed anything out of the ordinary.

The FBI man had his guy in handcuffs. Kate moved quickly through the room, putting flexible cuffs on the unconscious ones. Then she came to Angel, a smile on her pretty face.

"Guess I owe you a big thank-you," she said. She looked at him with an odd expression on her face.

"You're welcome." He waited. "Something wrong?"

She touched his forehead. "Guess not," she said. "At first, I thought . . . must have been a trick of the light. You okay?"

"Fine, I'm fine," he said. And then, anxious to change the subject, he added, "Glad I saw that guy's reflection in the glass. He—"

Reflections, he thought suddenly. *A trick of the light.*

"I have to go," he said. "Glad you're okay. Please

get outside and call off the troops so I can get out of here."

Kate went outside, hands held high, badge in one of them.

As soon as it was safe, Angel vanished into the night.

CHAPTER TWENTY

Finding a cab in L.A. was difficult under any circumstances. It was even more so in a not-particularly wealthy neighborhood, in the middle of the night.

Angel walked four long blocks to Figueroa, finally spotting one cruising slowly down that boulevard. He hailed it, climbed into the back, gave his address to the driver.

Reflections, he thought as the cab roared into the night. At the club, Hi-Gloss, with Karinna, when she'd disappeared on him. He'd circled the whole club, looking into the high mirrors to see out onto the dance floor. He'd still been looking into them when she came up behind him, touched his arm. He should have realized then that something was wrong, but he'd been relieved to find her, and it didn't sink in at the time.

Thinking back on that night, it wasn't that he didn't see anyone—if she had had no reflection at all, that would have tipped him off, he knew. So he had seen someone, or something. It just hadn't looked like Karinna.

Standing in the bank with Kate, things had suddenly fallen into place. Karinna never did her own makeup or hair. She wore heavy perfume—much more than most girls her age did.

She wasn't a vampire, Angel knew. He would have been able to sense that. What she was, he didn't know.

But what she wasn't, was human.

Add to that the sudden turnaround in the fortunes of Monument Pictures, and there was definitely something off in the Willits household.

When the cab pulled up in front of his building, Angel paid the driver and leaped up the front steps. He banged into the office, startling Cordelia and Doyle, both glued to Doyle's little TV.

"I need some help," Angel said.

"You—you're back," Cordelia said. "And we're glad."

"Me, too."

"We saw Kate on the tube," Doyle said. "She looked okay. Good. She looked good. The reports were kinda sketchy, though," Doyle continued. "Lackin' in detail, you might say. You . . . ?"

"Me," Angel replied. "I don't have a lot of time here. Listen . . ."

*   *   *

Forty-five minutes later Doyle dropped Angel in front of the Willits house and drove away. In Angel's coat pocket there was a book Doyle had scrounged up for him. In Angel's heart there was a deep anger. He let it carry him over their fence, up the drive, and to the front door.

He pounded on it three times. When there was no immediate answer, he reared back and kicked it, just below the knob. Wood splintered, metal screamed.

The door swung open.

Angel had been invited inside before, so that wasn't a problem. He went in.

"Jack Willits!" he called.

There was a moment of silence, and then a shuffling from deep in the house. After a couple of minutes Jack Willits emerged from the door he'd come through the first time Angel had been here.

"Don't you ever sleep?" Angel asked.

"Angel!" Jack ignored the question, a broad smile on his face. "My boy. Am I glad to see you. Wait till Karinna hears—we were worried about you, I don't mind saying—"

"Save it," Angel cut him off.

"Come on," Jack said. "I'm in the study, having a brandy. Join me."

"I don't want your brandy."

"Surely there's something you want." Willits glanced at the shattered door. "Quite the entrance."

"We need to talk," Angel said.

"Then let's talk." Willits led the way to his study, and Angel followed.

When they arrived there, Jack Willits went behind an ornate antique desk. On its surface there was a green glass-shaded lamp, a leather desk pad, and a scattering of writing implements and random papers. The room was huge, about the size of Angel's whole apartment, it seemed. A fire crackled in a fireplace almost tall enough to stand up in. On the mantel three Oscars gleamed. Jack waved toward a chair. Angel ignored him.

"You set me up," Angel said. "For Mordractus. You used your own daughter as bait."

"No," Willits protested.

"You're right, my mistake. She isn't your daughter. Or it wasn't. It just looked like her. What happened to the real Karinna?"

Jack Willits's face crumpled. He looked like a man whose world was falling apart, turning to dust before his eyes. No matter how much he tried to grab handfuls of the dust, it still slipped from between his fingers, and there was nothing he could do to stop it.

"I . . ." He sat down behind the desk, put his elbows on its surface, his face in his hands. "I don't know what to say."

"How about the truth? Or have you forgotten how to do that?"

"It's more complicated than you can know, Angel."

"Try me. I'm a very complex guy."

"I believe—"

"I said I was complex, not patient."

Willits choked back a sob. "He came to me, the day she died."

"Mordractus came to you?"

"That's right, that's his name. Mordractus."

"The day Karinna died. I want some detail here, Willits."

"Yes, *okay?* Yes, the day Karinna died!"

"How?"

"She was shot. She was out clubbing, as usual. She had escaped her bodyguards and was going with a couple of people, older people, adults. They should have known better, but they didn't. They were looking for a party. A friend of Karinna's told me all this, someone who didn't go with them. They left the club to look for this party, and I guess they were looking in the area where a nighttime bank robbery was taking place—you know, that gang that's been taking down banks all over town?"

"I've heard about them."

"So anyway, the bank robbers came out of the bank, I guess, and Karinna was out there with these other people. The robbers shot them, killed them all. I'm an important guy in this town, you understand that, don't you?" He looked at Angel with great sorrow in his red-rimmed eyes, as if it was very important that Angel be clear about his status.

Angel wouldn't even give him that. Jack went on.

"When the police realized who she was, they called me. She was a minor, her name wouldn't have been released to the press. I didn't even want it on the public records. My position at Monument was pretty tenuous, you know? Before, I mean. Before Mordractus. The last thing I needed was bad publicity.

"I don't know how he even knew about it, but he came to me, right there at the police station. I'd just been to the morgue, identified her body. They left me alone for a minute, and I turned around, and there he was. He was so soothing, so calm. He drew me into an empty office, and he started talking. He told me that no one ever had to know that she had died. That he could make sure her name wasn't on the records. That he could keep it out of the press.

"I would have agreed right there, but then he kept going. He could turn around Monument Pictures, he said. He could make sure I kept my job. Not only kept it, but improved it. All I've ever wanted to do was make movies, Angel. I didn't set out to be an executive, but if you make hit movies in this town, that's what happens. You keep getting kicked upstairs, until finally there is no more upstairs. You're as high as it gets. And when you're up there, you're a target. There's no shortage of people waiting for you to make a mistake, to tear you down. I didn't want to be torn down, but I was about to be."

Angel stood silently, watching as Jack Willits rambled on. He didn't even seem to know whether or not Angel was still in the room. A floodgate had been opened, and the words rushed out, a river of speech that would no longer be contained.

"Mordractus promised me that wouldn't happen. All I had to do was go along with his plan to keep Karinna's death a secret—and that was what I wanted, too, that was the beauty of it—and he'd make everything okay at Monument Pictures. And it worked, Angel. A few days ago I was history, dead meat. Now I'm back on top. I've got Blake Alten. No one can touch me. Everything Mordractus said he'd do, he did."

"Including using Karinna's likeness to draw me into a trap."

"I didn't know who you were, Angel. I didn't have any idea. Just some guy Mordractus wanted to get his hands on. He didn't give me any details about that, just said that you'd respond to Karinna, so I had to play along. I said I could do that. You have to understand, Angel, everything was at stake. Everything."

"Everything according to you."

"Well, that's life, isn't it? Human nature? We're selfish beasts, Angel. We look out for our own. We do what we need to do to further our own interests, right?"

"You do what you do to line your pockets, Jack.

Look around you. You could live—a dozen families could live—on what you could get by selling this house alone. You must have other investments. You don't need more than you have."

"It isn't just the money, Angel. It's making movies, don't you see? I don't want to give up making movies."

"When was the last time you made a movie, Jack? From what I hear, all you make is deals."

"That is making movies, Angel. If you think it's just about who's behind the camera, you're living in the past. It's about *deciding* who's behind the camera, and who's in front of it. Those are the decisions that count."

"And the final result is in how many tickets it sells, right? Not what's on the screen."

Jack looked at Angel again. He rose from his chair, went to a wall safe, and started to turn the dial. "You think I'm scum, Angel. I can see that. I can even understand it, to some extent. Maybe you're an old-fashioned guy. You don't get it, that's okay. But entertainment is business. Big business. You lose sight of that, you take your eye off that ball, you're yesterday's news. You're lower than the gum on the bottom of the theater seats. Do you have any idea of how much money we're talking about here, Angel? You think I'm talking about a few million?

"Billions, Angel. A hit picture. Ticket sales. International. Licensing. Video. Broadcast. One hit movie can make billions for the studio. There aren't many that do, but it can, and I've done it *three times*. I'm about to do it again. There aren't many people in this business who can say that. That's why I'm Jack Willits, Angel. That's why I'm on this planet. I make pictures."

"You used to," Angel said flatly.

Willits opened the safe. Angel could see bundles of cash inside it.

"We can make this go away, Angel," Jack replied. "Everyone's got a price. You've got a price. Whatever it is, I'll pay it. You can walk away from this, forget it ever happened."

He tossed one of the bundles to Angel. Angel caught it instinctively, glanced at it. Hundreds. A thousand of them. Jack threw him another, casually, like tossing a softball.

"Tell me when to stop, Angel," he said.

Angel stood next to the fireplace. He dropped the first bundle onto the flaming logs, then the next.

"Keep it coming," he said.

Willits tossed him two more bundles. They followed the first. This time Jack saw what he was doing.

"Hey, what . . . ? Are you crazy? That's money!"

"I know," Angel said calmly. "It doesn't burn very well. You've got to give it a few minutes."

Willits rushed toward him, panic in his eyes. "Get out of the way!" he insisted.

"You'll have to move me," Angel said.

"You can't do that! That's mine."

"You just gave it to me," Angel reminded him. "Mine now."

"Not if you're going to burn it!"

"It's not your concern anymore."

Jack stared at him with disbelief. "Fine," he said, grasping at a glimmer of hope. "But I wasn't giving it to you for nothing. You need to let this go. Walk away."

"I can't do that," Angel said. "You brought me into it. I'm in."

"It's over now," Jack reminded him. "You're still here. That must mean you beat Mordractus somehow, right? So it's ancient history."

"Not to me."

"Angel, what do you want from me?"

"I want you to recognize what you did, Jack. She's your daughter. You used your own dead daughter to keep your job. Do you see how sick that is?"

"She was dead!" Jack screamed. The tears welled up in his eyes then, tears of rage and sorrow and frustration. He pounded his fists against Angel's chest. "She was already dead! What did it cost me? Nothing!"

"It cost you everything, Jack," Angel told him quietly. "Everything."

"What do you mean? What are you talking about?"

"You want me to walk away. To forget this happened. I can't."

"But there's nothing you can . . . what can you . . ."

"Mordractus is gone, Jack. You don't have his protection anymore. You don't have his help."

Angel glanced at the fireplace. The money was finally starting to catch. There was more in the safe, though. Angel crossed the room, looked inside. A couple of bundles remained, and some envelopes. Documents of some kind, insurance policies. Angel ignored them.

There was something else. A small white rectangle of paper. Angel turned it over.

His business card.

But not the one Angel had given him. That had been dog-eared, with a phone number written in pen on the back. This one was pristine.

"Souvenir?" Angel asked.

"I forgot I had that," Jack said, between sobs. "He gave it to me. In case you didn't take the bait. I don't know how he knew you'd come to help Karinna, he never explained that. But he gave me the card. If you didn't show up, I was supposed to call you, hire you that way. Either way, you'd meet Karinna, agree to help her—he was sure you'd agree to help her."

"And I'd be so caught up in helping her that I'd lower my guard, let Mordractus get me." Angel turned to Jack's desk, where an old-fashioned paper

Rolodex was open. He flipped through the A's, found a card for Blake Alten, pocketed it. Jack, teary-eyed and distraught, didn't even seem to notice.

"That was the plan."

"The plan worked. That part of it, anyway. Mordractus was smart. But he underestimated me. So did you."

"Looks that way," Jack said.

"You won't do it again."

Jack slumped into his chair again, his face hidden in his hands, his body racked by sobs. Angel watched him for a moment, and as he did, he felt the anger that had driven him here fade.

It was replaced by something else, something he had a hard time putting a name to.

When he finally did, the closest he could come up with was "disgust."

"I came here because I wanted to hit you," Angel said. "I have never in my life wanted to do violence against a person the way I wanted to pound on you. I'm not proud of that impulse, but there it is. I wanted to wear out my fists on your face.

"But I can't do it, Jack. You aren't worth the effort."

"You can hate me if you want, Angel. Spit on me. Pity me. Just don't . . . don't do anything that's going to hurt my career. Don't hurt Monument Pictures. That's bigger than any of us."

"You're too late," Angel said. "Your values are too perverse. Karinna—whoever that was—told me you'd rank the movie business above your own family. I didn't believe it at the time. Now I see that she was right.

"All you're about, Jack, is greed. Greedy people collect what they're owed. And I owe you a debt, Jack. I owe you a big one."

"Angel, let it go," Jack sniffed. "You've got to just let it—"

"No, I don't, Jack. I can't. I won't."

"Angel . . ." Jack sobbed. "All right. Do what you have to do."

Angel turned and walked out of the study. Behind him, he heard Jack Willits, repeating himself over and over. "Do what you have to do," he said. "Do what you have to do."

Angel went to do it.

CHAPTER TWENTY-ONE

He found her upstairs, in her room. He pushed the door open, and she was sitting up in bed, smiling at him.

It wasn't a smile with any humor in it, or any good wishes. It was a smile full of cold, malicious evil.

Angel shivered, in spite of himself.

"I smelled you coming, vampire," she said, voice as chilly as that smile. "Smelled you all the way downstairs. Had a little chat with Jackie, did you?"

"Do I still call you Karinna?" Angel asked evenly. "Or do you want to tell me your true name?"

"If you don't know, I'm not going to give it to you, Angel."

"Sure, why make it easy on me?"

"You figured everything out, you think?"

"I think so."

"And what do you think you can do about it?"

"Send you away."

She scrunched up against her pillows. She still looked like Karinna, looked like a teenager, in spite of the horrible grin. Her room, strangely, didn't even look like a teenager's room, but like a little girl's. A *rich little girl's*, Angel corrected himself. Her bed was a queen-size white four-poster, much larger than a girl Karinna's size would need. The bedding, curtains, and carpeting were all in the same shade of pink, with white trim. The room's furniture and walls were all white—the bed, an armoire, vanity with a chair before it and a lighted mirror above.

"You don't even know what I am, vampire."

"I have a guess. You're a shapeshifting fairy. Rather prominent, in Celtic myth. And that's what Mordractus drew on, right? Creatures from Celtic myth and legend? Things most people didn't know ever existed, don't believe in? But he'd been around Ireland long enough to know there's more to that island than meets the eye."

"You're right there."

"So he brought you over from Faerie. Showed you Karinna. Dead Karinna. You took her shape, drew me into a trap. But you couldn't appear before a mirror, because mirrors can't be fooled. Your true self would be revealed. That was your mistake—I'm a little sensitive to mirrors myself."

"I told him I could just kill you. Begged him to let

me. But he wanted you alive. He was convinced that you had turned into some kind of do-gooder, that you'd rush to help poor Karinna. And that once he had distracted you, he could capture you alive. Obviously a fatal mistake on his part."

"I don't know if *fatal* is the word," Angel suggested. "But the consequences will definitely be long-lasting. Eternal, even."

Karinna's form shrugged. "Mistakes happen. Doesn't mean they can't be fixed."

"Meaning what?"

She sprang from the bed, suddenly, fingers hooked like claws. Angel barely had time to raise a defensive hand against her attack. Her fingernails scraped across his already-damaged cheek, tearing skin.

Angel shoved her backward. She hit the bed and came again.

This time he noticed, her hands didn't look like Karinna's. Her fingers were gnarled, the nails long and sharp.

"Showing your true colors?" he asked.

She snarled and slashed at him. He blocked her. She came again, and he pushed her back again.

With a young girl's legs, she climbed back onto the bed, squatted. Then she pushed herself off, and charged him with a demon's twisted claws, powerful jaws snapping at his throat. Her hair had turned white and stringy, her flesh mottled and creased. All resemblance to Karinna was gone now. This was her true face. This was what Angel had seen in the nightclub that night, for just the briefest of milliseconds.

He caught her wrists, held her at arm's length. Her strength was enormous, though, and he was tired. It seemed like days since he'd rested. Since before he'd been captured by Mordractus.

She writhed in his grip, snapping with sharp teeth. Angel gathered his strength and threw her back onto the bed. She bounced once, then hurled herself at him again.

This attack he met with a balled fist, driving it into her jaw. She stumbled, and he followed with a kick to her solar plexus.

She fell back, arms crossed over her middle, gasping for air. Angel snatched up the antique white chair that stood before Karinna's vanity, raised it over his head, and smashed it into her.

"Glad you changed faces," he told her unconscious form. "I would have had a hard time hitting Karinna. But I've got no problem clobbering you."

In the sudden quiet Angel drew the book from his pocket, flipped to the section Doyle had marked. "It's a simple banishin' spell," Doyle had said. "No muss, no fuss, no special equipment. If what you're tellin' me is right, you'll need to use it instead o' just killin' her outright."

The first section of it was in Latin, which Angel had learned as a boy.

When he spoke it, the room's lights dimmed and the shapeshifter stirred uncomfortably on the floor.

He turned a page. The next section was in English, or a version of it, anyway, and he read it aloud straight from the book, feeling a little like Mordractus with his grimoire.

" 'Begone, thou wretched beast from below,' " he read. " 'Thou hast outspent thy welcome in this place, and are cast away. Away! Return thee now to the realm from whence thou were summoned, without argument or insult, without threat or favor.' "

The shapeshifter's leg twitched. Angel glanced away from the page at her, and saw her eyes open, lock onto his.

"Think you're getting rid of me so easily?"

"I don't think there's a lot you can do about it."

"You'd be surprised."

Angel returned to the book.

" 'O, thou wicked and disobedient one, because thou hast not obeyed these words which I have spoken, I shall excommunicate thee, cast thee into the pit from whence there can be no return, where thou will burn in unquenchable fire. I shall destroy thy name and seal, unless thy obedience be forthcoming and immediate.' "

"Fat chance," the shapeshifter said. But she trembled and shook, and her skin seemed to have grown more pale, almost translucent. The spell was having some effect, Angel thought.

The room had grown cold without him noticing, but he noticed now. The lights had dimmed even more, but there was a glow beside Karinna's bed, an amorphous shape that seemed to coalesce even as he watched it.

It crystallized into the shape of Karinna. Not solid—Angel could see the wall right through her—but unmistakably her likeness. She didn't really stand on the floor, but hovered just above it. The insubstantial shapeshifter on the bed glared at it with hate in its eyes.

"Is this another trick?" Angel asked.

The Karinna-image didn't move, her mouth didn't open, but her voice was as clear as a bell.

"This is no trick, Angel. It's me, Karinna."

"The real one?"

"That's right. What's left of me, on this plane."

"But how . . . ?"

"The shapeshifter took my form before my body was even cold, much less buried," the ghostly Karinna explained. It felt strange to Angel to be talking to a dead girl whose voice seemed to come from nowhere, yet surround him completely. But Angel was no stranger to the strange. He tried to take it in stride.

"And everyone who knew me denied the fact of my death. My own father . . ." Her voice faltered, emotion reaching beyond the grave. "I was buried, but with no recognition, and my body—the shape of my body, my face—still walked the Earth. I could find no rest."

"Don't listen to her," the shapeshifter snarled. "She's nothing but a liar. Living inside her for a few days, I gotta tell you. Nasty."

"Shut up," Angel told the shapeshifter. "Go on, Karinna."

"She knows nothing about the real me," Karinna said. "She knew my form, nothing else. She couldn't know the pain of being dead but unable to rest, unable to complete the passage."

Realization dawned on Angel. One last element that had made no sense finally became clear. Why would Doyle have a vision that would lead Angel into a trap?

"So the vision that Doyle saw—that was you. The real Karinna. You were the one in trouble, the soul I was supposed to help. Doyle saw your face, but the vision wasn't clear enough to tell him that there were two of you with the same face."

"Yes," Karinna said, almost pleading. "I needed help. I *need* help. As long as she's here, I can't leave. By what you've done so far, beginning to banish her, you've allowed me to come back this much. But until she is gone, I can't continue my journey."

"Do you know what she did, Karinna? What your father did?"

"Yes. I'm ashamed of it. But where I'm going is beyond shame, beyond hurt, beyond the pain of betrayal. Please help me get there, Angel. Being in between like this, this is painful. More so than I can bear."

"Ignore her, Angel," the shapeshifter said. "She's dead, what can she offer you?"

"What can you?" Angel touched his cheek, split open by her raking claws. "You're not exactly taking the Congeniality prize."

"I can give you anything you want, Angel. With my abilities, my talents, we can have it all. We can have the world."

"Too greedy," Angel countered. "Too much responsibility. I'm happy with the tiny sliver of it that I've got." He looked at the Karinna-shape, floating just over the bed. "I'm sorry for your pain, Karinna. Sorry I can't do more for you."

"Just help me move on, Angel," she said. "That's all I ask of you. Help me to do that."

Angel nodded and raised the book. The next section was in Latin again. He read it.

As he did, the shapeshifter began to howl.

When he looked up at her, her image was even more indistinct than it had been. She convulsed in pain. Through her, Angel could see the end of Karinna's bed. The Karinna-shape hovering beside it seemed a little more substantial.

Angel kept reading.

The shapeshifter's howls became a single, anguished wail. It hurt Angel's ears. It sounded like all the pain in the world given voice by a single mouth.

Then it was gone.

She was gone.

Angel closed the book.

Karinna sat down on the bed, looking as solid as anyone.

"You're here?"

"Not really. Not to stay," she said.

"Then why?"

"I just wanted to thank you."

She climbed down from the bed. She was, Angel thought, more beautiful than the shapeshifter had been. There was something in her, some inner essence that came through, that made her more lovely still, and the shapeshifter hadn't been able to duplicate that.

With her red hair loose around her face, her clear eyes, her red lips curved into a shy smile, she looked more than ever like the young lady Angel had seen back in Tirgu Bals that time. Angel hadn't been able to help that woman, but he had helped this one.

Karinna came to him, wrapped her arms around him, strong and yet still girlish, and gave him a hug.

"Thanks, Angel," she said. "For everything."

"You're—you're welcome," he said. "Karinna."

She released him, took two steps backward, and gave him a smile that seemed to light the room.

And then she was gone.

❖   ❖   ❖

Angel was heading for the front door when he saw her. Marjorie Willits still looked fragile, as if a loud noise would shatter her to pieces. She peered at him from the doorway that led toward her husband's study.

"Angel?" she said hesitantly.

"Yes, Mrs. Willits?"

"It's over, isn't it?"

"It's all over, yes. I don't know how much you know. . . ."

"I know enough. Too much. Karinna . . ."

"Karinna is at peace, Mrs. Willits."

"Thank you for that."

"No need. I've been thanked."

"But still."

"You know what your husband did?"

"Yes, I know."

"And you're still here."

She nodded, gravely, and looked at her small hands.

"I wouldn't know where else to go."

"There are people," Angel said. "Services. Shelters. You have some money. You could get help figuring things out."

"I probably need help."

"Who doesn't?"

"But mostly what I need is strength. Jack needs strength, and I have to be the one to give it to him."

"You're staying with him?"

"He doesn't have anyone else."

"I'm not sure he deserves—"

"Never mind what he deserves, Angel. He may not be a good man, or a strong one, or a brave one. But whatever he's done, he is my husband and my responsibility, and I owe him."

"You're a better person than me, Mrs. Willits. I'd have been out the door long ago."

"I don't think it has anything to do with how good a person one is, Angel. Or how bad. We do what we have to do, all of us. Right or wrong."

"He said something very much like that to me."

"I'm not surprised." She glanced over her shoulder, as if he might emerge from behind her at any moment. "I think you've broken him, Angel. I don't know if he'll ever mend. I don't blame you for that, I'm just telling you what I believe. He's going to need my help. I'll be here for him."

"You're stronger than you look."

She graced him with a smile, and in it Angel could see traces of her daughter. It made him glad to think that there were aspects of Karinna left behind.

"Who isn't?"

"That's right," he said. "Who isn't."

He headed outside. In the doorway he stopped, turned, waved a hand at the ruined door. "Sorry about this," he said. "The door. It was . . . in my way."

"I understand, Angel."

"You'll probably want to get it fixed."

"Maybe we will. Maybe we'll just sell the house. We'll see."

"It was a pleasure meeting you, Mrs. Willits. And your daughter."

"And you, Angel. Pleasure meeting you."

She went back inside, toward the study and her husband. Angel went down the front steps. His dented GTX was parked in the drive, keys in the ignition.

He climbed in, started it, and left Bel Air, heading for home. But on the way he had another thought. He looked at the time. An hour of darkness left. Plenty of time for one more stop. The address he'd taken from Jack's office wasn't too far away.

EPILOGUE

Angel slept most of the day and spent the night resting as well. At around ten the following morning, he and Doyle were sitting in the outer office, talking about anything except Karinna Willits and her father and the trouble they brought to Angel, when Cordelia walked through the front door waggling the Hollywood trades.

"Your boss is all over the news," she said, "and none of it's good. At least, for him."

"He's not my boss anymore," Angel pointed out.

"Whatever, you know who I mean, right? Jack Willits."

"He made the papers, huh?"

"They're calling it the fastest career crash in Hollywood history," Cordelia said. "Except since they're the trade papers, they use headlines like 'Ex-exec Checks Neck.'"

"What happened to him?" Doyle asked.

"What didn't?" Cordelia replied. "He's been fired."

"That was fast," Angel said.

"Hey, those multinational corporations smell blood when it's in the water," Cordelia said. "And they want to make sure it's not their own. Why, when I was working at Monument, I—"

"For, like, twenty minutes?" Doyle interrupted. "You been tapped to take over his job?"

"Never mind," Cordelia said. "There's a place and a time for sarcasm, and this isn't it."

"When is it?"

"When it's coming out of my mouth."

"Go ahead, Cordy," Angel said. "He's been fired. Is there more?"

She looked at Doyle and then deliberately turned away. "You know how most of those big Hollywood execs have golden parachute deals, so even if they do a terrible job and get canned, they still walk away with millions of dollars? Willits had a golden parachute—maybe a platinum one—but he doesn't get it. The corporation that owns the studio says it has proof that he was cheating the studio. There's even a hint that maybe he was embezzling, although of course they don't come right out and say that, because that'd make them look bad."

"Cheatin' how?" Doyle asked.

"You know all that stuff about Blake Alten doing a

picture for them, for almost no money? Never happened, Alten says. He never agreed to any deal like that, and if he had, he would have had to have been hypnotized because he would *never* agree to any such deal. Especially with Monument Pictures, he says. Especially with a Monument Pictures headed by Jack Willits, for whom he has absolutely zero respect."

"Ouch," Doyle said.

"So Alten says that Jack was lying about the deal. And the corporation backs Alten. They say they've been through all of Jack's paperwork, and there is no deal. There's no contract, no letter of intent, no sign that there were ever any discussions. They think Jack floated the Blake Alten story to hang on to his job, to boost his own profile long enough to sell off his shares of Monument Pictures stock while it was up. The SEC, whatever that is, is looking into those charges."

"Securities and Exchange Commission," Angel said.

"They enforce laws relating to the stock market," Doyle added. "Why I keep out of the market. Too much regulation."

"If bookies sold stock, you'd be in the market," Angel said. "Legitimate gambling scares you."

"Harsh words, my friend," Doyle said. "You wound me."

"I thought we were talking about me," Cordelia said. "Or at least, paying attention to me."

"You mean there's more?" Angel asked.

"It's a long story," she replied. "I couldn't even read the whole thing at one time. I was afraid it would make my eyes bloodshot, so I put drops in them. How do they look?"

"Red-free," Angel said. "What else?"

"The corporation has not only fired Jack Willits, they're thinking about suing him. Breach of trust, breach of promise, stock manipulation, yadda yadda yadda. A lot of business talk that didn't really mean much. Basically, what it boils down to is that, not only is he out of a job, he's stepped in a mountain of doodoo."

"I think that sums it up nicely," Doyle offered.

"Thank you." Cordelia smiled and did a little curtsy.

"I wonder if Blake Alten really was hypnotized," she went on. "That would explain how he was able to ignore me. I was having a great hair day that day, so—"

"That's probably it," Doyle said. "You're right. Your hair was fabulous."

"Do they say who's taking over Willits's job?" Angel asked, desperately trying to keep the conversation on-topic.

Cordelia thumbed through some pages, ran her finger down a column of type.

"They're looking for someone, considering a number of candidates, it says. In the interim, the law firm of Wolfram and Hart will be running things."

"Terrific," Angel said. "New meaning to the phrase 'Hollywood sharks.' "

"I didn't know there was a phrase," Doyle said.

"I wonder what Blake Alten would have thought of me if he hadn't been in a trance," Cordelia said. "I wonder if he'd have wanted me to co-star in his next picture."

"Almost undoubtedly."

"Do you think so? What kind of a guy do you think he is?"

"Seems nice enough," Angel said. "Nice house, too."

"Because, I'm sure I could arrange to meet him again, if you really think he'd like me. I mean, what's not to like, right? Look at me."

"I'm lookin'," Doyle assured her with a grin.

"I didn't mean you. I meant, the universal 'look at me.' "

"The universe ain't here, Cordy. So I was lookin' for 'em."

"Oh. Well, okay, then. Thanks."

Angel rose from the couch. Those two could go on for another hour and not hear a single word he said. He headed for his private office.

"You know the female lead in a Blake Alten movie can pull in something like five or six million dollars, right?" Cordelia was saying.

"I didn't know that."

"It's true. Even a relative unknown, like Julie

Williams in *Trouble Happy*. Blake saw her in a soup commercial, and the next thing you know, she's cashing a check for seven figures. Do you know what I could *do* with five million bucks?"

Angel swung the door to his office closed.

Doyle and Cordelia looked at each other. Doyle shrugged.

"What's up with him?" Cordelia asked.

"Hard day, maybe."

"Hard day? I mean, sure, he works hard. Battling demons and all takes a lot out of you, I guess. But when was the last time five million dollars vanished from *his* bank account because a movie star was sleepwalking? I could've really used that money. Really, some people just need to get their priorities straight."

"I'm with ya, Cordy," Doyle said. "I'm right there."

"So anyway," Cordelia continued. "Five million big ones . . ."

About the Author

Jeff Mariotte writes comic books such as *Desperadoes* and *Countdown,* edits comic books for WildStorm Productions, is co-owner of Mysterious Galaxy, a specialty bookstore, and writes books, including *The Xander Years, Vol. 2,* and *Gen 13: Time and Chance* (with Scott Ciencin). He and his family live in a book-filled house in San Diego with various book-loving animals. There seems to be one constant in his life.

Everyone's got his demons....

ANGEL™

If it takes an eternity, he will make amends.

Original stories based on the
TV show created by Joss Whedon
& David Greenwalt

New titles every second month

Available from Pocket Pulse
Published by Pocket Books

"Wish me monsters."

—Buffy, "Living Conditions"

Vampires, werewolves, witches, demons of nonspecific origin...

They're all here in this extensive guide to the monsters of *Buffy* and their mythological, literary, and cultural origins.

Includes interviews with the show's writers and creator Joss Whedon

THE MONSTER BOOK

By
Christopher Golden
(co-author of THE WATCHER'S GUIDE)
Stephen R. Bissett
Thomas E. Sniegoski

FROM

POCKET BOOKS

2809